Come Back Home

WILL THIEMAN

PAGE PUBLISHING, INC.
Conneaut Lake, PA

First originally published by Page Publishing 2020

ISBN 978-1-64701-711-8 (pbk)
ISBN 978-1-66240-586-0 (hc)
ISBN 978-1-64701-712-5 (digital)

Printed in the United States of America

CHAPTER 1

2015

An elderly man walked into a suburban high school a few miles from the city of Columbus, Ohio. It happened to be November 11, 2015, or, rather more importantly, Veterans Day. The school principal asked this man to come speak to the student body. He reluctantly accepted. He was honored by the request, but he was worried about the reaction of the students. This elderly man didn't think the students would understand the story he was to share, nor did he think they would care. And this troubled him deeply.

As he loathed the request, he was actually shocked that he received a call from the school, because he was never a military man. He was a small child when the war was occurring, but he had a vivid memory of everything that happened. It was a strange time, but a more appropriate word to describe it would be *horrific* time. World War II was the deadliest conflict in human history. By the time the war ended in 1945, more than forty-five million people lost their lives.

When he sat down in his seat, it was almost time for the special afternoon assembly to commence. The alumnus of Arlington Heights High School was sitting in the front row, trembling with nerves. He knew that the beginning of the lecture was the most important part.

When he was a charming high school student, he would practically be on a different planet if the speaker was boring. As the principal was walking across the stage, he tried to figure out a way to engage his young audience.

"Good afternoon, everyone. As all you should know, today is Veterans Day. Veterans Day began after World War I. It always falls on November 11, which marks the end of the First Great War. The armistice was called on the eleventh day of the eleventh month of the eleventh hour," said the principal of the school, who looked like a man in charge. He wore something seldom people wear often: suspenders, glasses, and a bow tie. This principal liked to stand out because he believed it exerted more authority. "I think it is very important to honor every man and woman who has served for this great nation. As a result, we have a fellow Arlington Heights Golden Bear to speak about his experiences during World War II. Please help me give a warm welcome to a person who once sat in the same chair as you all do today."

After the principal directed the elderly man to come onstage, the gentleman waltzed right up there. He shook the principle's hand and grabbed the microphone. "Thank you for inviting me here. I was honored when I received a call from Principal Whaley," the man said. "Do you all know Paul Olsen? Stand up, Paul."

Paul stood up from his seat, and the students started cheering.

"Pauly is my grandson. I'll do my best not to embarrass you here today."

Before he wanted to start telling war stories, he desired to engage this young audience. But how could he engage them? By asking them questions? It wasn't a bad idea. "How many people here are eighteen years old or close to that age?" the man asked. Almost 20 percent of the audience raised their hands. "Imagine it's 1942 and American soldiers are shipping off to Europe like clockwork. Your birthday gets randomly drawn in the Selective Service draft. Would you be ready to fight in Europe?" asked the man standing onstage. "Now, raise your hand if you would be willing to fight in Europe." Most of the hands went down, but a few remained. The elderly man called upon one of the boys with his hand raised. As he was about to call on him,

4

the man noticed the boy looking down. His eyesight was poor, but not poor enough to see the young lad playing with his phone.

"They didn't have iPhones back in 1941," said the man. The auditorium roared with laughter. The alumnus of Arlington Heights was not amused. It seemed disrespectful.

"I'm sorry," the boy said.

"It's okay. You see, it may be a generational thing, but in my eyes, I see it as disrespectful. Let me ask you something. Do you have friends?"

"Yes."

"Do you have parents, brothers, and sisters?"

"I live with my mom and dad. I also have two younger sisters."

The man stared the boy in the eyes and asked him one more question. "Do you have a girlfriend? And if so, do you care deeply about her? I'm not trying to put you on the spot. I promise you, this is the last question."

The young student didn't hesitate again. "I have a girlfriend. If it tells you how we feel about each other, we're going to the same college next year," said the young man in front of the entire school.

"Are you prepared, right now, to tell your friends goodbye, your family goodbye, and your girlfriend goodbye? Are you prepared to never see them again?" said the old man.

"I never thought about it that way. I'm not sure I would ever be prepared for that," said the young man.

The alumnus of Arlington Heights let the students think about the scenario. People that didn't live through a total war have no understanding of what it means to fight overseas, especially during the Second World War. The closest they have come to war is through Call of Duty: Modern Warfare on Xbox.

Once he felt the students were ready to listen, he began talking again. "I'm not going to stand up here, lecturing you about the history of World War II. You have the best teachers in the state to teach you about the war. Instead I want to share a story about a few people who were your age when the war was in full rage. But before I begin, I want to ask you about the motivations of young people who volunteered for war."

One student raised her hand, so he called on her. "To remove Hitler from power."

The man collected his thoughts before he responded. "The short answer is yes. But it's more complicated than that. The men and women who volunteered wanted to fight for humanity, no matter the cost. And unfortunately, some of these young people paid the ultimate price. You see, when tyranny and aggression rise up and are more powerful than freedom, some force needs to push it back down."

* * *

1943

After watching his father fly planes while growing up, all Walter Wilson wanted to do was be up in the cockpit and soar through the blue skies. Walter's father, Bill, flew planes during World War I and flew alongside Eddie Rickenbacker, who was also from Columbus, Ohio. Rickenbacker received a medal of honor for his heroics and became a colonel. And his fame didn't end with his war victories, as Eddie Rickenbacker owned and operated the Indianapolis Motor Speedway after the Great War.

When the war ended for Bill Wilson, he returned to Ohio and met his wife, Allison. Bill raised his family in a little town outside Columbus, Ohio. The town was called Arlington Heights, and it rested about two miles northwest of the capital city between the Olentangy and Scioto Rivers. Arlington Heights was a great place to settle down, and a great town to raise children. Many other families felt the same way, so there was an abundance of children running around with Walter. Since he had a good support system around him, Walter Wilson and his sister, Mallie, had all the opportunities they had ever dreamed. Both of them were avid tennis players, and Walter's career was highlighted with a state championship his senior year of high school.

Walter was offered a scholarship to play at Ohio Wesleyan University, which was a small liberal arts school north of the capital city. He was all set to enroll at Ohio Wesleyan in the fall, but in 1943, war was ongoing throughout the world. Hitler was in aggression mode and poised to conquer Europe. Even though Walter dreamed of playing tennis in college, he wanted to weigh his options of whether to join the fight.

Although Walter always dreamed of playing tennis in college, he had also always wanted to become a fighter pilot in the United States Marines. He had heard stories of fighter pilots from his dad and read about the heroics of the fighter pilots who fought in the Battle of Britain. The United Kingdom would have fallen if not for the pilots of Britain in the summer of 1940. Walter wanted to make an impact like the British fighter pilots; he wanted to save the world from tyranny and contribute to stopping the Nazi regime.

But the trouble was telling his folks. Bill Wilson did not want his son to become a pilot; he wanted his son to attend school and become a lawyer. Bill made the choice of enlisting in the military during the First Great War. While it was an honor to serve his country, he missed out on the opportunity of acquiring an education. After the war, he was supposed to attend the Ohio State University, but he fell in love with Allison and she became pregnant. He was forced to forgo his education and support his family through a job as a factory worker.

Walter planned on telling his family while they were sitting down for dinner in their two-story brick house. Walter was comforted with the smell of candles sitting on the table. He yearned to find the opportune moment to express his intent and was enthused when his sister, Mallie, began talking about her summer. Mallie was a year younger than Walter and looked a lot like him. Mallie was like many girls her age. She longed for attention and enjoyed hanging around her friends. "I plan to have an absolute ball of a time this summer. I'll be at the pool every day. I need to be a bronze goddess by July," said Mallie.

"Why do you want to be tan, sweetheart," said Mrs. Wilson.

"All the girls in school want to be tan. That's how the boys like us," said Mallie.

Mrs. Wilson shook her head. "Times sure have changed. When I was your age, all the girls wanted to be pale." When Mrs. Wilson was younger, it was more desirable to have pale skin. The pale skin symbolized wealth, and it signified that a girl wasn't from the working class. Connecting the dots, if girls were tan, it meant they worked in the sun.

"No tennis?" Mr. Wilson asked.

"Ahh, maybe a little. I'm kinda tired of playing tennis. Sorry, Dad," Mallie said.

Bill nodded and said it was fine. But inside, he was the opposite of fine, and the whole family knew that he was disappointed. Hell, the whole community knew Bill would be disappointed. Everyone in Arlington Heights was well aware that Bill wanted his children to be really good tennis players.

As Walter was prepared to divulge the plan to enroll in officer school, he felt similar to horses awaiting the gates at the Kentucky Derby. He was ready to race, but he wondered how his family would react. Walter was eighteen years old and a legal adult, but he wasn't quite sure if his father would try to forbid him from joining the military. While everyone was quietly chomping on dinner, the gates opened, and it was time for him to gallop.

"I have something to tell everyone," said Walter.

Walter's mom, dad, and sister turned to him and gazed right into his blue eyes. Feeling the weight of Ohio Stadium on his shoulders, he said, "I'm not going to Ohio Wesleyan in the fall. I plan on enrolling in officer school in the United States Marines on September 1. I want to become a fighter pilot."

The only noise that could be heard in the dining room was the candles burning and the wind blowing through the windows. His father didn't know what to say. He had some idea this was coming but chose not to see it because he was a World War I veteran. Before the First Great War, war was a romantic idea, men riding off into the sunset and fighting for a patriotic cause. They would return to their countries as heroes, greeted by a crowd of people and beautiful women lusting over the chance of marrying a war hero. However, the Great War had changed that notion of a romantic idea, because people suffered. Men came back crippled, blinded, wounded, and traumatized. Bill Wilson couldn't understand why anyone wanted to fight in this new world war.

"Walter, I don't know what to say. I really don't want you to go. You have a good life here. College awaits you, son, and you have a very bright future at Ohio Wesleyan. I just don't understand," said Bill.

"Well, Dad, you don't have to understand. Ever since I was young, all I wanted to do was be a pilot. I do want to go to Ohio Wesleyan or some college someday. Just not right now. I want to fly planes in the Marines. I want to be in this war and make a difference."

Bill gasped. "You still are young. You're still a kid. You're *my* kid."

"I'm eighteen," said Walter.

"Then you're still a kid," said Bill.

"Oh, Walter, please don't do this. It would have me worried. Young boys aren't coming home, and I just don't want you to do this. Please don't do it."

After Mrs. Wilson's plea, the only noise that could be heard was the summer night's wind coming in through the window. After about ten minutes of silence, Walter was getting out of his seat to leave the table. His father told him to sit back down.

"Now, listen, I clearly won't be able to talk you out of it, so I guess I'm going to have to support you on this decision," said Bill. "Listen, son, my father never supported me when I signed up during the Great War, and I resented that. I don't want to make the same decision."

Walter shook his father's hand and exhaled a huge sigh of relief. When the handshake ended, Walter went to the kitchen to put his plate in the sink. As he came back out to the dining room, his mother asked him if he had any exciting plans for the summer. "My plan is exactly the same as if I were going to Ohio Wesleyan. I'm going to be coaching tennis at Beechum Park until early August. I plan on shipping out to basic training on September 1. I want to have one last summer of fun."

Mallie broke free from her silence and said, "That's trouble! Are you teaching tennis with Randall?" After Walter nodded to her question, Mallie told him not to get into too much trouble.

Randall Moore and Walter had grown up playing tennis together and had been best friends ever since. The boys had taught tennis every summer together since they had been fifteen years old. It seemed as if Walter was itching to join the armed forces, but Randall might have been the reason Walter waited. It was always an adventure, and Walter wanted one more before joining the military.

While Walter was rinsing his dish off in the sink, he was thinking about the previous summer. Every day Randall and Walter would teach tennis until midafternoon. After tennis clinics, they would be free the rest of the day. On some days, they would go swimming at the pool right next to the courts. Those days were refreshing, as it was a great way to cool down after a hot day in the sun.

Another option would be to play tennis. It sounded crazy, but Walter and Randall didn't get enough tennis just teaching. They were driven to be the best tennis players in the state of Ohio. In order to pursue that dream, they drove to a public park a few miles away from the tennis club where they taught. Even though the club manager allowed them to play after teaching, they refused to play at the club. The boys didn't agree with the dress code at Beechum Park. It was hard for them to believe, but the club actually had a policy where players were required to wear shirts. That policy didn't bode well with them. When the shirts came off, they believed they could attract all the beautiful girls that often wandered around the tennis courts.

The third option, Walter and Randall would head to one of the local establishments in Arlington Heights. There was a pub not too far from the tennis club, so some days they would walk over to the restaurant called the Old Pub. Randall and Walter would cool off from a hot summer day with a couple of Cokes, but on other days, they would refresh themselves with a couple of ice-cold beers.

The boys' favorite memory spent at the Old Pub was with one of their coworkers, Hughe Denning. Mr. Denning had a wife and two kids. He taught tennis with the boys one summer.

At first glance, Walter and Randall thought Mr. Denning was a serious man, especially with his thick mustache. However, that sentiment changed when Mr. Denning overheard the two boys talking about drinking on Memorial Day. "It's a great excuse to drink," said Walter.

Mr. Denning then turned to them, saying, "You boys can start at my house. We'll play some fun drinking games, and my wife can cook for us."

Both Randall and Walter just looked at each other and weren't sure whether he was serious. As it turned out, Mr. Denning was dead serious. After tennis one day, Mr. Denning suggested that the boys drink with him at the Old Pub. They agreed and had a great time. After a few drinks, Mr. Denning invited them back to his house. "What do ya say we keep this party rolling? I have plenty of beer at my house, and my wife's making dinner. Do you boys want to come back to my house?" asked Mr. Denning.

Memories such as meeting Mr. Denning, teaching tennis, bumming around, and chasing girls made Walter crave a great summer before he started his life as a pilot. And moments like the ones Walter had during the summers forced him to wait until the end of the summer to enroll in officer school. The young man said to himself that maybe the summer in Arlington Heights, Ohio, would alter his decision about joining the military.

"No way," he said under his breath.

CHAPTER 2

The next day, Walter woke up around 8:00 am. He peeked out the window and saw sunny skies. It was a perfect day to begin his summer of teaching tennis. As any excited teenager on the first day of summer, he raced down the stairs for breakfast. His mom was waiting in the kitchen for him and said, "Breakfast is ready!" Walter's mom almost never made breakfast, so he thought something was wrong.

Walter poured himself a glass of fresh orange juice and helped himself to his favorite breakfast: chocolate chip pancakes, bacon, and scrambled eggs. The chocolate chip pancakes looked delicious, as the chocolate chips had begun to melt over the pancakes. It tasted just as good as it looked. Although Walter couldn't savor the taste to the fullest because his busy morning awaited him, and it was almost time to pick up Randall for their day of teaching tennis.

Walter stood up from his chair at the kitchen table and was ready to sprint out the door. However, his mom said, "Walter, would you mind sitting back down? I really need to talk to you."

Walter nodded, but he only had a few minutes.

"Are you joining the military to get back at me?"

Walter didn't answer right away; he pondered his next sentence because he didn't want to tell his mother the truth.

Walter and his mother had had a distant relationship ever since he was about ten years old. When Walter reached that age, his mother had started drinking. She would constantly take trips to the kitchen and fill up her glass with bourbon. Her field trips to the cabinet began in the morning and did not end until after dusk.

Walter and his sister, Mallie, learned at a young age that their mother had two sides to her: sober and drunk. These sides motivated Walter to give his mother names inspired by the hit movie *The Wizard of Oz*. While drunk, Allison was like the Wicked Witch of the West, cruel, mean, and condescending. However, she was quite the opposite when she was sober. When sober, Walter called her Glinda, the Good Witch of the East. She was nice, caring, and friendly. Unfortunately, the Wicked Witch of the West appeared more times than Glinda, the Good Witch. One memory of the Wicked Witch stuck out in particular to Walter.

* * *

It seemed like a regular morning when Walter was a young boy. Walter remembered that it was a cold winter morning and snow had fallen on the ground. When he woke up, he looked out the window and saw snow in front of his house and hoped it was a snow day. He ran downstairs, almost as excited as a little kid on Christmas. "Mama, do we have school today?" Walter asked.

"I'm sorry, dear. You do have school."

"It's okay. Where's Daddy?"

"He left for work a few minutes ago."

"What did you make us, Mama?"

"I made oatmeal this morning. Go upstairs and get ready for school and then come back down for breakfast," Allison told her son.

Walter ran up the stairs and prepared himself for school. He stepped into a pair of slacks and pulled a shirt and sweater over his head. When he was changed, he walked down the stairs to the dining room. As he approached the table, he saw his sister sitting down at the table. "Good morning, Mallie."

"Good morning, Walter. After school, do you want to build a snowman? I want to build the biggest snowman in Arlington Heights!"

"Yes, I would like that. Let's do it right after school," Walter said.

Allison walked back into the dining room holding three bowls of oatmeal. She put the bowls down on the table, and both Walter and Mallie could see the steam rising from the bowl. "It's hot, so be careful. Oh, wait, I forgot the brown sugar. I'll get it from the kitchen," Allison said. When she returned from the kitchen, she placed the brown sugar on the table.

"What do we do with the brown sugar?" asked Walter.

"You pour it in the oatmeal, sweetheart. I forgot you have never had oatmeal before. Your daddy hates it, so that's why we have never had it."

Allison left her children in the dining room while she went to freshen up. Walter and Mallie both were quick to scoop the brown sugar in the bowl and dump it in their bowls. Once the brown sugar was on top of their oatmeal, both Walter and Mallie mixed it around with their oatmeal. Walter tried the first bite and said, "Hmm, this is really good, Mallie. The brown sugar makes it so good."

"It is really good, Walter," said Mallie.

The Wilson children ate their oatmeal in record time. When Mallie finished her last bite, she said, "Walter, let's go make snow angels."

"Okay, but we can't be too long. I want to be at the table when Mama comes back."

Walter took Mallie's hand and led her outside. They lay on their backs and swung their arms and legs to create the snow angels. When Walter was finished, he jumped up. He then pulled Mallie up by the arm so her snow angel was perfectly shaped and no scuffs appeared.

"We did good," said Mallie.

"We sure did. Good job," said Walter.

The pair of siblings walked back into the house and sat down at the table. Mrs. Wilson marched downstairs a few minutes later and appeared to be upset. "How did this snow get in the house?" Mrs. Wilson asked as she saw the trail of snow leading from the door to the table.

Walter took the blame; he didn't want his sister to be in trouble. The young boy was always protecting his younger sister. "I'm sorry, Mama. I wanted to build a snow angel. It was me."

"Well, now my floor is all wet," Allison Wilson said.

"I'm sorry, it won't happen again," said Walter with his head slouched down.

"I'm sorry too, Walter. I didn't raise a son to be so disrespectful. There will be consequences, and you will find those out after school. I'm going to drive you to school now. Get in the car. Don't make me tell you again," said Allison Wilson. Her children didn't want to disappoint her again, so they hurried to the car as fast as possible.

School couldn't go by any slower. The voice of Walter's teacher was going through one ear and out of the other. He might have physically been at school, but he was mentally somewhere far away. All he could think about was how ashamed he felt. Could he do anything right? Could he ever have his mother's approval?

After school, Allison Wilson picked up her children from school. It was the moment Walter was dreading since he began the school day. It was judgment time, and he finally was able to find out what would be his punishment. He hopped in the car first, and Mallie was right behind him. She closed the door to the black Ford, and Allison began to drive back to the Wilson house.

When they were pulling into the driveway, Mallie noticed that there was still snow on the ground. "Walter, Walter, Walter!" Mallie said.

"What do you want, Mallie?" said Walter.

"Let's build a snowman. Mommy, do you have carrots for the nose?"

"Yes, I sure do, sweetie. I'll grab some carrots from the kitchen, and we will build a snowman," Allison Wilson said.

"What about Walter, Mommy?" asked Mallie.

"Walter will be waiting in his room until suppertime. He needs to learn about respect," Allison said.

Walter's head sank to the ground. He wanted to cry, but he didn't want to show emotion in front of his sister and mother. As soon as Walter walked in the door, he climbed the stairs to his room.

He lay on his bed crying for several minutes. He looked out his bedroom window and saw his sister and mom building a snowman. He wanted more than anything to be with them at that very moment. He asked himself many questions that day. *Why didn't she love me? Why is she harder on me than Mallie?* Even though he knew that answer.

* * *

That particular story of his mother disappeared from his mind quicker than a cup of water after a hard workout on the tennis court. His focus returned to the breakfast table with Allison. He turned to his mother and said, "No. I'm making this decision for me. I told you that I forgave you a long time ago. It's not about you anymore. It's about me. I'll let you know if I change my mind, but for now, I plan on enrolling in officer school."

"Very well, then. It's your life," replied Allison Wilson.

"Yes, it sure is," said Walter.

Allison Wilson grasped the information that Walter expressed and was upset, but happy. She was happy that Walter expressed how he had forgiven her. Obviously, she was upset that he was still insisting on joining the war. However, Allison realized that she had lost the right to give Walter life advice a long time ago.

Allison wished her son a good day, and Walter walked out the door to his black 1936 Ford Coupe so he could drive to Randall's house. Randall was an only child and lived with his mom, Nancy. Randall's father left them when he was very young, and it had been just Randall and Nancy ever since his departure.

When Walter pulled into the driveway, he jumped out of his car and walked up to the small blue American foursquare house. He was about to open the door, but Mrs. Moore beat him to it.

"Good morning, Walter. How are you doing today?"

"I'm good. Just ready to teach some tennis," replied Walter as he walked into the house.

Nancy nodded and asked Walter if he wanted anything for breakfast. "I'm fine. My mom made me breakfast today," said Walter as he sat down on the white couch in the living room.

Walter always showed up early to help motivate Randall to be on time. Randall had a habit of showing up so late that sometimes the manager of the club would come knock on his door to ensure he was punctual. Randall didn't appreciate the gesture, but it did motivate him not to dillydally in the mornings.

Nancy walked into the room and sat on the chair adjacent from where Walter was sitting on the couch. She turned to him and asked, "How are your parents? Did you tell them you're thinking about joining the military?"

"Yes, I did. They handled the news better than I had anticipated. My mom tried being the center of attention as usual."

"I wouldn't worry about her. You did the right thing."

Walter and Nancy had a very good relationship. Nancy was instrumental in helping Walter get through the dark days when his mother was drinking. She would always tell him, "It's darkest just before the dawn," or "Keep your head up and hang in there." Whenever he needed someone to talk to, she was one of the very first people he called.

Nancy got up from her seat and left the room. A few moments later, a confident and borderline-cocky eighteen-year-old kid came strolling down the wooden stairs. His cheekbones were as high as ever. Some people thought his confidence was the only thing higher.

"You ready, chief?"

"Am I ready? I've been waiting for you for almost ten minutes! You're always on Moore time!" Walter said. Walter came up with Moore time to tease Randall about his tardiness.

"Let's get outta here," said Randall.

The boys walked to the car and drove to the tennis courts. Beechum Park, where the boys taught tennis, was a short drive from Randall's house. It was in the center of Arlington Heights, and the tennis club was a staple of the community; it was located in the center of a three-acre park. Many tennis legends had grown up playing at this club, including Walter and Randall. Walter would always brag that he was one of the best to ever play at Beechum Park. Whether it was true or not, Walter and Randall played for hours at the club, trying to gain an edge.

Walter and Randall walked up to the tennis courts with no time to spare. The head pro, Thomas Heines, was sitting in the club shop, flipping through the pages of the *Columbus Dispatch*. Even though he was in charge, Coach Heines was always the last pro on the courts.

"Nice of you ladies to show up today," said Coach Heines. "I assigned you guys to courts 3 and 4."

Coach Heines had been the coach at Beechum Park for the last decade. Randall and Walter enjoyed working for Coach Heines. He was down-to-earth and was the kind of boss that wouldn't expect you to do anything he wasn't willing to do himself. And plus, Coach Heines had been the boys' coach since they were young lads.

The tennis clinic that they were teaching was a group of about twenty kids from ages ten to seventeen years old. This drill session consisted of four teaching professionals, so each instructor had five players on a court. Walter began coaching some boys who were about thirteen years in age who were good players.

Walter didn't teach these skilled kids for very long that day, or very long during the summer. "They're missing out getting coached by the best here," Walter would say under his breath. Thomas Heines would prefer them to be on his court and would coach them for the majority of the drill session. Only a few minutes into the drill session, Coach Heines yelled, "Rotate!" and all the players switched courts directly to the right.

As the players rotated to Walter's court, he noticed that this group was younger and some of them had yet to reach double digits in age. Walter sighed, as he couldn't stand teaching little kids. He thought they were so annoying. Walter went through the motions until Coach Heines yelled for a water break.

During the next water break, Walter headed in the direction of Randall. As he was walking toward Randall, his eyes wandered to a group of girls that were playing doubles. One girl in particular stood out to him, and Walter couldn't quite understand why he couldn't take his eyes off her. He was drawn to her. This girl couldn't stop chatting with her friends. She had smooth, silky hair, and the color was the most beautiful shade of black he had ever seen. This girl's pale skin complemented her hair color on the same level as cream and sugar do to coffee. Her complexion reminded him of Snow White, and he caught himself asking, "Where are the seven dwarfs?"

"Walter! Are you okay?" said Randall, waving his hand in front of Walter's face.

"Who is that down there playing doubles? You know, the girl with dark hair? She's really cute," said Walter.

"Looks like someone has love in his sights," said Randall.

"Very funny. Just tell me the girl's name," said Walter as he took a sip of water.

"Ahh, sport, that's Abby Walker. She'll be a senior at Oakhaven School for Girls. Gorgeous, isn't she?"

Walter looked over to where she was standing. She was sipping on water and chatting among her friends. All the girls were looking at Abby like their fearless leader, as if she were Al Capone. He had never been drawn to a girl quite like Abby Walker. Walter perceived his crush on Abby in the same sense as when someone finds the perfect Christmas tree in a lot full of Colorado spruce trees. Once you see that perfect tree, no other tree would suffice.

Walter taught three more hours and didn't think much about tennis or how to improve the students he was coaching. He could only think of Abby. He was frustrated with his feelings because she was a member of the tennis club and extracurricular activities with members were strictly forbidden. He'd have to find a way to interact with her outside the club and do so in secret.

After the workday of teaching tennis finished, Walter and Randall left the club together. Before they went home for the night, they took a dip in the pool. It was refreshing, as they had been in the sun for several hours. They hadn't adjusted to spending a good amount of time under the hot sun, so they were exhausted. Both of them decided to return to their respective homes for the night and recharge their batteries.

When Walter was exhausted, he didn't want to be around anyone. So when he returned home, the young man went straight to his room. That night consisted of reading fiction novels and listening to the radio. On the radio, the newscaster talked about the victory in North Africa during the previous month. The Allies were able to upset the Germans, who were led by their best field commander, Erwin Rommel.

However, that night the news was like an ocean. Similar to how waves come into the shore and bounce back to the ocean, the news traveled through one ear and bounced back through the other. He was engulfed with the same train of thought he had had most of the day. His mind was pondering about getting to know Abby. Hopefully, Walter could ask her out sooner rather than later, because, after all, he was considering the military soon.

CHAPTER 3

Walter was excited for the first weekend of summer, and the chances of running into Abby were as high as ever. On the first Saturday of June, the annual community fair was held at Beechum Park. Everyone in Arlington Heights attended the event, and this year would be no exception. Many people would come to the community fair to get their mind off the war.

Walter was walking out the door to meet Randall at the fair while Mallie was walking into the house. "Where are you going?" asked Mallie.

"I'm going to the community fair tonight. What are your plans?"

"I'm not really sure. I may check out Beechum Park and hang out at the fair later tonight. I've heard it's supposed to be fun. Everyone will be there," Mallie said before stepping into the house.

"Well, hopefully, I'll see you there. Just don't get into trouble tonight. I'll keep my eyes open for you," said Walter, winking to his sister. He then hopped in his black Ford Coupe and drove to the community fair. When Walter arrived, he saw Randall standing by the park entrance.

"What's up, chief? I've been waiting here ten minutes for you," said Randall.

"I ran into Mallie on the way out the door. I just assumed you would be on Moore time and be a few minutes late!" said Walter as he shook Randall's hand.

The two boys ventured into the community fair as the sun began to set over Arlington Heights. Walter looked at Randall and said, "What's the plan tonight?"

"Well, sport, I'm happy you asked. Let's sit at that picnic table and decide."

The boys walked over to the red picnic table in the center of the park. In front of them was a stage and a man playing guitar. "Let's just listen to music for a while," said Randall.

"That's fine with me," Walter said.

"It would be better only if we had a couple of girls to spend the evening with," said Randall.

Walter nodded and smiled and continued listening to the live music. After a while of listening to music, Walter became restless. He glanced to his right and saw a few carnival games. "Randall, let's check out that game over there," Walter said.

"Ahh, sport, I'm okay. You go, and I'll stay here."

Walter walked over to the game where the objective was to throw a lightweight white ball into a gold cup. When he reached the game tent, there were almost fifteen people in line. While standing in line, he began to strategize the best way to win. A few minutes into drawing up a plan, he looked behind him because there was a scent of roses and tulips in the summer air. To his amazement, Abby Walker was standing behind him in a gorgeous purple dress with white polka dots. He couldn't stop staring at the most beautiful thing he'd ever seen. He awoke from his daze and began talking to the young girl.

"Hi, Abby. It's nice to see you," said Walter.

"Do I know you?" replied Abby, who looked confused.

If Walter had a hammer, his head would have taken a beating by his own right hand. Walter totally forgot that he hadn't met her yet. He would have to dig deep in his bag of tricks to not look like a moron.

"We met a couple of summers ago at Beechum Park," said Walter, hoping that it could potentially save him, even though it was a lie.

"I was in Maine two summers ago," replied Abby.

Damn it! Walter thought to himself.

"Truth be told, I saw you playing the other day and someone told me who you are. I'm Walter Wilson," said Walter, hoping the truth would pay off.

"Oh, hi, Walter. I do recognize you from the tennis club. I didn't recognize you without your tennis clothes on. How has your night been?"

"I can't complain. It's been a good night. But it just got a whole lot better," said Walter without any hesitation.

"And why would that be?" said Abby.

"Well, because now I'm in front of something truly beautiful," said Walter. "This fair is something else, isn't it? What a beautiful night."

"It is a beautiful night. You're right, nothing could be more beautiful," said Abby. She had hoped that he was talking about her, because Abby did find him attractive—how could anyone not? He had sandy-blond hair and the body of a track star. Not to mention, he had a couple of the cutest freckles under his eyes that she had ever seen.

"I'm glad we can agree on something. Do you see those prizes they're handing out for winning this game?" Walter said while he was looking in Abby's stunning blue eyes.

"Yes, I do."

"Well, I'm going to win something for you. Which prize do you want?" asked Walter.

"You're pretty cocky," said Abby. "I want the stuffed bear."

"Not cocky, but rather confident," said Walter. "I'll be winning your bear soon."

An elderly man with a white mustache was running the game tent. "Step right up, son. Try your luck."

Walter, displaying confidence, whispered under his breath how he didn't need luck and that he planned on sinking the first shot. The young man from Arlington Heights received three chances to throw the ball in the gold cup, but Walter knew he only needed one chance. On the first try, he missed badly. It didn't even make it onto the platform of the one hundred cups.

"I shouldn't hold my breath for that bear," said Abby while laughing.

"Don't worry. That was just my warm-up shot. The bear will be in your arms soon enough," said Walter.

The second time, he was closer to winning the game. The ball rimmed in and out of the cup and landed in one of the plain white cups next to the gold one.

"That's just unlucky," said Abby while smiling.

Walter ignored that comment and cocked his arm back for the final throw. He released the ball, and it landed in the gold cup. Everyone in line erupted with a small cheer, as they were excited to see someone win. Under his breath, Walter said, "Game over."

The elderly man with the mustache handed him his prize. When Abby was finished with her three throws, he handed her the bear. "Thank you, Walter. I didn't doubt you for a second."

"Oh, it was no problem. It was pretty easy," said Walter.

"What are you trying to say about my abilities?" said Abby.

"I think I'm trying to say you need to work on your tossing skills."

"Since you are so good, maybe you can teach me sometime," said Abby.

"I would really like that," said Walter.

"Anyway, I need to go hang with my friends. I hope to see you around," smiled Abby, as she walked toward her friends.

As she disappeared into the busy crowd, Walter began searching for Randall. He returned to the picnic table, but Randall wasn't sitting there. "I wonder where that boy is," Walter said to himself. After looking for several minutes, he found Randall talking to his sister and her friends.

"Randall, what are you doing?" said Walter.

"I ran into Mallie and her friends, and we began chatting," said Randall.

"Oh, well, I've been looking for you. Mallie, did you just get here?" said Walter while looking at his sister.

"We were just asking Randall if there was anything fun here. He told us we should try out the Ferris wheel," said Mallie.

"Well, carry on. I'll see you at home later," Walter said. Randall and Walter said goodbye to Mallie and her friend. The four of them separated. Walter and Randall returned to the picnic table, and Mallie and Sarah ventured over to the Ferris wheel.

Walter and Randall sat at the picnic table, listening to music, for almost another hour. They were ready to return home, but the boys wanted to take a Ferris wheel ride before they left. They wandered over to the red-and-white ride named after the creator, George Ferris. And as luck would have it for Walter, Abby was standing in the back of the line. This time, she was not alone, but with a friend. The friend was just as cute as Abby, but with blond hair.

Without even hesitating, Randall initiated a conversation. "Well, hello there, ladies. Beautiful night, isn't it?" Randall said toward the girls.

Both of them turned toward him. "It sure is. My name is Martha, and this is my friend Abby," the girl with blond hair said.

Of course, Randall took charge and introduced him and Walter.

While Randall was busy trying to impress Martha, Walter said to Abby, "It seems that you're following me."

"Well, it would actually appear that *you're* following me. I was standing in line before you."

"Well, I guess great minds think alike?"

"Oh, are you saying that I'm great?" Abby said while looking into Walter's eyes.

"You're great in some ways. I mean, you can't be great at everything. Especially tossing balls into small cups."

"You've only seen me in a crowd. I'm so much better one-on-one," said Abby.

"Is that a challenge?" asked Walter.

"You seem smart enough to figure it out," said Abby as she gave Walter a half-smile.

Walter and Abby playfully talked to each other until it was time to hop on the Ferris wheel. There was one last buggy that had room for four people, so Randall, Martha, Walter, and Abby jumped on the Ferris wheel together. It seemed like the stars were aligning.

The four young adults continued with their conversation on the Ferris wheel. Trying to impress the young ladies, Walter and Randall bragged about their tennis accomplishments. "Do you remember that time we won nationals in Nashville?" Randall asked Walter.

"Are you kidding me? Of course I do! We came back to win the match," Walter said.

"Was that a great match or what? We almost received a bid to the US Open because of it. I guess that win just wasn't convincing enough," said Randall.

Walter and Randall might have won a state title together and might have been damn good tennis players, but they never won any national tournaments, nor were they close to gaining any entry into the US Open. They were like any other guys just trying to impress a couple of cute girls.

Before he knew it, the ride ended. The two groups said bye to each other. As Walter and Randall headed toward Walter's car, Walter heard a distant voice in the background. "Wait up," said Abby.

Walter turned around and saw Abby walking toward them. He was again giddy as a little boy on Christmas morning. "What are you doing right now? Martha and I wanted to see if you boys want to come over to my house? We'll have a fire and share stories," said Abby.

Walter couldn't believe it, and he didn't waste any time confirming that he would come.

"Awesome! I'll see you in a few minutes. I live at 2234 Shady Grove road. It's the big yellow house behind Millener Farms."

CHAPTER 4

When Walter and Randall arrived, Abby and Martha were waiting for them on the front porch. Walter stepped out of his car, and Abby raced to meet him.

"I have to check with my parents to make sure we're allowed, but it should be fine. I'll meet you in the back of my house," said Abby.

While Abby and Martha vanished inside, the boys walked up the long driveway. Walter couldn't help but notice the large house Abby lived in. It was a yellow Victorian. "This must be the biggest house in Arlington Heights, huh, sport?" Randall said as he tapped Walter on the shoulder.

"It must be. I've never seen a house so big," said Walter.

After thinking for a few moments, Walter turned to Randall and said, "I wonder if Abby is James Millener's granddaughter. They live right behind Millener Farms, and she does live in a big house."

Randall nodded to Walter and said that it was plausible.

"It's more than plausible," Walter said to himself.

James Millener was an icon of Arlington Heights, Ohio. It was debatable that Mr. Millener was more powerful than the governor of Ohio. He was the first mayor of Arlington Heights and owned most of the land in the town. Along with all the land he owned, James Millener also owned many businesses around Columbus and

Arlington Heights. These businesses ranged from restaurants to shipping companies.

Finally, after the long walk up the fifty-yard driveway and to the back of the house, Walter and Randall arrived; they didn't even break a sweat. Abby and Martha were there to greet them.

"My parents said that we can build a fire in our pit. They did tell me that the boys need to be gone by midnight."

"That won't be a problem. I'm glad your parents are allowing us to be here," said Walter.

The four of them began gathering logs, leaves, and sticks to place in the firepit. While the boys were gathering logs and sticks, Martha and Abby grabbed two benches from the shed. When the girls returned with the benches, the fire was big and strong and reached about four feet into the night sky.

Abby and Martha put the two benches down by the fire, and they each sat on one. Walter squatted on the bench next to Abby, and Randall sat down next to Martha.

"So, boys, I assume you go to Arlington Heights High School," said Martha.

"Well, we did. We just graduated a few weeks ago. We were on the tennis team together," said Randall.

"Yes, and you were the best players on the team, and no one in Ohio could ever come close to beating the great Randall and Walter," said Martha.

"Something like that," said Walter. "We worked hard and put ourselves in a position to be great."

"Who's better, you or Randall?" asked Abby.

"Walter is a little better," said Randall.

The fire began to decrease in size, and all that was left were ashes rising in the night sky. "I'll get some more logs, sticks, and whatever I can find," Randall said. He then stood up from the bench and went on to say, "Martha, do you want to come with me?" Martha proceeded to walk with Randall to find sticks near the Walker house.

Walter Wilson sat alone with Abby Walker. As the fire was dwindling, Abby became cold, so she curled up as close as possible to Walter. Walter's reaction to her movement was to place his arm around her and bring her even closer to him.

"I hope you know that I wasn't talking about the night when I mentioned the word *beautiful* at the fair earlier," said Walter.

"I know you weren't."

"So what do you think I was talking about?" Walter asked.

"I think we've played enough games for one night. And besides, you know I'm not very good at games."

Walter smiled and put his arm tighter around Abby. "God, you are so beautiful."

Abby looked at him with a stare full of happiness. She lowered her head back down and rested it on his shoulders. The two young adults sat on the bench alone together until their friends came back with more sticks. "Well, this should do it," Randall said as he put a pile of rigid brown sticks in the firepit.

"Well, Randall, maybe we should have given them more time alone together," Martha said while smiling at Abby.

Randall leaned over to be closer to the new and improved fire. As his body became warmer from the vicinity to the fire, he responded to Martha's comment. "I'm with ya, Martha. Hey, sport, do you want Martha and me to look for logs in Cincinnati next time?" Randall said as he looked over in Walter's direction.

Walter laughed at his friend's joke. "I think that would be a good idea, Randall. I heard the logs are denser in southern Ohio. It could be better for maintaining a fire," said Walter.

"Oh, yeah, we learned about that in science class. The logs have increased density ratio per pound of log due to the warmer temperatures. Isn't that right, Walter?" said Randall while cracking a big smile.

"I think my legs are becoming restless. Abby, would you maybe want to walk around? You can show me around Millener Farms."

Abby stood up and said, "I would love to."

After leaving their friends by the firepit, Abby and Walter walked around Millener Farms. Millener Farms was a big but diverse plot of land. Millener Farms consisted of a farm, a tennis court, swimming pool, barn, and two houses. The tennis court and swimming pool were in between the two houses. Walter was curious about why two houses existed on Millener Farms. "Abby, why are there two houses on Millener Farms?"

"I should have explained it when you first arrived. I live in the yellow one, and my grandfather lives in the gray house on the edge of the property."

Walter hesitated before he responded, "Who is your grandfather? Is it James Millener?"

"Yeah, James Millener is my grandfather."

Walter had a mixed reaction when Abby told him James Millener was her grandfather. He enjoyed strolling around an elegant house, talking to Abby; however, he was intimidated by her family. Abby's family were some of the most influential people in town. For one, there was no doubt her parents would want her to date someone of elite stature, not some middle-class farm boy. Second, if they caught Walter sneaking around with Abby, there would be consequences.

The wealth of the Millener family was intimidating, but he was not going to let it dictate how he felt about Abby. He remained calm and asked her about James Millener and what it was like to grow up a Millener.

"So how does it feel to be the granddaughter of James Millener?"

"Honestly, it feels no different than anyone else's relationship with their grandfather." She wanted to change the subject, so she asked Walter about his tennis game. "So how did you end up becoming so good at tennis?"

Knowing it was going to be a long response, Walter took a couple of deep breaths and then answered her question. "Well, my father is the one who first got me involved in tennis. He put a racket in my hand at an early age and taught me everything I needed to know. From there, I was driven to become the best. I love to compete."

"Well, you are really good," said Abby.

"I'm actually not that talented. I may be good, but not as talented compared to a lot of people. You see, tennis is like a chess match. It's like a boxing match. You have to put your strengths up against your opponent's weaknesses. If you can do that, you have a chance to beat anyone who is far more talented than you," Walter said, even though he wasn't sure if Abby understood.

"So you're saying you should be a boxer," said Abby, grinning.

"That's exactly what I'm saying. James Braddock has nothing on me," said Walter. Walter was referring to the former heavyweight champion of the world.

"I think my grandfather may know him. Should I arrange that fight?" said Abby.

"Oh, boy, I don't think I'm ready." Walter laughed.

"I thought you said you loved to compete." Abby smiled.

"It wouldn't be much of a competition," Walter said, then sighed. "I know he's serving right now, but if he's not too busy, I would love to meet him after the war."

Walter got a lot of inspiration from James Braddock. He was the definition of a fighter, one who fought through injuries and poverty to become a champion. He was glad a man like that was representing the United States military, and was hoping that many soldiers had the same spirit as Braddock.

Even though Walter didn't want to talk anymore about tennis, the young man felt obligated to ask her why she played tennis. "How did you get into tennis?"

"Mom and Dad both play a bit, so they wanted me to learn. After I learned, it was something to do with my friends. It's just a social thing for me," she said.

While they were circling the big red barn, they heard horses coming from the stalls. Walter loved horses and enjoyed walking around the farm. He asked Abby what it was like to grow up on such a big farm.

"Ahh, it can be great at times, but you can feel isolated. I'm an only child, so it can get very lonely. It's a big house, it's a big piece of land, but it can become very quiet."

"That makes sense. The house I grew up in wasn't quite as big as this one," Walter said while chuckling.

Walter didn't want to talk about money and houses. It was something he didn't care too much about, at least not at this point in his life. The first thing he could think of was asking her about future plans, which became a mistake.

"So do you have any plans for the future? Will you go to college next year?" asked Walter.

"That's the plan. My dad has been gearing me up for school since I've been a little girl. He always has hired tutors to help me with my schoolwork. The expectations are high in my family," she said to Walter. Abby then asked what Walter had in mind in for the future.

"I was thinking about either going to college or joining the military and serving our country. We're in the middle of a war against the biggest tyrant in the history of mankind, and I believe I could be of help. But I've been going back and forth about whether to pull the trigger," said Walter.

"What's holding you back?"

"I've had dreams of playing college tennis. I know I'll go back to school even if I join the military, but I'm not sure I'd play tennis."

Abby didn't know what to think. She was starting to have feelings for him the more the night continued, yet she also almost ended the night with young Walter Wilson. It would have been hard for her to spend time with him and then see him go off to war, but she thought it could be possible that the more time they spent together, the more and more he would not want to join the fight against Hitler and the Nazis.

Just the thought about him going to war made her scared, and it was something that boggled her mind. Why was she scared? She had just met him. Whatever the reason happened to be, she grabbed his hand and held it tight. She didn't want to let go until the night was over.

While Abby grabbed Walter's hand, they were passing the tennis court built by James Millener. "So that's your own personal tennis court, huh?" asked Walter.

Abby nodded, saying, "Yes." She went on to say, while pointing in the direction beyond the tennis court, "And the pool's over there."

"That's quite a setup," said Walter. "Maybe I'll have to come over and give you a private tennis lesson," Walter said while smiling.

"I would really like that."

They continued to walk around Millener Farms. It was a perfect summer's night for a walk: stars shining bright, full moon on display, and a temperature that was just right.

Abby asked Walter about his favorite vacation. She wanted to ask him something other than his future.

"I would have to say going to my grandmother's lake house in Michigan. It's pretty much my favorite place in the world," said Walter. "What was your favorite vacation?"

"My grandfather has a house down in Florida. Do you know Naples, Florida?" asked Abby.

Walter shook his head, so she continued her story. "When I was a little girl, we would make a trip to Florida every year. My dad would take me to the beach for hours, and hours. I don't think I'll ever forget those memories."

After they talked about their favorite vacations, Walter thought he'd ask about her favorite movie. "I love *The Wizard of Oz*. I could watch that every day and wouldn't be tired of it."

"*The Wizard of Oz*, huh? Do you like it because you're as pretty as Dorothy?"

Abby blushed. She didn't answer the question but looked up at Walter and smiled. She wasn't used to many compliments. Most of the men she talked to believed they were too good to compliment her. Walter was different. Even though they had spent only one night together, she observed that he cared far more about his happiness and feelings than how much money he was worth. She liked that about him.

After walking around the farm for over an hour, Walter looked at his watch. It was almost midnight. "Abby, we probably should walk back to the firepit. It's almost midnight."

Abby shook her head, and she and Walter began walking in the direction of the firepit. When they reached the firepit, Abby and Walter noticed two things. The fire had burned out, and their friends were gone.

"I wonder where Martha and Randall went," said Abby.

"I'm not sure, but I bet they're all right. Maybe they both went home," said Walter.

It was just about midnight, so it was time for Walter to drive back to his house. While they were still holding hands, Abby walked Walter to his car down the long driveway. The walk down the driveway seemed too short for the both of them.

Once they arrived at the car, Walter hugged Abby goodbye. Before the hug was over, they shared a long and passionate kiss. "When can I see you next?" Walter asked.

"Not soon enough," Abby said with a smile.

CHAPTER 5

Abby came from money, and Walter did not. It seemed as if Abby was destined for college, and Walter was intrigued by the military. With those two contrasting ideas, it appeared as if the relationship was doomed from the start. And secretly, both of them knew it deep down but couldn't have cared less. After their time by the campfire, the two couldn't be separated.

Even though they were never apart, the two youths were seldom alone at the Walker house together. The only time the two were alone was when Walter was giving Abby a tennis lesson. Walter and Abby always wondered how Abby's parents didn't catch on during these tennis lessons. There was more flirting than hitting during the hour-long instruction.

During these tennis lessons, Walter had the pleasure of meeting Christopher and Ann Walker, Abby's parents. Mr. Walker insisted on watching every lesson. He tried giving Walter tips on how to coach, and advice for Abby on how to play. Walter wasn't pleased with his on-court presence, especially because Christopher Walker knew nothing about tennis. However, he never said anything to the man about his little knowledge of the game. He learned at a young age that sometimes it's best to just roll with the punches and fight the battles that are worth fighting. And correcting Mr. Walker on the tactics of tennis was hardly worth the fight.

Even though Walter wished Mr. Walker weren't present to watch his tennis instruction, he was able to learn a lot about the character of Christopher Walker. Abby's father wanted her to strive to be the best at everything. Walter looked at Mr. Walker's view another way: nothing was ever good enough for this man regarding his daughter. For example, Abby knifed a backhand winner down the line, and her father thought it could have been a better shot. "Abigail, you could have managed to hit that shot closer to the line," said Mr. Walker.

When Mr. Walker made that statement, it was hard to envision Walter would ever be good enough for Abby's father. He grew up in a modest middle-class family, nowhere near the standards of the Walkers or Milleners, the family that founded Arlington Heights, Ohio.

When they were not playing tennis together, Abby and Walter were hanging around Randall and Martha. The four of them would play tennis and then go swimming afterward. They played tennis and swam so much they coined the term "tennis and swimming exhibition." Abby's parents caught on during these "tennis and swimming exhibitions." After the third or fourth exhibition, Mr. Walker would stand by the window with his tobacco pipe and watch his daughter swim with young Walter Wilson. It seemed as if every time Walter glanced up at the window, Abby's father was staring at him. Walter wasn't sure whether the stare was that of "I'm going to hurt you if you touch my daughter" or "What is going on between this farm boy and my daughter?"

As Mr. Walker discovered the courtship, it became evident that he didn't appreciate Walter in his daughter's life. Whenever the two would talk, Mr. Walker would keep the conversations short and cold. Christopher Walker's body language wasn't any more positive; Abby's father would never smile. To make matters worse for Walter, Randall tried hard to impress Mr. Walker whenever he had the opportunity. One time, while Mr. Walker was waxing Abby's Mercury Deluxe, Randall said to him, "Abby's really lucky she has a father who waxes her car. I actually wax my own car."

And from that showboat comment forward, Mr. Walker was always respectful to Randall. Whenever the boys came to pick up the girls, Christopher Walker would say, "It's always nice to see you, Randall," while shaking his hand. There was no handshake of any kind to Walter. One time, Mr. Walker even let Randall drive his brand-new Cadillac LaSalle to the cinema.

Although Mr. Walker didn't like the thought of Walter and his daughter dating, he never prohibited his daughter from seeing Walter. Abby was even allowed to invite him to her lake house at Buckeye Lake for a weekend. This lake was an hour away from the city, and the Walkers spent time there to get away for the weekend. Columbus might have been a small city, but it was always nice fleeing for a nice, quiet weekend away from all the hustle and bustle.

When she learned about her lake trip, Abby invited Randall and Martha for the weekend. The four of them left on a Friday afternoon once Randall and Walter were finished teaching tennis. They might have driven by themselves, but they were met at the lake house by Abby's parents.

Walter drove his black Ford Coupe, and he pulled up to the lake around seven o'clock in the evening. The house was a two-story cottage and had a wraparound front porch looking over the lake. In the back of the house was a two-room shack where the help would sometimes stay. That shack would be Walter and Randall's quarters for the weekend. Mr. Walker was old-fashioned, and he didn't believe that single boys should be staying under the same roof as single girls.

As soon as Walter and Randall placed their bags in the garage apartment, they raced to the front of the house. "This is going to be a great weekend!" said Walter.

The two of them wandered out to the dock in front of the house. "Someday, I'm going to have a house on this lake," said Randall, gazing into the lake.

"Yeah, it sure is beautiful," said Walter.

Once the boys were finished looking at the lake, Randall and Walter ventured into the main house. Everyone was already sitting down in the dining room, waiting for dinner. Walter sat down in the smooth wooden chair next to Abby, and Randall sat next to Martha. Right after Walter and Randall sat down, Mrs. Walker carried the food to the table.

Mrs. Walker cooked chicken, broccoli, and mashed potatoes. As everyone was passing the food around the round wooden table, Abby realized that this was the first time Walter had been in a formal setting with her father. Even if Walter didn't know what he was in for, she certainly did. Christopher was going to see what this boy was made of tonight. Abby knew that her father would interrogate Walter on the same level a detective does to a suspect.

"Well, Walter, what are your plans for the fall?" asked Mr. Walker.

After a deep breath, Walter said, "I'm thinking about joining the military. But I'm not quite sure. I do have a college offer to play tennis at Ohio Wesleyan, but I want to serve my country. And honestly, sir, I'm not sure I'm ready for college just yet."

Mr. Walker took another sip of his red wine and leaned back in his chair. He was like a judge ready to deliberate his opinion. "Well, young man, I think you are plenty ready for college. It just takes some discipline."

"Well, I think it took a lot of discipline to win a state championship," said Walter.

"That's a different kind of discipline."

"How is it different?" Walter asked with a rather-impolite tone. He wanted to use more of a sarcastic pitch, but it wasn't worth it. Abby wouldn't have been happy, and plus, he already knew the answer. He was just baiting Mr. Walker into saying something along the lines of "intelligence discipline" versus "physical discipline."

"Oh, never mind, son, never mind," said Mr. Walker.

Walter didn't push it but didn't quite understand, because he thought of all his achievements from state tennis champion to scholar athlete. Walter just had one thing that was a blemish to Mr. Walker: his parents didn't have money.

"Who wants dessert?" Mrs. Walker asked.

Serving dessert prevented a standoff between Walter and Mr. Walker. Ann Walker got up from the table and went into the kitchen. Not long after, Abby jumped up from her chair and raced into the kitchen. "Mom, I need to talk to you."

"What is it, dear?" asked Abby's mother as she was slicing the cake.

"Why is Dad acting like this?" Abby asked in a very upset tone.

"Your father is just trying to do what's best for you. You'll understand someday," said Ann, who desperately wanted to end the conversation.

"But, Mom."

"I'm finished with this conversation, young lady. Talk to your father after dinner," said Mrs. Walker as she was walking back into the dining room with the chocolate cake.

As she was already upset with her father, she became disappointed with her mother. Her father was lashing out at Walter, and her mom would do nothing about it. In Abby's eyes, she was just as guilty as her father.

It had been an exhausting day, and all four of them wanted to wake up bright and early to take advantage of the lake. When dinner adjourned, Walter kissed Abby good night and he and Randall walked across the road to the shack that was called the guesthouse.

Walter needed something to lighten the mood, so he looked in the refrigerator and noticed it was stocked with Pabst Blue Ribbon beer. Randall saw the PBRs, too, and cracked open two cans of beer, handing one to Walter. "Here ya go, buddy. You really need one of these after a dinner like that," said Randall.

"I'm glad it wasn't just me who could tell the guy was such an ass. You have permission to beat me if I ever act like that when we have children," said Walter.

Walter and Randall began drinking their PBRs and talking about how much fun they would have on the lake tomorrow. Suddenly, Randall heard something from outside. It sounded like Abby's voice. He walked closer to the window. Abby and her father were talking between the guesthouse and the lake house. Walter heard it as well, so he ventured over to the window next to Randall.

"Abby, what are you doing dating Walter?" Mr. Walker asked Abby. "I am not thrilled you are seeing a boy like him."

Abby was upset by the line of questioning but wasn't going to back down. "A guy like what?" she said.

"Do I need to spell it out for you? He's not like us. He will always be a no-name middle-class person. You, my daughter, are better than that," said Mr. Walker.

"Well, I don't really care what you think," Abby said toward her father.

Both Mr. Walker and Abby were astonished that she spoke to him in such a condescending tone. He paused for a moment before responding. "You're going to get in a lot of trouble talking to me like that. I'm a very understanding person, but this is not how I wish my daughter speaking to me."

"Understanding?" Abby said. "Do you understand...that I'm in love with him? I don't care who he is or how much money he can make. I'm happy with him, and that's all I really care about."

Abby couldn't believe that she told her father she was in love with Walter. It just slipped out. Mr. Walker was just as surprised by Abby's statement, so he just went back into the house. Time was a necessity to him, and he needed to sleep on the conversation. After Mr. Walker went into the house, Abby stayed a few more minutes outside. As she looked up at the garage apartment, she realized the magnitude of her words.

Abby returned to the house, allowing Walter and Randall to take a step back from the window. They heard every word of the conversation between Abby and Mr. Walker. "Honestly, Randall, I don't know what to say," Walter said.

Randall took a seat on the bed because he could tell it would be a long conversation. "How do you feel about her, sport?" he asked.

"I don't know. I really, really like her. I just don't know if it's love. I don't know what love is," Walter said, sounding stressed out.

On one hand, he really liked her and hadn't had stronger feelings toward anyone before in his life. On the other hand, he was contemplating joining the military and didn't want to break her heart.

Randall wanted to help his friend. "Walter, I think you're just scared," said Randall. "I think you just don't trust many people, especially girls."

"I wonder why that is," Walter said.

"Maybe it's because of your mom. You've never trusted her, so you may be skeptical of girls. I wouldn't let that dictate your feelings about everyone, though. You should go for it, sport," said Randall, tapping Walter on the shoulder.

"Ahh, you may be right."

"I know I'm right," Randall said.

"Well, I have a confession to make. Ever since I've been hanging around Abby, I've been less and less motivated to become a pilot."

"Really?" asked Randall.

"It's the most dangerous job in the military. I want to help out, but not in combat. Maybe I'll join the National Guard or something," said Walter. "Do you think that makes me a coward?"

"Absolutely not. You're one of the bravest people I know. And you still want to serve your country," said Randall.

"Thank you, Randall."

"Do I hear wedding bells?" asked Randall, laughing.

"Let's not jump ahead of ourselves. But maybe someday. I'm not sure Mr. Walker would be too thrilled about the idea as we are," said Walter while smiling.

The two boys finished their serious conversation and then went to bed. While Walter was falling asleep, he couldn't help but think about how excited he was for his future. He realized that he was in love with Abby. The last thing that entered Walter's mind before he went to sleep was the thought of telling Abby about his plans not to become a pilot. He couldn't wait to see her face light up when she heard the news. Walter was actually surprised he was able to fall asleep, considering his excitement level was at an all-time high.

The next morning, Walter woke up and jumped out of bed. He looked at the top bunk and didn't see Randall. Walter stepped into a pair of shorts, threw on a shirt, and opened the door.

"Good morning, son," said Mr. Walker.

Mr. Walker was sitting in a lawn chair and relaxing like it was the Fourth of July. Abby's father was reading the newspaper in his hands, and had a tobacco pipe in his mouth.

"Top of the morning to you, sir," said Walter.

"Yes, yes. It's a beautiful morning. I love coming to this lake," said Christopher Walker. "Does your family have a lake house?"

"No, sir," said Walter.

"I'm sorry to hear that, son. I'm from the East Coast, and we had a beach house. And Mrs. Walker grew up on this lake," said Mr. Walker.

"That must have been nice."

Walter couldn't have cared less whether the man grew up in the king of Scotland's palace. He wanted to end the conversation so he could enjoy time with Mr. Walker's daughter.

"Yes, it was nice. Both of our families have power and influence," Mr. Walker said while looking at Walter in the eye. "Well, have a good time."

If something looked like a duck, quacked like a duck, and waddled like a duck, odds were it was a duck. The same paralleled with Mr. Walker's conversation. It looked like a threat, smelled like a threat, and sounded like a threat. It was definitely a threat, and so Walter said good day to Mr. Walker as fast as a speeding bullet and got out of dodge. And before he knew it, Walter was standing in the kitchen next to Abby. He didn't want to worry her, so he didn't mention his conversation with Mr. Walker.

"Good morning," said Abby. "We cooked you and Randall breakfast today."

Walter looked at the food sitting on the dining room table. Everything looked so delicious, and he could smell the chocolate chips melting onto the pancakes.

"You remembered I like chocolate chip pancakes," said Walter.

"Of course I did. How could I forget?" said Abby. "I'm teasing you. Don't get mad, but it was just a coincidence!"

"I can't get mad at you after making me breakfast," said Walter as he took a bite.

The four of them scarfed down the breakfast in order to spend more time on the lake. It couldn't have been a more beautiful day to spend on the water. The sun was shining bright, the skies were blue, and the water was warm.

Fishing was first activity the four of them decided to try. Abby claimed that the fish nibbled more in the morning. However, that could not have been further from the truth when the teenagers cast their rods. The fish didn't take many bites on the worm, and Martha was the only person to catch fish. "Should we cook it for dinner?" asked Martha after she reeled in a bass.

"No. Catch and release. In honor of the fish," Randall said as he took it off the hook and threw it back in the water.

Once they were done fishing, the four of them went canoeing. Abby's family owned two canoes, so Abby and Walter shared one and Martha and Randall shared the other canoe. They paddled to a little channel located in the island of the lake.

It might have been a long canoe trip to the island, but the channel in the island was gorgeous. The channel consisted of rocks and lily pads. Many turtles were sunbathing on several of the large rocks. Some of them were snapping turtles, and some were hardbacks. The hardback turtles were very colorful, and they had a number of different colors naturally painted on their chest. The surrounding of the channel added on to the beauty. Several houses were in this little channel. The array of houses consisted of small and big houses, and a few of the houses were shaped in the letter A and were called A-frame houses.

Abby looked at the A-frame house and said, "I want to live in a house like that someday. It's shaped in an A for *Abby*."

"Well, you can live in the A-shaped house by yourself," said Walter.

"Hey! That's not very nice," said Abby.

"It's too small with the way the house is shaped." Walter laughed.

Abby smiled, and the lake crew paddled back to the house for the last activity of the day, swimming. Swimming was saved for last because, as Randall pointed out, you gotta save the best for last.

The water was perfect; it was clear with a blue tint and maintained a temperature of about eighty degrees. It was so perfect that the four of them swam until it was dusk. In the Walker summer home, the custom was that dusk signaled suppertime.

As dusk arrived, the four of them climbed out of the lake onto the dock. Abby and Martha walked into the main house to get ready for dinner. While Abby was walking into the cottage, she looked back at Randall and Walter, who were trembling slowly around the house. "Meet us in the main house when you're ready for dinner," said Abby.

When Abby was finished changing, she came out of her room. Her mom was walking out of the door and was wearing a nice formal dress.

"Mama, where are you going?" asked Abby.

"Your father and I are having dinner in town. There is chicken that you can cook, dear."

"Okay. I'll see you later," Abby said.

"Don't get into any trouble," Abby's mom said as she left the house.

After talking with her mom, Abby looked in the refrigerator for food. "Check," she muttered to herself, confirming there was plenty of food for tonight. She had started getting the food out of the cabinet and refrigerator when Walter grabbed her from behind.

"What's cookin', good lookin'?" said Walter, wrapping his arms around Abby.

Abby turned around and kissed him on the lips. She almost forgot that he asked a question—the kiss felt so good. "Just prepping for dinner. We're by ourselves tonight. Mom and Dad are eating in town," said Abby.

"How about that! I didn't think there would be a snowball's chance in hell that Mr. Walker would leave his daughter alone with a charming young man such as myself."

"He loves his whiskey, and there is none in the house. He's willing to take a chance," said Abby as she gave him a wink.

"I better not mess up, or I will never see you again. Hell, I'll never see the light of day again," said Walter. "Anyway, where is the grill? I'll get it started."

Even though he laughed at his joke, he was serious, especially rewinding his earlier conversation with Mr. Walker. If Walter so far as blinked the wrong way, Mr. Walker would ship him to a place like Timbuktu.

It took about an hour to make dinner and less than the snap of fingers to eat it. Everyone was practically starving. "This chicken is awesome, boys!" said Abby.

Walter thanked her for the compliment. He went on to say, while smiling, "Grilling is the only way I'll make dinner. The rest of the time, it's all you."

"Does that seem fair?" asked Abby.

"More than fair." Walter smiled. "Most men won't even do that."

"Fair enough," said Abby while smiling.

When the four friends were done eating, Walter asked, "What's next on the agenda?"

"Let's see…we could go night swimming," said Abby.

"Isn't it too dark? Won't that be dangerous?" asked Martha.

"Martha, come on! It will be fun. There's no danger in swimming at night," said Randall. "Lakes don't have sharks."

"Okay, fine."

Martha agreed, and the four of them changed into their bathing suits and met at the dock. Once they were all there, Walter and Randall sprinted down the long wooden dock and dived headfirst into the water. When Walter popped his head above the surface after his leap, he noticed that the girls were still standing on land.

"What are you waiting for? Are you waiting for summer to end?" Walter asked.

"Hey! We're coming. Don't rush us!" shouted Abby.

Not more than a minute passed before the girls jumped into the water. Abby reached the surface of the water and started shivering. "It's colder now than during the daytime."

"Well, aren't you the rocket scientist today!" said Randall.

Walter swam over to Abby and put his arms around her in the water. "Here, I hope I can make you warmer."

"You always make me warmer," she said while smiling.

They put their arms around each other and began kissing. Abby and Walter were like two peas in a pod, and Martha and Randall didn't seem to care about their open affection.

It was pretty evident Martha and Randall didn't care about their friends' romance in the water, but Mr. Walker cared. He must have had a trait of impeccable timing, because he stood at the end of the dock a few minutes after Abby and Walter began kissing each other.

"Fun time is over!" shouted Mr. Walker, who was stumbling around.

Mr. Walker was drunk. Everyone could smell the whiskey from his breath. He was drunk, and he was mad. The combination of gasoline and fire isn't as explosive as Mr. Walker's mood was that night.

"Dad, we are getting out of the water," said Abby.

"That would be a wise decision. It would also be a wise decision to not waste any time. I'm turning in for the night, and I expect everyone to be in bed in the next ten minutes," Mr. Walker said as he walked into his house.

Abby, Martha, Walter, and Randall climbed out of the water. Walter and Randall began walking toward their hut when Abby stopped them. "Walter!"

Walter stopped to see what Abby wanted from him, while Randall kept on walking toward their assigned bedrooms. "Yes, sweetheart?" said Walter.

"Meet me at the end of the dock in an hour."

Walter put his arms around Abby and said, "I think we should just say good night right here."

Abby kissed him on the lips for a second and started walking toward her house. As she was walking in the side door, she looked at him and said, "I'll see you in an hour."

Walter returned to the guest quarters. He saw his bed, and it looked appealing. He was exhausted after a long day on the lake. Plus, he didn't want to further anger Mr. Walker. He certainly didn't have that luxury. "Maybe I should just sleep instead. I'm sure Abby will understand," he said to himself.

While Walter was sitting on his bed, Randall was pulling the covers over himself. "Sport, aren't you getting some shut-eye?" asked Randall.

"Apparently, Abby wants me to meet her on the dock soon."

"Well, looks like someone will lose his virginity tonight," Randall said with a huge grin on his face.

Walter was quick to shoot down that suggestion. Of course he wanted to make love to Abby, but he didn't want to rush anything. "No, not tonight. But soon, real soon. So do you think I should meet her?"

"Does the pope preach in the Vatican?" Randall smiled.

"Of course," said Walter.

"Then you should go, sport. It's not even something to think about," said Randall. "But I'm getting some sleep. Good luck."

Randall fell asleep, and Walter was forced to pass the time alone, which was hard. He succeeded in staying awake and walked over to the dock. Walter arrived a few minutes after Abby did. As he was approaching the wooden pier, Walter saw Abby lying under a blanket. Once he was close to her, Walter said, "Hey, beautiful. Long time no see."

"Hi. I wasn't sure if you would actually come," said Abby.

"Of course I would come. I can never turn down a chance to spend time with you," said Walter.

He knelt down on the dock to lie with her. Walter smelled the same scent he sensed at the community fair, a combination of tulips and roses. *God, she looks so beautiful tonight,* Walter thought to himself. She was wearing her dark-purple nightgown and had her hair straight down. It seemed as if she was glowing. He wrapped his arms around her.

"I missed you," said Abby.

"I missed you too. But you saw me an hour ago," said Walter.

"I know. I have to give you a big hug and kiss since I haven't seen you in a very, very long time," Abby said into his ear.

They proceeded to lie next to each on the pier and talk for hours. It was a beautiful night. The sky was clear, so they were able to see the moon and stars. Nothing could be better.

After a while, Abby kissed him on the forehead. Before she knew it, her mouth opened and her lips began to move. "I love you."

Walter's eyes became big and wide, and he smiled. He was so happy that she expressed her feelings toward him. Right away, he responded with, "I love you too."

For Walter, the whole night, and the whole relationship, seemed surreal. Just weeks ago, he was watching her from afar hit a forehand at Beechum Park. The moment he saw those beautiful blue eyes, he knew she was special, and was on a quest to find out why. He found out why, all right: she was fun, beautiful, smart, and kind. Once Walter discovered what made her special, he didn't want to spend a day without her. And he had hoped Abby felt the same way.

Even though this was the happiest she had been in a while, Abby started feeling sad. She realized he would be enlisting to become a pilot soon, and she didn't want him to fight over in Europe. She looked up and said, "We hugged for a while when we didn't see each other for an hour. Can you imagine how long we will hold on to each other when you're back from the Army? I'll never want to let you go again."

"We won't be hugging for very long," Walter said with a smirk on his face.

"What do you mean? You won't want to see me?" she asked.

"I don't want to become a pilot anymore. Don't get me wrong, I want to serve my country, but in another way. I want to join the National Guard."

Abby couldn't believe it. She was stunned. She thought it was too good to be true and that maybe she was in a dream.

"Are you serious?" Abby said. "Why did you change your mind?"

"I'm so serious. And I changed my mind because I love my country but I love you more. I found a way to help my country and be with you at the same time."

"That makes me so happy! You have no idea," said Abby.

Walter had an idea of how happy his decision made her. The joy of his announcement could be seen through a smile on her face and the glow in her eyes. The biggest indicator of her happiness was that she couldn't stop kissing him. They kissed for hours, until they fell asleep together.

It was almost dawn, and the sun was beginning to rise over the lake. Diamonds could be seen forming over the water. Abby and Walter were still asleep on the dock. Abby suddenly woke up and realized her parents would be awake soon. She nudged Walter, saying, "Get up! We have to get back. My parents may wake up soon, and we would be dead if they caught us."

Both of them didn't want to be caught, so they began walking toward the house. Walter jetted off and climbed back into bed. He hoped Mr. Walker did not wake up.

Abby did the same and attempted to reach her room undetected. As she was walking in the front door, her father was waiting for her on the porch. "Where have you been, young lady?" Mr. Walker asked.

"Uhhhh," she mumbled, as no words came out of her mouth.

"I saw you two out by the pier. There will be consequences. Get some rest," said Mr. Walker.

Abby listened to her father and went upstairs to bed. She couldn't help but wonder what her father meant when he said *consequences*. Before she fell asleep, she made the decision not to tell Walter about the encounter with her father. He would be too worried, and she didn't want to ruin the special night that they had had together.

The next morning, the four young adults ate breakfast and enjoyed the lake for the remainder of the trip. After some fun in the sun, they loaded up the car and left for Columbus. Everyone had a fun weekend, especially Abby and Walter. Both of them discovered that their relationship was special. They could enjoy the rest of the summer, as Walter decided against becoming a pilot.

CHAPTER 6

Several weeks had passed since the trip to the lake. Abby's relationship with Walter was blossoming, yet she was worried. She wasn't worried about her connection with Walter but with what her father had mentioned to her at the lake house. He had made a remark about "consequences." What worried Abby the most was that she knew something would happen, but she didn't know when and what. That absolutely terrified her.

However, she could not focus on the past, and she certainly couldn't worry about what was out of her control. It was the Fourth of July, and she was invited to the Wilson house for dinner. After dinner, Walter and Abby planned to watch the community fireworks at Beechum Park. She couldn't have imagined a better Fourth of July.

Abby was expected at Walter's around 5:30 p.m., so she began getting ready around 4:00 p.m. She hopped in the shower and did her makeup and hair. She was almost dressed when her mom knocked on the door. "Are you almost ready, dear?" her mom asked in a soft voice.

"Just give me a moment," said Abby. Mrs. Walker said okay and walked downstairs to wait for her daughter.

When Abby came downstairs in a blue sundress, her parents had a feeling that she would not be part of their plans. "What's the occasion for dressing up? We're just going to the neighbors and then the fireworks," said Mr. Walker, smoking tobacco through his wooden pipe.

"I'm actually having dinner with Walter and his family. I'll probably meet you at the fireworks," Abby said to her parents.

"Oh, when were you planning on running this by us?" asked Mr. Walker. "I have half of my mind telling me to not let you go."

"I'm practically an adult. I think I can make my own plans," said Abby.

Christopher Walker was not amused by his daughter's sassy attitude, and it infuriated him. He took his tobacco pipe out of his mouth. "You're not an adult, and you still live under my house. I am still your father, and you will obey me."

"Oh yeah? What are you going to do about it, Christopher?"

"What did you just call me, young lady?" shouted Christopher Walker.

"Christopher—isn't that your name?" Abby smirked.

Mrs. Walker looked at her daughter, then turned to her husband. She desperately wanted to prevent a standoff between her husband and only daughter. "Chris, she should be allowed out with Walter," said Mrs. Walker. "Sweetheart, have fun tonight. Hopefully, we will see you at the fireworks."

Abby's mom was more levelheaded than her father. Mrs. Walker knew that it was important to pick and choose the battles, and not letting her daughter spend time with her boyfriend was not a battle she wished to fight.

As the conversation with her parents ended, she raced over to Walter's house. She couldn't wait to see him. She had yet to meet Walter's parents, so she was full of jitters. Abby was either 90 percent excited and 10 percent scared, or 90 percent scared and 10 percent excited, but she couldn't figure out which way the scale dropped.

She arrived at the small brick house on Edington Road and was walking up the driveway. The door opened, and Abby was hoping it was Walter. However, to her dismay, it was his mom and sister. "I'm Walter's mom. And this is his sister, Mallie. You can call me Allison," Mrs. Wilson said. She was wearing an apron.

"It's nice to meet you too. I've heard so much about you."

"Come on in! Walter and his father are out back, grilling," Alison said.

Abby walked in the door with Mallie and Mrs. Wilson, and her nerves were washed away like pebbles on a beach. They were nice and gave her a tour of the house. It was much smaller than the house she grew up in, but much cozier.

When the tour was finished, Abby sat down at the table with Walter's sister and mom. "So, Abby, what year are you in school?" Walter's mom asked.

"I'll be a senior," said Abby.

"Do you attend Arlington Heights High School?"

"No. I go to Oakhaven School for Girls. I really like it there," said Abby, hoping that they did not think she was a snob for attending a private school.

"That's a really good school. I've heard nothing but good things," said Allison.

Abby was relieved that Allison Wilson was accepting of her private school education. When some people discovered she went to a private school, they thought differently of her, and most of the time, different was never positive.

Before Mallie could get in a word to Abby, Walter and his father walked in with the chicken. "That looks so good," said Mallie.

Mr. Wilson put the plate of grilled chicken on the table and walked over toward Abby. "You must be Abby. Walter has told me all about you. I'm Bill, Walter's father."

"It's really nice to meet you. Walter also told me so much about you as well," said Abby as she shook Mr. Wilson's hand.

The five of them ate dinner and had a pleasant conversation. It was nothing like the dinner Walter endured at the Walker lake house. Walter's family asked Abby all kinds of questions, from how she liked playing tennis to what her favorite books were to read. At no point in time did they ask what her plans were in the future. Walter's mom did ask if she planned on having children, which made Abby uncomfortable. She was practically a child herself. Abby responded to that question by saying, "I'm seventeen. I haven't really thought about it. I would like to, though, eventually."

Abby wanted to make an effort to get to know Walter's family, so she began talking to Mallie, who was sitting in the seat next to her. "So, Mallie, how old are you?" asked Abby.

"Seventeen. I'm a year younger than Walter."

"How has your summer been so far?" asked Abby.

"It's good. I've been swimming a lot and spending time with my friends," said Mallie. She went on to say, "How has your summer been?"

"It's been the best summer so far. I've been spending time with your brother, I've been swimming, and I've been playing tennis," said Abby.

"I bet you've spent a lot of time with Randall, then. They aren't apart very often," said Mallie.

"Yeah, he's really funny. We haven't seen him much in the last week. I think he's spending more time with my friend Martha, but I'm not sure," said Abby.

"Yeah, maybe," Mallie said, sounding that she wasn't convinced by Abby's theory. "Are you sad that Walter will become a pilot at the end of the summer?"

Walter caught Mallie's last comment and realized that he forgot to tell his family about his decision. Walter stood up and raised his water glass. "Everyone, I've decided not to become a pilot. I'll be joining the National Guard instead."

"I'm so glad, Walter!" Mallie said. Mallie had always looked up to Walter as a role model and didn't want him leaving.

"Are you sure this is what you want, son?" asked Bill Wilson.

"I am certain. I've never been more sure."

"Well, we are proud of you, no matter what you decide," Allison Wilson said.

Walter didn't acknowledge his mother's comment; instead, he brushed it off. He acted like she didn't exist. It was normal for Walter to ignore his mother, so his family failed to notice. Although Abby noticed and was confused as to why Walter could be so distant toward the woman that carried him in a womb.

It was getting late, and the fireworks were scheduled to launch in ninety minutes. Abby and Walter were about ready to depart the

Wilson home when Mrs. Wilson stepped out of the kitchen with apple pie. The dining room smelled like fresh cinnamon and ripe apples. Abby and Walter couldn't leave quite yet; the dessert looked too good to pass up.

"Do you want to stay for dessert?" Alison Wilson asked. "It's Granny Nanny's recipe," Alison went on to say, referring to her mother's pie recipe. Walter and Abby both looked at each other and agreed to delay the drive to the fireworks.

"I never asked, What are your plans tonight?" said Mr. Wilson as he looked at young Abigail.

"I think," Walter started saying, until his father cut him off.

"I'm not talking to you, son. I was asking Abby," said Mr. Wilson.

"I think we're going to the fireworks. We may meet up with my parents. And then I'm not sure what we will do," said Abby.

"That's a good plan. We may see you at the fireworks. We would love to meet your parents," said Bill.

"They would really like that," said Abby.

That last remark was a lie, and Abby knew it as soon as the words left her tongue. Abby's parents had no desire at all to meet Walter's parents. They would rather have a meeting with the queen of Sheba.

As Walter took his last bite of apple pie, he and Abby stood up and walked out the door and into the beautiful July night. The couple was about to drive off when Bill came sprinting down the driveway like a madman. Walter rolled down the window of his Ford Coupe and asked what his father wanted. "One last thing. Can you keep an eye on Mallie tonight? I think she's watching the fireworks with some young man tonight," Bill said.

"Yeah. I'll keep an eye on her. I'll see you later."

Beechum Park was busy with patriotic people, so they had to park a few blocks away. Walter parked and opened the door for Abby. "You're such a gentleman, opening the door for me."

"My princess deserves nothing but the best," Walter said with a smirk across his face as they walked toward the park.

Showing up at the fireworks in Arlington Heights was close to mandatory. The Fourth of July festivities included fireworks, music, and food. There was a live band at the center of the park. It was similar to the community fair, but it was a bigger event.

One of the first things that caught Abby's and Walter's eye was a station selling cold beer. They picked up a couple of beers and walked around the park. While they were walking around the park, the first person that they bumped into was Randall's mom, Nancy. She gave Walter a hug and said, "Happy Fourth of July!" She then looked at Abby and said, "You must be Abby. Walter has told me so much about you."

The three of them chatted for a few minutes. Mrs. Moore was enlightening Abby and Walter how fun the parade was this morning. "It was the best one yet."

The parade was an annual Arlington Heights tradition. It consisted of many floats with bands and veterans walking down the main street of Arlington Heights, twirling flags and banners. Needless to say, Walter and Abby didn't wake up in time. They weren't too upset about it either, because every parade was almost identical. "How can it be the best one yet? It's the same every year," said Walter with a sly grin on his face.

"We must agree to disagree, then. Anyway, how come Randall isn't with you tonight?"

Walter looked puzzled by this question. Last night, Walter was hanging out with Randall and Randall told him that his mom needed help getting ready for their relatives. "I thought he was cleaning the house to get ready for your mom coming over tomorrow," said Walter.

"Getting ready for my mom?" Mrs. Moore asked as a rhetorical question. "My mom isn't coming over tomorrow. She's in Wisconsin."

"Huh, I wonder what he's up to, then," Walter said. "Strange to keep things from your best friend. Well, if you see him, tell him he's got some explaining to do."

After they talked with Mrs. Moore, they started walking toward where they wanted to sit. They eyed their spot and were almost there when Abby's parents strolled up to them. "Well, well, now, fancy seeing you two here," said Mr. Walker. Abby and Walter both looked at each other and wondered if he was serious. Before they could say anything, he said, "Are you enjoying the Fourth together?"

They both didn't know what to say, but Abby struck first. "It's been great so far. It was nice meeting Walter's parents. Walter's mom made a delicious dinner."

Mr. Walker had a great big smile on his face. "Wow. I'm so glad you've had a good time. Well, enjoy your night. We are watching the show with the Coles." Mr. and Mrs. Walker proceeded to convene with Mr. and Mrs. Cole. Mr. Cole had been Mr. Walker's business partner for the last ten years.

When their encounter with Abby's parents ended, Abby and Walter walked in silence to a spot where they wanted to watch the show. They put down their blanket on the grass and sat down. Both of them were wondering why Mr. Walker was so nice. Was he drunk? Was he just in a good mood because of the Fourth? He had been nagging on Walter for weeks.

"What happened? Your father was awfully friendly. He must be up to something," Walter said as he took a sip of his beer.

"Maybe he's changing his ways. You never know," said Abby. Deep down, though, she didn't believe her father was nice for the sake of being nice. She knew for certain he was acting like a magician. He was waiting for the opportune moment to unveil his final act and reveal what was rolled up his sleeve.

Before the fireworks began, Abby wanted to ask Walter what had been on her mind ever since the dinner at the Wilson house. "How come you and your mom don't get along?" asked Abby.

"Could you tell?"

"Yes. If you don't want to tell me about it, that's fine. I just want us to share everything," said Abby.

"Okay, it will ruin your night, though," said Walter.

"A night with you can never be ruined."

"It all started when my brother died," Walter said, tears almost forming in his eyes.

* * *

56

It was 1933 and just a normal hot and humid summer day in Arlington Heights, Ohio. The Wilson brothers had walked two miles to fish at the river. It was a daily summer routine for Walter and Bill Jr., or Billy. Billy was four years older than his younger brother. Every day, they would fish in the morning and go home for lunch around noon. After lunch, they would throw the baseball together and then jump in the pool to cool off before supper.

Within the first hour of fishing, Walter caught a big fish. When he reeled it in, it looked like a trout, but the Wilson boys weren't sure of the type of fish.

"Wow, that's a huge fish, buddy. Good work. You'll be better at catching fish than me and Dad combined!" Bill Jr. said to his brother.

"You really think so, Billy?" said Walter.

"I know so, pal. Should we keep it and cook it for dinner, or throw it back in and keep fishing?" asked Billy.

"Let's keep fishing, Billy," Walter said. Walter really wanted to keep the fish and cook it for dinner. However, his brother was his idol, and he wanted to spend as much time as possible with him, so he wanted to continue fishing.

Throwing the fish back into the river might have been a mistake, because neither Walter nor Billy caught another fish. When it was almost noon, the boys headed home for lunch. By the time they arrived home, it was almost ninety degrees, and it felt like one hundred degrees, stemming from the humidity. Walter and Billy could taste the water in the air.

"How are my boys doing?" asked Allison Wilson when the boys walked into the small brick house.

"We are having fun, Mama," said Walter.

"Oh, yes, we are, Mom. Walter caught a fish, but we threw it back in the water," said Billy.

"Walter, I'm so proud of you. How come you threw it back?" asked Mrs. Wilson.

"We caught it early, and we wanted to fish more. I assumed that Walter would catch more than one," said Billy.

"I'm sorry, Billy," said Walter.

"Walter, I'm kidding. You did good, pal, you did good," Billy said while patting his brother's back.

The boys washed up for lunch. Walter and Billy rinsed their hands with soap in the kitchen sink and then sat at the table. They were practically starving.

"What's for lunch, Mama?" asked Walter.

Allison Wilson walked back from the kitchen, holding a plate of sandwiches in one hand and her daughter, Mallie, in the other. "Mallie and I prepared you some turkey sandwiches."

"Thank you so much, Mallie," said Billy, giving his sister and mother a kiss on the cheek.

"Thank you, Mallie. Thank you, Mama," Walter said. Walter waited until his sister and mother were sitting down to kiss them on the cheek, because he couldn't reach them standing up. With Billy and Walter, it was like "monkey see, monkey do."

Still sitting at the kitchen table, Billy asked Walter if they could skip baseball. "Walter, pal, would you mind if we skip baseball? Let's go straight to swimming," said Billy.

"But, Billy, I really want to play baseball."

Without hesitation, Billy agreed to play baseball. He was the most caring twelve-year-old boy and thought of others before himself. "Of course we can. We have to work hard for you to become the next Babe Ruth."

The boys put their plates in the sink and grabbed their baseball gloves. As they were walking out the door, they could hear their mom say, "Have fun, boys. Make sure you're in the house by suppertime."

Walter and Billy jogged to the baseball field, which was a few blocks away from the Wilson house. When they arrived, Walter almost regretted not skipping baseball for the pool—it was so hot and muggy. But he loved sports and wanted to be great.

They played for a couple of hours. "All right, Walter, let's throw it a couple of more times, then let's go swimming," said Billy.

"Deal," said Walter.

"These have to be the best throws of the day. Show me that you want to be the best baseball player in America someday," Billy said.

"Here goes," Walter said while launching the ball over Billy's head.

The next few moments would always be a blur to Walter. Billy went running after the ball, which landed across the street. As he was jogging to recover the ball, Walter heard a loud noise. He looked over, and a car had struck Billy.

Billy was rushed to the hospital, but he died on the way to the emergency room. He was only twelve years old. Walter was devastated. His older brother, role model, and best friend had been killed. Even worse, as an eight-year-old kid, he blamed himself.

Allison Wilson was just as devastated by the accident. Shortly after, she began drinking. And even though she never said it, she placed the blame on Walter. No one really knew if she believed it while sober, but she believed it while on booze. Regardless, it created a memorable childhood for Walter.

* * *

After hearing the story of Walter's brother, Abby placed her hand over her mouth as a reaction to her shock. She then wrapped both her arms around Walter. "Walter, I'm so sorry. Sweetheart, I had no idea you had a brother. I'm so sorry. I wish there were something I can do," said Abby.

"You already have, Abby. I haven't felt this alive or happy since my brother died almost ten years ago. No one has loved me quite like you have. You have made me feel special, just like Billy did. He would be smiling if he were here."

Abby tried holding back her tears. That was the best compliment someone had ever given her. "That's what I love about you. Even when you're hurting, you always think of other people," Abby said as she kissed Walter on the cheek.

Walter smiled. "Now, if only we can get your father to have the same perspective."

Abby smiled too. "I'm sure he will. Just give it time."

The fireworks began shooting off from the cannon located on the far side of the park. Both Abby and Walter held on tight to each other, enjoyed the night, enjoyed the show, and most of all, enjoyed each other.

When the show was over, the night seemed like it was coming to an end. The young adults picked up their blanket and walked to the car. "Should I just drop you off at your house?" Walter asked.

"I'll go home in a couple of hours. Dad seemed awfully chipper tonight. I don't think he'll mind if I'm out later."

Walter nodded. "Whatever you say," he said as he turned the key in the ignition.

They almost reached Walter's house, but Walter wanted to investigate why Randall was absent from the Fourth of July festivities. "Let's drive over to Randall's. I want to see where that boy was tonight."

Abby agreed, and they drove toward the Moore house. Once they were there, they hopped out of the car and walked up the driveway. Walter knocked on the door of the little blue house, but no one answered. Walter and Randall had an open-door policy at their houses, so he and Abby walked inside the house.

"Hello!" yelled Walter. No one answered, so they went to the living room in the back of the house. The sight in the living room shocked Walter, and it surprised Abby. They saw Randall and Mallie asleep on the couch together. It was clear a romance had blossomed.

"What the hell is going on?" said Walter.

Both Mallie and Randall woke up, startled. Randall and Mallie had not a clue what to say, so they said nothing. "I can't believe it," said Walter. "You are like a brother to me. How could you do this?"

Neither Randall nor Mallie could form any words. Randall wanted to defend himself, but he just didn't know what to say. Walter then looked at Mallie and said, "I'll see you at home."

Mallie didn't look too happy. She didn't want her brother to find out like this, but she did want him to know about Randall. Randall meant a lot to her, and there was nothing he could say to change her feelings. "Walter, I'm sorry. I didn't want you to find out like this," said Mallie.

Walter shook his head in disappointment, and he stormed out of the house like a violent hurricane. He was walking to his black

Ford Coupe while Randall sprinted down the driveway. "Sport... Walter, hold on a minute. Let me talk to you," said Randall.

"What do you want, Randall? I just saw you with my sister. I thought that was off-limits?"

"I didn't mean for this to happen. It just did. We started talking at the fair a few weeks ago, and things escalated from there. For real, man, I love her."

"Wow. You *love* her. Okay I guess you can live happily ever after. I just can't be part of this. I feel like you betrayed me," said Walter.

"Walter, you're my best friend! I'm sorry I held the truth from you," said Randall.

"Well, I don't know what to say," said Walter. "Let me have time to think."

"Fair enough."

Abby and Walter drove off. Abby could tell that Walter was really upset. He just stared at the road while breathing heavily. She attempted to make him feel better or, at the very least, attempt to see his point of view. "Walter, I'm really sorry about what just happened. I know it must be hard."

Walter took a few deep breaths, then said, "I don't know what to think." In all honesty, Walter wasn't sure how he felt about it. Even though Walter and Randall chased girls for every summer since they were fourteen, he knew that Randall was a good man and his sister would be lucky to have him. On the other hand, it was his sister. No one could have his sister.

They drove around Arlington Heights at least three times. He needed to blow off steam before he dropped Abby at her house. Once he felt calm, they decided to drive to Millener Farms. When they pulled in the driveway, Mr. and Mrs. Walker were waiting for them on the front porch. Mr. Walker came to the car and said, "Walter, why don't you come inside for a while? My wife made a pot of tea."

Walter said yes, and everyone gathered in the living room to share a pot of tea. Mr. Walker asked Walter a lot about his tennis career.

"How did you become so good at tennis, young man?" asked Mr. Walker.

"I worked really, really hard. I wanted to be as good as Bill Talbert someday. I've reached my ceiling, and I won't live up to his standards, but I never stopped trying."

"Ahh, yes, Bill Talbert. He just won the US Open, if I'm not mistaken. He's an Ohio man, too, born in the Queen City. He's a good man to look up to," Mr. Walker said as he took a sip of his tea. "You may not be as good as Bill Talbert, but you did win a state title, did you not?"

"Yes, sir, we did. Everyone on our team battled. It was an amazing feeling, and it was amazing sharing that moment with my best friend, Randall."

"Well, young man, I bet it was a fine moment," Mr. Walker said as he yawned. "Well, it's too bad your career is ending. Ann and I would have loved to see you compete."

Walter smiled at Abby and said, "Maybe it won't. I hope the National Guard lets me go to school and play tennis."

Mr. and Mrs. Walker looked dazed at this comment. They didn't understand. They believed Walter was enlisting to become a pilot. Even though they were worried about his social class, Abby's parents were more concerned about him getting shot down and leaving their daughter heartbroken. As a result of the confusion, Mr. Walker asked, "I don't understand. I thought you were becoming a pilot. Is this not true?"

Again, with a smile on his face, Walter said, "Well, no."

"He decided to join the National Guard!" shouted Abby, who was sitting next to Walter at the table.

"Well, then, if you are playing tennis next year, we will have to come watch you play," said Mrs. Walker. By their reaction to Walter's change of plan, it was obvious they were hiding something.

After social hour was over, Walter went home. It was late, and even though there was drama centered on his relationship with Randall and his sister, he was still planning on playing tennis with Randall in the morning. "Well, I better get going. I have an early day tomorrow. Thanks for having me," Walter said. The Walkers said goodbye, and Abby offered to walk Walter out to his car. Once he was at his car, Abby kissed him goodbye and strolled back into her house.

Abby walked into the house and went straight to sleep. It had been a long day for her, but it had also been a great day. She was able to meet Walter's parents and spend time with him. Even though her parents acted strange after Walter said he wouldn't become a flyboy, they did have a quality conversation with him. She was convinced that her parents were warming up to him and that it was only a matter of time until they realized how much he meant to her.

The drive home seemed very short; it went by so fast because all he could think about was the reaction of the Walkers when they found out he wouldn't be flying the skies in Europe. It was puzzling. He felt as if his head were in a Chinese pretzel. However, Walter decided that the moment he walked in his house, he would not use one brain cell to think about Mr. Walker. The only thoughts about the Walker family he would have would be with Abby and Abby alone.

As he walked into the door, he noticed there was an envelope in the mailbox. *Weird,* Walter thought to himself. He was confused as to why there was mail on July 4; the post office was closed on a national holiday. However, he looked at the date, and it was postmarked July 2. The enveloped was addressed to Walter F. Wilson, so he opened it.

> *Dear Walter Wilson,*
> *This letter is to inform you that you have been chosen for the Selective Service. As of right now, you are scheduled to report to Fort Hayes near Columbus, Ohio, by July 13, 1943. Only bring with you a few personal items. Failure to appear will result in prosecution.*

Walter couldn't believe his eyes. He was convinced that it was a bad dream, and he was hoping to wake up. Even though he knew it wasn't a dream, the first thing he thought was, *This must be a joke.* He felt crushed. It certainly was ironic that the moment he decided not to become a pilot, he was drafted into the Army.

It was troubling that he was forced to report in a week. How would he tell Abby? How would he tell his family? How would he tell Randall? How would he tell his friends? It was after midnight, so everyone was asleep. He would have to wait until morning to deliver the devastating news.

CHAPTER 7

Walter woke up the next day and still had no idea how he would tell his parents the news. When he came downstairs, both of his parents were sitting at the table for breakfast. His father was drinking coffee and reading the newspaper, while his mom was reading a book. It seemed to be the opportune moment to tell his parents about the letter he received last night.

Walter poured himself a cup of hot coffee and sat down at the table with Allison and Bill Wilson. He took a few deep breaths. "Is there anything wrong, son?" Mr. Wilson asked.

The young man took a few more deep sighs and said, "There is no easy way to say this. I received my draft notice last night. I ship out in a week."

Everyone at the kitchen table looked sad; they looked defeated. Walter's mom started sobbing. His father held his mom and said, "I'm really sorry, Walter. I know you changed your mind about fighting in Europe, and you were handed a bad deck."

"Bad deck? That's an understatement. The moment I change my mind, I get drafted. I just don't understand."

Allison grabbed her son and pulled him close. It was the first time she had put her arm around him in ten years. "Walter, I'm so sorry. You're the strongest person I know. You'll be fine."

Walter's father put his hand on his son's shoulder. "Well, your mother and I are sorry. But we will be behind you the entire way."

Suddenly, the front door swung open. It was Randall and Mallie, and they came right in. "We're here," said Mallie.

After hearing voices coming from the kitchen, they wandered in and saw Mrs. Wilson sobbing. "What's wrong, Mom?" asked Mallie.

Before she could answer, Bill said, "Your brother has been drafted. He ships out in a week."

Mallie didn't take the news very well, and she began crying. She sprinted to Walter and put her arms around him. Everyone at the Wilson house didn't know what to say, and the house was as quiet as a morgue.

Walter went on the back porch to get some air and to think about his situation. He pulled out a lawn chair from the shed and started pondering. His father's words about a bad deck were shaking through his brain. Walter had always been unsure of himself, and that was evident in the swaying back and forth like a seesaw about whether to join the military. But as of recently, he had seen more clarity in his life than ever before. He wanted to join the National Guard and, if permitted, play tennis for the Ohio Wesleyan Battling Bishops. He could also get a good education so he and Abby could have a good life together. Both an education and Abby seemed far in the rearview mirror now, even though they were so close in proximity.

"Hey, sport, mind if I join you?" asked Randall as he walked outside.

"It's a free country," Walter said.

Randall sat down next to his friend and ignored the condescending remark. He wasn't sure whether it was from the draft notice or the fact that he was sleeping with his sister. Either way, the tone was more than justified.

"I'm sorry about everything," said Randall.

"What exactly are you sorry for? Are you sorry for becoming romantically involved with my sister, or sorry that I got drafted?" asked Walter. "You should only be sorry for one of those."

Randall wasn't sure which one he should be sorry for. He assumed it was for dating his sister. "I'm sorry about how I got involved with your sister. I should have come to you first or maybe should have never started."

Walter cracked a smile. "Randall apologizing, now that's not something you hear every day. And I've heard it two days in a row. If I didn't have the worst luck in the world right now, I would say that I'm one lucky man."

The smile must have been as contagious as a common cold, because Randall began grinning. "It's not very often that I'm wrong."

Walter stopped smiling and cleared his throat. "Randall, you should only be sorry for the fact that I was drafted. You've been like a brother to me, and you're a good man. My sister is lucky to have you," Walter said, patting Randall on the back.

The truth of the matter was that Walter's world had shifted. It was like the North Pole becoming the South Pole, as his thought process had turned upside down. His animosity toward his best friend converted to gratefulness. Walter was grateful that his best friend was there for his sister, because he might be gone from her life forever.

"Thanks, sport. You have no idea how much that means to me. I'm sure it will make your sister happy," Randall said.

I'm sure it will, Walter thought to himself. *I'm glad they're happy,* he silently added to himself again. He wanted them to be happy, but he was envious. And how could he not be jealous? They would be able to see movies, eat ice cream, and just be together, while Walter was on the front lines, defending humanity from Fascism.

"When are you going to tell Abby?" Randall asked.

"Soon. Today."

"She's going to be devastated."

Walter sighed. "I know."

Walter didn't know what to do. Abby would be hurt and would be worrying about him. She would be up nights, sweating and rolling around in her bed about whether he was coming home. Walter wasn't sure he could do that to Abby.

"Randall, I need your opinion on something," Walter said. Randall nodded, so he continued. "I'm thinking about breaking it off with Abby. I think it will be better for her. I love her so much, and I think this is what's best for her."

Randall pondered Walter's theory for a few minutes, then responded. "She loves you. I'm not sure that would be the best for her," said Randall. "Maybe you should talk to her about it."

"If I ask her, she'll want to stick it out with me. She's a beautiful and smart girl. I'm sure she'll find someone like me, if not better."

"Sport, you don't give yourself enough credit. You're a great man, and anyone would be lucky to have you. Just think about it before you make any decisions." Randall then stood up from his chair and left Walter to think about his dilemma.

Walter didn't need any more time to think about his decision. His mind was made up. He grabbed the keys to his Ford Coupe and walked out of the door. The engine started right up, and he was off to Abby's house.

It felt like eternity until he arrived at Millener Farms, because he was dreading his conversation with Abby. It felt like he was his own executioner and that he would be the one shattering his own world. As he pulled into her driveway, he said to himself, "Be strong, you're doing the right thing."

When he climbed out of the car, he trembled up the driveway. Mr. Walker was sitting on the porch, smoking a pipe and reading the newspaper. He had the same smell as usual, a combination of tobacco and mints. Mr. Walker must have liked the taste of mints, because he wasn't trying to cover the smell of tobacco. And why would he? Christopher Walker had the same level of confidence as a world champion boxer.

"Walter, how are you doing today? It's such a beautiful day, isn't it?" Mr. Walker said, smoke coming out of his throat.

"Yes, sir. Ohio is beautiful in the summer."

"I used to spend my summers in Maine, and Ohio doesn't come close. But I still can't complain," Mr. Walker said. "I'm guessing you're not here to chat about the weather with me. Abby is inside."

"Okay, thanks," Walter said as he stepped inside the Walker home.

Walter couldn't believe how pleasant Mr. Walker was to him. He usually acted as an artist protecting his prized possession. Sometimes it was difficult to even enter the house. He laughed and said to himself, "timing is a bitch."

Abby was sitting at the kitchen table, drinking some orange juice. She was glowing as bright as a firework on the Fourth of July. The young girl had a great time last night, and this was the happiest she had been in her young life. When she saw him enter the kitchen, she sprinted toward him and wrapped her arms around him. "I missed you."

"I missed you, too, but we just saw each other twelve hours ago."

"That's twelve hours too long," said Abby as she kissed him on the cheek.

If this wasn't hard enough, she was making it much more difficult. Tears began streaming down his face like a waterfall.

"Sweetheart, what's wrong?" Abby asked.

Walter could barely move the muscles of his mouth. He finally managed to speak, though, but it was hard. "I got drafted."

Abby broke down crying. She couldn't believe the news, and she almost fainted from shock. One minute she was at the top of the mountain, and the next she was at the very bottom.

"Umm, Abby, listen, I don't know how to say this, so I'm just going to say it. I think it would be best if we broke it off. There's a good chance I won't return. And I don't want you to be worried about whether I'm coming home or not."

Abby didn't take kindly to the news and wouldn't let Walter go without a fight. It was hard enough hearing about him getting drafted, and she couldn't bear to lose him altogether. "You can't do this," she said. "I love you, and that won't ever change."

"I love you too. And I probably always will," said Walter.

"Then don't do it."

"I have to. I couldn't live with myself."

She began sobbing uncontrollably, and Walter let her cry for a few minutes. "You will find someone better than me. You're smart, funny, and beautiful. Any man would be lucky to have you. You'll be just fine."

Abby continued to cry, and Walter was standing there, not knowing what to do. His arms were flailing by his hips. There was nothing to say. It was hard for both of them.

"Well, Abby, I think I'm going to head home now," Walter said. "I'll always love you," he said while walking out of the door.

"I'll always love you too."

Those were the only words that Abby managed to say. She saw the man she wanted to spend the rest of her life with walk out the door. For a seventeen-year-old girl, it seemed worse than Armageddon.

CHAPTER 8

I t had been two days since Walter had broken off the relationship with Abby, but it seemed like two years. And since the breakup, she had been a mess. She didn't leave her house, not once. Abby barely left her room, and the only time she strolled downstairs was for breakfast, lunch, and dinner. The rest of the time, she spent in her bed, sobbing.

"Abigail, dear, I made a good breakfast for you. Why don't you come down and join your father and me?" Ann Walker said while waking her daughter.

Abby slowly lifted her head above her pillow. There were bags under her eyes, as she had been crying the entire night. "I'll be down in a few minutes."

Mrs. Walker closed the door to her daughter's bedroom and went downstairs to rejoin her husband for breakfast. "Is she coming down soon?" asked Mr. Walker.

"Yes, she'll will be down in a few minutes," said Ann Walker. "Please be nice."

"Sweetheart, do you think she will be okay? She's been in her room ever since she broke up with that young man," said Mr. Walker as he took a sip of his coffee.

"She's heartbroken. To her, it seems like her world just ended. Just give her time."

"I will certainly keep that in mind. Even though I didn't care for that young man, I do feel for her. It breaks my heart hearing her cry like that," said Mr. Walker.

"It's a good thing he's not in my life anymore. I bet you're happy," Abby said while she was walking down the stairs.

Abby heard most of her parents' conversation from the top of the stairs. She was at least happy that her parents understood what she was going through. It was hard that they didn't understand the way she felt about Walter, but at least her parents had some sense of her heartbreak.

"What's for breakfast, Mama?" asked Abby.

"Belgian waffles and fruit," said Mrs. Walker. "They're homemade."

"Who catered them?" Abby smirked.

"Very funny, young lady," said Mrs. Walker, who was glad her daughter had a sense of humor for the first time in forty-eight hours.

Before she knew it, Abby had grabbed a plate and filled it with a couple of waffles and some fruit. She then untwisted the cap of the maple syrup and poured it all over her waffles. Within a few minutes, the waffles and fresh strawberries disappeared. Abby had been hungry, as she had barely eaten in the last couple of days. She was like someone in the desert looking for water and the food quenched her thirst.

"Hungry, huh?" said Mrs. Walker.

"How did you know?" Abby said while smiling.

"A mother's intuition," said Ann Walker. "Your father and I were thinking about playing tennis. It's such a beautiful day. Would you care to join us?"

"I would, but I already made plans with Martha."

The truth was, Abby hadn't made any plans with Martha, but she didn't want to spend time with her parents. She still resented them for how they treated Walter, especially now that he was gone. On the flip side, her parents didn't mind; they were just happy that she was doing something other than crying in her room.

As everyone finished breakfast, Abby returned to her room. She waited until her parents had left to play tennis at the country club before coming out of confinement. When she heard the engine of her father's Cadillac convertible, she telephoned Martha.

"Hello," answered Martha.

"Hey, it's me, Abby. I was calling to see if you were busy today."

"Kind of. I'm shopping for a dress. Why don't you come with me? You can help me pick one out. I'll pick you up in an hour?"

"Perfect. I'll see you soon," said Abby before she put the receiver down.

After she hung up the phone, Abby returned to the second floor of the house. She realized that she hadn't taken a shower in a couple of days, so she turned the water on and hopped in. Once she finished bathing herself, she threw on an old dress and waited for Martha.

Martha appeared at the Walker residence almost an hour after the girls' phone conversation. She honked the horn of her black Plymouth Roadking to signal for Abby to come out.

"Hey, Martha," Abby said as she closed the car door.

"Hi, Abby. How are you holding up?"

"Okay," she said.

By the one-word response, Martha assumed she wasn't okay. "Well, hang in there," Martha said as she started the engine and drove off. "Where do you think we should go to buy my dress?"

Abby thought about the question for a few moments. Even though they were going dress shopping, that was the last thing on her mind. "Jeanine's Fashion always has a good selection. It's on Arlington Avenue, next to Jake's Burgers."

"That sounds perfect. We'll grab lunch at Jake's after."

It took less than two minutes to arrive at the dress shop. Both of the girls unlatched the door handle and stepped out of the car. When they were walking into the store, a woman whose hair matched the dress she was wearing greeted them. "Welcome to Jeanine's," said the woman with the hair color of a fox's fur. "Is there anything in particular you're looking for?"

"I'll be attending a dance tomorrow night at the country club with probably the most handsome guy in town, and I need to find a dress," said Martha.

"Well, you've come to the right place. Let me know if you need any help," the woman said and then disappeared into the back of the store.

"She was helpful," said Abby.

The two girls laughed, and Martha began trying on dresses. Martha was rather particular, so she went through many dresses before she found the one she wanted. "How about this one?" Martha asked, twirling in front of Abby.

"I really like that one," Abby said about the red-colored dress. "Whom are you going to this dance with, anyway?"

"Tom Willis," Martha said as she stepped out of the dress. "It's going to be a lot of a fun. You should come."

"I don't think so. I have no one to go with," said Abby.

"I'll find you someone," said Martha.

"No, it's perfectly okay. You and Tom will have fun. He seems like a nice boy."

Martha dropped the conversation when the "helpful" employee that looked like a fox processed her for the transaction. Abby didn't want to attend a dance with another boy. She would rather hear someone scratching a chalkboard than dance with someone other than Walter.

After the girls walked out of the dress shop, they headed straight for Jake's Burgers. Jake's had the best burgers and shakes in town, and if something could help Abby's mood, it was a cold chocolate shake and a juicy burger.

"What can I get for you, ma'am?" said the girl working at Jake's.

Before Abby could order, Martha interrupted her. "We'll have two burgers, two fries, and two shakes," said Martha. Abby pulled out a couple of dollars, but Martha slapped her hand. "You helped me pick out my dress, so lunch is on me."

The girls sat down at one of the five tables at Jake's until their food was cooked. Most of the orders were for carry-out, so Jake's didn't have too many tables in the restaurant. "Order up," said one of the cooks from the back.

"Ma'am, your food is ready," said the same girl that took Abby and Martha's order. "Why don't y'all stop talking and come get it?"

Martha stood up from her chair and walked over to grab their food from the counter before the employee threw the burgers at them. She placed the burgers, fries, and shakes in front of Abby. Abby took her food and started munching. Even though Abby ate a big breakfast a few hours earlier, she was still hungry.

Once Abby and Martha were finished with their lunch, Abby tried standing up with her chocolate shake in one hand. "Sit back down, Abby. Let's hang out here for a few more minutes while we drink our shakes."

Abby hesitated because she wanted to return home. But after a mini stare-down with Martha, she took a seat in her chair. "Abby, I know you and Walter have broken it off, but what exactly happened?" asked Martha.

"He was drafted," said Abby. "He told me that he didn't want to leave me heartbroken. He said that he didn't want me to be worried about him while he was away and that there was a chance he may not come back."

Martha took another sip of her shake. "How do you feel about it?"

"I don't like it at all. I would have worried every second of the day until he returned even if there was only a small chance of him returning. I care about him that much."

"Did you say this to him?" asked Martha.

"I just told him that I didn't want to break it off with him. I was in such shock that I couldn't really comprehend the situation."

There was chocolate on Abby's face from the milkshake, so Martha pointed it out to her. "You're such a little kid when you drink a shake," said Martha. "Anyway, I think you should talk to him."

"I don't know. He was pretty set on breaking it off."

"You obviously know this more than anyone, but everything he does is for other people. You need to convince him that you will be better off staying with him through the war. Just do whatever it takes. You know what buttons to press with him."

Abby cracked a smile. Martha was right, and Abby was determined to put things back together with Walter. She would not take no for an answer. "Whatever it takes," Abby said to herself.

Martha stood up from the table and threw her cup in the trash can. "Come on, let's go. I'll drop you off at Walter's so you can reunite with Prince Charming"

When Abby arrived at Walter's house, she rang the doorbell. "Well, hi, Abby. How are you doing today? Walter's out back with Randall," said Mrs. Wilson.

Abby said hello to Walter's mother and trembled the short distance to the back porch. She was nervous, and it felt like her heart was beating a million miles an hour. As she slid the back door open and walked out onto the porch, Abby walked into the unknown.

"Abby," said Walter. "What are you doing here?"

She knew it was a fair question, but it took her by surprise. Anything he said was bound to surprise her. "Umm, I was wondering if I could talk to you?" asked Abby as she looked over in Walter's direction.

Walter nodded at Randall, who was sitting beside him in a lawn chair. "Well, I better get going. Mallie is expecting me to go to some museum with her. You can't say I don't care about her, because I hate museums," Randall said while laughing. "It was nice to see you, Abby."

"What do you want, Abby?" said Walter. He thought he had been clear about breaking it off. Although Walter was rather curious as to why she had come to his house. His heart hoped that she came over to try to patch things up, but his brain wanted to still be apart.

"I wasn't prepared to hear that you were drafted," said Abby.

"Well, I was surprised too."

"Now that I've had time to think about it, I wanted to tell you how I feel," said Abby.

Walter didn't count his chickens before they hatched. He figured that he wouldn't have to see Abby until after the war. He knew it would be too hard to see her before he left because he was still in love with her. His love for her might never change, but at least Walter felt he would be prepared to face it when he returned. "Let me hear it, Abby. How do you feel about me going to war?"

"I hate it. It isn't fair," said Abby.

"Yeah, tell me about it. Life isn't fair."

Abby brushed up on Walter's shoulder. "Please, let me continue." Walter stopped talking and looked at her. He was as silent as a slippery eel found in the Atlantic Ocean. "You may be right about being better off without you and that I would be okay finding someone else."

"Why are you telling me this?"

"Let me continue," Abby said, and Walter stopped talking once again. "I may be okay, but I want to be more than okay. I want to be happy, and I would be happiest with you. And even if there's a small chance that we can be happy together, I'm going to take it."

"Well, how would you know you would be happiest with me? Surely, that's not true," Walter said.

"Because I've never been happier in my life. I want to spend every minute of the day with you."

"I just don't know, Abby. If anything ever happened to me, I would feel terrible," said Walter.

"You're the kindest, sweetest person I know. You're always thinking of other people. But now it's time to start thinking about you. I want to worry about you every second of the day while you're gone, even if there's a chance you won't come home. I want to be the first one to meet you at the base. I love you," said Abby. She then got on one knee in front of his chair. "What do ya say? Will you be my boyfriend again?"

Walter couldn't help but smile. Abby was right. Since before he could remember, he had always been thinking about other people. It was time to start being selfish. "I suppose."

"What did you say?" Abby smiled as she inched her lips closer to Walter's lips.

"I suppose."

"You what?" Abby said, her lips now only a few inches away from his lips.

"I suppo—"

Walter only managed to say so little before Abby attacked him with her lips and climbed on to his lap.

The two young adults began kissing each other like a couple of schoolkids playing spin the bottle. And they didn't stop even when Walter's mom came outside, carrying a tray of freshly squeezed lemonade. They were trying to make up for lost time from their forty-eight hours of separation, and the lost time they would suffer during Walter's service in Europe.

"I'm sorry, sweetheart. We should have talked before I made the decision that affected both of our lives," Walter said before he kissed her forehead.

"It doesn't matter now. Let's just try to cherish the few days that we have together," Abby said as she was sitting on Walter's lap.

While Walter and Abby were sitting in peace, the sliding door swung open. "Hey, sport, I see you have love in your sights again. It's good to see you back in the saddle," said Randall as he and Mallie walked outside.

"It does feel kinda nice, doesn't it, Abby?" said Walter, looking at Abby. "Did you already see the museum?"

"Nah, it was closed. It's too bad, because I was really looking forward to it," said Randall, giving Walter a wink.

"Yeah, I bet. And did you hear? Pigs are starting to fly, and dogs have begun to speak French," said Walter.

"If dogs spoke French, I could never get one. I can't stand the French," said Randall.

"Why's that?" Walter laughed.

"Because they think they're better than us in everything!" replied Randall.

"They obviously aren't very good at defending their country," said Walter with a grin.

Abby hopped off Walter's lap. "Mallie, let's go inside. I'm getting really hot out here."

The girls proceeded to skip inside while Randall sat down in the same chair he had been sitting in hours previously. Randall then stared at Walter with an all-too-familiar face. It was a face that Randall would give Walter when he had a crazy idea. "I don't think I can make you go alone."

"I don't think I can either. I want Abby, you, and Mallie to drop me off at the base," said Walter. He knew damn well what Randall had meant but wanted to brush it off as a joke.

"In all seriousness, I want to come with you."

"You're not going with me," said Walter.

"Walter, I want to come with you. I want to fight by your side. I want to serve my country."

"No, Randall, I can't let you come. You have Mallie to think of. I won't let you follow me. Not this time," said Walter.

"Come on, Walter. You know I've secretly wanted to join the military. Let's fight Hitler together. You are safer with me there, and vice versa. If we stick together, we'll both come back to our girls in one piece. Think of Abby!"

Walter would love for Randall to come with him, and it was true, he would feel much safer. Instead of him being scared and alone, it would turn into an adventure. Randall was right; he would be better suited to return home to the people of Arlington Heights, his friends, his family, and of course, Abby. Walter could imagine returning with Randall greeted by a parade of people throwing confetti. He cracked a smile just thinking about that image. It gave him chills up and down his spine.

It might have given him chills, but he didn't think he could live with himself if anything ever happened to his best friend. Walter thought of two important people in his life, Mallie and Mrs. Moore. What would both of them think if he let Randall follow him to war? They wouldn't be very happy, and on the contrary, they would be scared, worried, and upset. Every day they would wonder if Randall would be coming home. Walter still had an open mind about it, but for now, it was still a no, but a soft no.

"I'm sorry. I just don't think I can let you do this. The more I think about it, the more it doesn't make sense. Again, what about Mallie? What about your mom? I love those people so much, and they would be a wreck if you went," said Walter.

Randall looked Walter in the eye and said, "Yes, they would be worried, but you also mean a lot to both of them. You are like a son to my mom, sport. She will still be a wreck thinking about you. And

Mallie, for God's sakes, are you kidding me? She would be sad about me leaving, but she would understand. You're her brother, and you have a better chance of returning home if I'm watching your back."

Walter took a sip of water. He knew deep down Randall had a point. Walter looked back at Randall and stated, "Let me think for a few minutes."

Walter took a few minutes to contemplate his decision. He looked up at the sunny blue sky and began to ponder about the many pros and cons associated with Randall joining him. His heart wanted Randall to come, and desperately, but his brain told him that Randall shouldn't join him.

After about five minutes, Walter was ready to make a decision. "You can come with me, but you have to clear it with both Mallie and your mom," Walter said.

Randall had a huge smile on his face and said with joy in his eyes, "Thank you, chief. We are going to take down those Nazis!"

Walter's heart won the battle against his brain, and he hoped he made the right decision. If anything happened to Randall, he would have guilt for the rest of his life.

Abby and Mallie came outside, carrying cookies, just as Randall and Walter were finishing their conversation. Mallie dropped the plate of cookies.

"You're what?" Mallie screamed. "I never want to talk to you again!"

CHAPTER 9

I t didn't take long for Mallie and Randall to become two peas in a pod again. Mallie forgave him because she understood why he needed to join the military. She couldn't imagine a world without him, and if that meant Randall had to be away from her for a while, then so be it.

And once Randall and Mallie patched things up, the four of them cherished what little time they had with each other. They continued to play tennis, attend movies, have bonfires, and lie under the stars. It was a special five days.

The day that everyone had been dreading had come. It was July 12, 1943, the day before Walter and Randall would leave for the Army. This was the final day Abby and Walter would be able to spend with each other until after the war. Walter woke up early to pick up Abby from her house. When he arrived, Abby was sitting with her parents in the living room.

"Good morning, Mr. and Mrs. Walker," Walter said.

"Good morning, young man," said Mr. Walker as he flipped a page of the newspaper.

"Walter, are you ready for tomorrow?" asked Mrs. Walker.

"I'm as ready as I'll ever be," said Walter.

"I'm sure you are," responded Mrs. Walker.

It appeared as if Mrs. Walker was going to say more, but Abby grabbed Walter's arm and dragged him toward the door. As they were walking out the house, Abby mentioned to her parents that she would be back the next day. Mr. and Mrs. Walker weren't the type of parents to allow their daughter to spend the night at a boy's house. However, they had hearts and relented to the request.

Once they left, Abby asked where they were headed. "I want to go see Randall's mom before I leave tomorrow," responded Walter.

"Have you seen her since Randall decided to join you in the war?"

Walter was ashamed of himself because he hadn't seen Mrs. Moore since the Fourth of July. "I haven't. I was too afraid what she may think of me for allowing her son to join me."

When they arrived at Randall's house, Abby and Walter walked to the door and went in. The open-door policy had not changed, especially now that they were joining the military together. As they walked in, Mrs. Moore was sobbing. "I don't know what I'll do. It was hard that one of my boys was heading overseas, but now both of you are," said Mrs. Moore as she tried hard to stop crying.

Walter put his arms around her and told her it would be okay. "I tried talking him out of it."

"When Randall makes up his mind, there's no going back," Mrs. Moore said. "He explained everything, and I may be sad, but he's brave. He's right too. You boys are better off when you're together. I know you will both make it back. Everything will be all right."

They tried comforting her but had little success. She was distraught, as well as she should be. The two people she cared about most in the world were going off to war.

After a while, Abby and Walter said their goodbyes to Nancy Moore. There was enough hugging and crying to last a lifetime. As they were walking out of the door, Mrs. Moore called Walter back.

"Please come back safely," said Mrs. Moore while giving Walter one last hug.

"Randall and I will come back home. I promise."

As the young couple left the Moore house, they drove to Walter's house. With the help of Abby, Walter packed for his journey into the military. He was only permitted to take a few personal items. Most of these items included pictures of important people in his life: his family and friends. Walter picked up a picture of Abby from his bed. "I'll be carrying this one in my pocket at all times."

"You better. I'll be your good-luck charm."

He smiled at her and continued packing. Once they were done packing, Abby and Walter just lay on his bed. They were both exhausted.

Mallie came inside the house, crying. Walter knew why she was crying; he didn't need to be a rocket scientist to figure out why his sister was upset. The concept of Randall leaving for the war had begun sinking in. Mallie wouldn't stop crying, so Walter went downstairs to talk to her. "Mallie, what's wrong?" asked Walter.

"I'm just really sad you and Randall are leaving tomorrow," said Mallie.

Walter put his arm around his sister. He could imagine the pain she was going through, because he was experiencing the same hardship. "I know it's hard, but I promise you we will come back. In the end, it will make your relationship stronger with Randall."

Walter's effort to console his sister was commendable, but it didn't stop the tears from rolling down Mallie's cheeks. Mallie continued to cry, but Walter did indeed have good news to tell her. "I have a surprise for you," Walter said with a smile on his face.

"What is it?" Mallie asked while she was attempting to wipe her tears away. "We are all going to the quarry tonight. You, Randall, Abby, and me. The plan is to bring some blankets and pillows and sleep there. You and Abby can drive us to the base tomorrow."

That caught Mallie's attention, and a sudden smile appeared on her face, much like a rainbow during a thunderstorm. "When are we meeting him?"

"In about an hour. I just have to say bye to Mom and Dad," said Walter.

While Walter was downstairs, consoling Mallie, Abby slipped a note she had written to Walter into his bag. When she heard Walter coming up the stairs, she sat on his bed.

Walter checked his watch, and it was time to leave his house and leave his parents. Abby and Walter walked down the stairs, and his parents were sitting in the living room. Mrs. Wilson was crying, and

Mr. Wilson was trying to make her feel better about the situation. "Well, I'm off," said Walter.

He then proceeded to shake his dad's hand and give his mom a hug. "You be careful out there, ya hear?" said Bill Wilson.

"I love you, Walter. Be safe," Allison Wilson said, trying to hold back the tears.

"I'll be back. I promise," Walters said as he gave his mom a long hug.

Walter told his parents that they didn't need to worry and that he would be back after the war. It was hard saying goodbye to them, but he was confident that he would see them again.

Randall was waiting for them at the quarry, and once they had parked, Mallie ran out to greet him. He had a bag of hot dogs, beer, and chips in his hands. "I brought the food, sport."

"Good. Let's have one last hoorah before we leave tomorrow," said Walter.

Randall then cracked open beers for all of them and toasted, "To a night none of us will forget! To a night Walter and I will be thinking about during our journey ahead!"

After Randall finished toasting, the four of them started grilling hot dogs on the grills supplied by the state park. "How would you like your 'dog cooked?"

"I like mine pretty burnt, Mr. Moore."

The girls had no preference. They hated hot dogs. However, it was Randall and Walter's last night in Arlington Heights, so they ignored the enjoyment of Abby and Mallie for just one night. Hot dogs were an American tradition, and Walter and Randall wanted good, old-fashioned American dogs before they left for the patriotic cause.

As dinner finished, Abby and Walter retreated from Randall and Mallie. "All right, Randall, we'll see you in the morning," said Walter as he walked away from his friend.

"Just wake me up in the morning. Let's make this night count. It will be our last one until the war is over," said Randall.

Walter proceeded to lie down on a blanket with Abby. They cuddled and talked under the stars for hours. They talked about their future after the war. "I'm coming home, and we're getting a house on Abington Road. Randall can live down the street, but at least a hundred yards," said Walter.

"Abington, huh?" said Mallie. With a smile on her face, Abby went on to say, "What if I don't want to live on Abington?"

"It's a great location. Right near Beechum Park and the Old Pub. We'll have a white picket fence and a golden retriever," said Walter.

"You've sold me with the golden retriever. But you have to promise me that we'll have a patio. I want to host summer parties," said Abby.

"Is there anything else you want, princess?" Walter smiled.

Abby didn't hesitate to answer, because there were a few things she desired for her dream home. "Pink's my favorite color, so I want a pink front door," said Abby.

Before she could continue her wish list, Walter interrupted. "A pink door? Are you kidding me?"

"I want a pink door. I also want a nice big kitchen overlooking the backyard," Abby said as she climbed onto Walter's lap. "I want to see the kids playing when I'm cooking dinner."

Abby couldn't be more excited about her long-term future. But the short-term future seemed bleak. Walter was leaving for boot camp tomorrow, and she had a wide range of emotions. She was scared, worried, nervous, and proud. She was proud of him for serving this country with honor; she was nervous and worried that he wouldn't return home.

Right before she was about to fall asleep, Abby asked, "How often will you be thinking of me?"

Puzzled by the question, Walter said, "Is that a serious question?" Walter went on to say, "I'll be thinking of you all the time. When I wake up, I'll be wishing I were waking up next to you. Once I'm awake, I'll be thinking about you throughout the day. And when I go to sleep, I'll be wishing I could kiss you good night," said Walter.

"That's good, then. I really want you to come back to me, so can you do that? Can you come back?"

"I will do my best. I don't want to jinx it by saying it's 100 percent. Every day, though, I will treat as if it's one more day closer to seeing you," said Walter.

Both of them stayed awake as long as they could, looking at the beautiful night sky full of stars. They would kiss each other, look at the stars, kiss each other, and look at the stars. They cycled through that while fighting waves of exhaustion. They couldn't fight forever, however, and they fell asleep.

The next morning, Walter woke up as the sun was rising over Arlington Heights. It was beautiful—the sun reflecting off the water, the sweet smell of the morning dew, and the chilly morning temperature. This sunrise would be the last he would watch over his hometown until after the war. To Walter's dismay, he couldn't see the entire sunrise. He shook Randall and told him it was time to leave.

"How are we getting to Fort Hayes?" Randall asked.

"Mallie will drive my car and drop us off. Let's go," Walter said.

Randall and Walter woke up Mallie and Abby, and they hit the road. Mallie opened the driver's side door and climbed in. As a result, Walter and Abby rode in the back while Randall took shotgun. "You need to step on it, Mallie. We can't be late on the first day," said Walter.

Mallie listened to her older brother and picked up her speed. They arrived at the base near downtown Columbus with a few minutes to spare. All four of them got out of the car and walked to the gates of Fort Hayes, where two guards were stationed in front.

"You're late. You must report immediately," said one of the guards.

"Can we say bye to our girls?" said Randall.

"Out of the question," said the same guard.

The second guard looked at his partner. "It will only take a few minutes, Jonny. Let them have a few minutes to say goodbye," said the soldier. "We wouldn't want them to have low morale before they even stepped on base."

As soon as the uptight guard waved his hand, Walter wrapped his arms around Abby and she whispered into his ear, "Come back home. Come back to me."

"I will. I love you. I'll try to write you every day," said Walter as he and Randall headed into base.

Randall and Walter walked into the military base and out of sight from Abby and Mallie. Even though they dreamed of it, it was unknown whether Randall and Walter would ever step foot in their hometown again.

When Abby and Mallie saw the boys disappear into the military base, they walked back to the car. Both of them opened the door in complete silence and hopped inside. Abby noticed a note addressed to her on the seat.

> *Dear Abby,*
>
> *I'm sorry I have to be away from you for an extended period of time. It will certainly feel like eternity, because every minute not spending with you seems so long. I can't tell you how happy I am right now, and even a war can't change that. We had the most special time together this summer, and I will be thinking about it every night before I go to bed. Even though physically I won't be able to see you, you'll always be in my heart, so therefore, you will always be with me. I love you so much, and I know I'll see you again.*
>
> *Love,*
> *Walter*

CHAPTER 10

A few weeks had passed, and Abby started her senior year of high school. While she walked the narrow white halls of the all-girls school, her fellow classmates looked at her with pity.

Abby's classmates didn't give her nearly as much stress as some of her classes. She could barely handle her history class. The first topic of the school year was the origins of the Great War. The teacher, Mrs. Wilcox, hated Germany. All she talked about was how Germany was the cause of the last world war. She believed that the harsh sanctions against Germany were more than justified. After Germany unconditionally surrendered to the Allies, France was on a mission to cripple Germany. England and the United States didn't want to throw a crushing blow at Germany; France wanted to force Germany to reduce her military to a maximum of one hundred thousand soldiers, strip them of territory, force them to pay all the war damages, and demilitarize the Rhineland. As history shows, France wouldn't bend to the wishes of the United States and Great Britain, and Germany was punished to a massive extent.

"Do you really think it was all Germany's fault?" asked one student.

"Oh, absolutely. Germany handed Austria a *blank check*," said Mrs. Wilcox.

In the aftermath of the Black Hand assassination of the archduke Franz Ferdinand, who was the heir to the Austro-Hungarian throne, Germany offered Austria-Hungary unconditional support in their pursuit of justice against Serbia.

"But wasn't it the alliance system? It wasn't all Germany's fault. Everyone had some blame in the war," said a girl with brown hair sitting a few rows from Abby.

The girl was referring to the infamous alliance system that entangled Europe in the late nineteenth century and early twentieth century. Countries made agreements and formed alliances. Austria-Hungary and Germany formed the Dual Alliance in 1879 to protect themselves against Russia. The Triple Entente was established in 1907 between France, Russia, and Great Britain in fear of the threat against Germany.

After the heir to the Austrian Hungarian throne was assassinated by a Serbian nationalist group, Austria-Hungary handed down unconditional and unreasonable demands to Serbia. Serbia was backed by Russia, and with the Dual Alliance, Germany backed Austria-Hungary. When Austria-Hungary invaded Serbia, the alliance system fell into place, and Europe was engulfed in war.

Mrs. Wilcox paused at the question. She didn't think anyone would question her. "I guess you're right," said Mrs. Wilcox. "Well, class is adjourned for today. I will see all of you tomorrow."

All the students filed out of the room one by one. Abby had almost reached the door when Mrs. Wilcox stopped her. "Can I talk to you?"

Abby nodded and agreed to stay and talk with her teacher. "Your father told me about Walter. I just wanted to let you know that if you need someone to talk with, I'm always here for you. My husband was killed in the Great War, so I know what you're going through."

Abby didn't have much to say but thanked her for being kind. She understood why her teacher had so much animosity toward the Germans. She hoped to never have the same resentment as her teacher had, because that would mean Walter wouldn't have come home.

After her conversation with Mrs. Wilcox, Abby sprinted to lunch to meet up with her friends. Martha was sitting at one of the long lunch tables, so she pulled up a chair next to her. "Hi, Martha. How are you doing today?" asked Abby.

"I'm doing okay. I had math this morning, and I can't stand math. The teacher is so boring and talks in such a monotone voice," said Martha.

"Oh, Mr. Buckley. He puts me to sleep at least three days a week," said Abby. "What class do you have after lunch?"

"History with Mrs. Wilcox," said Martha.

"You're in for a real treat," said Abby.

Martha asked, "Why?"

Abby took a sip of her water and then answered the question. "She hates the Germans and thinks they're the reason for the Great War. Her husband died in the war, so it explains her hostility."

They talked for a few more minutes, and then the afternoon bell rang, signaling the start of afternoon classes. For Abby, it was biology. Biology was not her strong subject, so she wasn't looking forward to it. Abby walked to the class and took her seat. Once in biology, she mentally checked out of school for the rest of the day. Abby couldn't quite understand how, while the world was at war, people were going about their normal day. It didn't make sense to her.

When classes adjourned for the day, she zipped home in her red Mercury Deluxe as fast as she could. It was her senior year, and it was supposed to be the best time of her life—hanging out with her friends and making plans for the future. But on the contrary, she was miserable. She didn't think it was right that she was able to spend her days having fun with her friends while Walter was off serving his country.

When she returned home, her mother was waiting in the kitchen. "How was school, dear?"

"It was fine. Same as usual. I'll be reading in my room if you need me," Abby said.

"You've been spending a lot of time upstairs," Mrs. Walker said as a rhetorical question.

"I've been reading a good book."

Abby was walking up the stairs, but her mother called her back down. "What's the matter, Mom?" asked Abby.

"Your father's friend Mr. Baker will be joining us for dinner tonight. I expect you to be on your best behavior, young lady."

"Aren't I always?" Abby said.

After about an hour of reading her book, she heard a knock on her door. "Dinner's almost ready," said her mom. "Be down in five minutes."

Abby complied with her mom's wishes. As she slithered down the steps like a snake, she saw her father sitting at the table with Mr. Baker. Mr. Baker came from a wealthy family and was a proper gentleman. He showed up to dinner wearing a white shirt, black pants, and a red bow tie. This man had been a friend with Abby's father for a long time. "Hello, Mr. Baker," said Abby.

"Well, hi, Abby. It's pleasure to see you," said Mr. Baker. Once they had exchanged greetings, Mr. Baker continued his conversation with Mr. Walker.

Since her father and Mr. Baker were engaged in what looked to be a serious conversation, Abby decided to see if her mom needed help in the kitchen. "Do you need any help?"

"That would be great, dear. Would you mind taking the chicken out of the oven?" said Mrs. Walker.

Abby agreed and grabbed two red oven mitts from the cabinet. Mrs. Walker also asked her to set the table, and even though Abby really didn't want to, she agreed. She carried plates, silverware, and glasses to the oak-colored dining room table.

Once the table was set, Abby and her mom brought the food out to the dining table. "Everything looks delicious," Mr. Baker said.

"It will be delicious. My wife is a great cook," said Mr. Walker.

Mr. Baker seemed like a nice man, but Abby felt so out of place. Her parents and Mr. Baker kept talking about their friends, their finances, and everything else that had no relevance to her. She finally felt part of the conversation when Mr. Baker said something about the war.

"So have you heard any new developments in the war?" Mr. Baker asked.

"Well, the Allies just took Sicily about a month ago. I heard the Germans will attempt to rescue Mussolini," said Mr. Walker, taking a sip of wine.

"I heard that as well. It's looking good for the Allies. The tide is turning in our favor," said Mr. Baker.

"Not necessarily," said Mr. Walker. "France is still under German occupation. No victory will happen without a liberated France. It just won't happen," said Mr. Walker.

Abby's mom took a sip of her wine and joined the fray. "I can't believe that it's been almost two years since we entered the war. I still remember where I was the day of Pearl Harbor. What an awful event!" said Mrs. Walker.

Pearl Harbor was the most infamous event in the United States military history. Early in the morning on December 7, 1941, Japan delivered a surprise torpedo attack on the naval base Pearl Harbor off the island of Hawaii. All eight of the US battleships were sunk, and over two thousand American soldiers lost their lives. The next day, President Franklin D. Roosevelt asked Congress to declare war on Japan.

"I believe we all know where we were the day of Pearl Harbor. I was sitting at the old Cup of Jaba, grabbing a cup of joe. What a tragic event. So many young men lost their lives that day. The Japanese made a grave mistake," said Mr. Baker.

"I can recall when President Roosevelt made that passionate speech in front of Congress the day after Pearl Harbor. I have faith we will end this war victoriously. It's just hard to say how long it will take," said Mr. Walker as he grabbed a roll from the bowl.

Mrs. Walker leaned over and asked, "How long do you think it will take to end the war?"

"If I had to make an educated guess, I would say 1946. This war will drag out. Germany will fight at all cost," said Mr. Walker.

"I wholeheartedly disagree, my friend. Six months. In my estimation, we are six months away from a German surrender," said Mr. Baker.

Abby had a huge smile on her face, and she lit up like a Christmas tree. "Really. Six months?"

"I hope so. So much for your father sending Walter away," said Mr. Baker.

"Who's ready for dessert?" Mr. Walker asked, interrupting Mr. Baker before he could answer the question. Mr. Walker then walked into the kitchen to grab the chocolate cake Mrs. Walker had baked.

Abby's mind was going in every direction. It felt like she was on a merry-go-round spinning out of control, bobbing up and down way too fast. She wasn't sure what she heard, but it sounded like Mr. Baker indicated that her father sent Walter away to the war. But how could that have been possible? Could her father have caused Walter to be drafted? It just didn't seem plausible. As her father left the room, she seized the opportunity to ask Mr. Baker about the situation.

"So my father sent Walter away to the war, Mr. Baker?" asked Abby.

"I thought you knew. He called the War Office and pulled a few strings. He didn't want you dating Walter. He figured that Walter was enlisting in September, anyway, so he didn't think that sending the young man into the military a couple of months earlier would harm anyone," said Mr. Baker.

"Walter was going to join the National Guard. He decided to stay here for me, and he planned to enroll at Ohio Wesleyan. Get your facts straight!" screamed Abby.

After Abby lashed out at Mr. Baker, she started to cry. While she was crying, Mr. Walker walked back into the dining room and realized what had happened. "Mr. Baker, I think it would be best if you left. We have a lot to talk about," said Mr. Walker.

"Well, thank you so much for dinner. It was delicious, as always. Have a pleasant evening," said Mr. Baker, already walking out the door.

Once Mr. Baker left, the screaming match began. "How could you?" said Abby. "You knew how I felt. I'll never forgive you!"

"I know you're upset, and I'm sorry. I really thought he wanted to fight in Europe, and thought it would be best if he left before you had your heart broken. I did it for your own good. Once I realized that he was an ambitious young man and wasn't going to Europe, I tried fixing what I had done. Unfortunately, I couldn't undo what I did. And for that, I am truly sorry," said Mr. Walker.

There was nothing for Abby to say. She was speechless. She didn't know what to think. Maybe it would have been better if she had never met him. Walter would not have been drafted and would be safe at home.

Abby just sat there, and Mrs. Walker tried consoling her. "I'm so sorry, dear."

The apology didn't work. Mrs. Walker might not have been involved in her husband's affairs, but she did nothing to prevent it. And for that, in Abby's eyes, she was just as guilty. "Can you just leave me alone tonight? I need time to think," said Abby, tears still running down her cheek.

The rest of the night, Abby just thought about Walter and cried. She thought more about Walter and cried. The young girl just didn't understand why her father would send Walter away to the war. He could have gotten rid of him another way. She stayed up about an hour after her parents went to bed.

The next morning, Abby woke up, ate breakfast, and went to school. When she arrived, school couldn't have gone by any slower. In history class, the teacher continued talking about the Great War. All Abby could think about was Walter and how terrible she felt about what happened.

"Do any of you girls know on what day the Germans surrendered to the Allies?" Mrs. Wilcox asked.

No student raised her hand.

"Anyone?" she asked as a question. "Abby, do you know?"

Abby started crying. She was sad about Walter, but she couldn't understand why she was sobbing in the middle of class. Mrs. Wilcox cared for Abby and felt sorry for her. "Why don't we talk after class?"

"It was November 11, 1918," said another girl.

"You are absolutely correct, young lady," said Mrs. Wilcox. The Germans unconditionally surrendered to the Allies on the eleventh hour of the eleventh day in the eleventh month in the year 1918.

After the period ended, Abby stayed behind and sat in her desk. Mrs. Wilcox shut the door and walked toward Abby. "What's wrong?

I saw you crying in class earlier. You can talk to me," said Abby's teacher.

Abby wanted to talk to someone about her circumstance, so she went ahead and shared what had happened. "My dad pulled some strings and had Walter drafted."

"What do you mean?" Mrs. Wilcox asked.

"He knows some people who could get Walter drafted. That's all I really know," said Abby.

"I'm really sorry, Abby," said Mrs. Wilcox. "Have you talked to your grandfather about it?"

"No. He's in Florida. I think I want to move out when I'm eighteen, which is in a week. I can't be around my parents anymore," said Abby.

"I understand. What are you going to do?" asked Mrs. Wilcox.

"I don't know. I just want to get out of here," said Abby.

"Well, I'll be here if you need me. You are welcome to stay at my house the day you turn eighteen," said Mrs. Wilcox. Mrs. Wilcox wasn't as nice to everyone as she was to Abby. Abby reminded Mrs. Wilcox of herself when she was a young girl.

Abby finished talking to Mrs. Wilcox and went to lunch with Martha. Abby told her best friend what had happened. "I'm so sorry, Abby. If there's anything I can do, just let me know. I'm always here for you," said Martha.

Abby thanked her and told Martha that she didn't want to talk about it anymore. They went back to talking about school and music.

The afternoon bell rang at noon, but Abby decided not to attend biology. Instead, she decided to skip school. The young girl went straight home, and her mom was sitting in the living room. "Is everything okay?" asked Mrs. Walker.

"I just didn't feel like going to school. And by the way, I'm moving out in a week. So you have one more week to see me and then I'm gone," Abby said to her mother.

"Abby...dear, I know your father messed up, but it's no reason to ruin your life," said Mrs. Walker.

"I'm not messing up my life. I'm trying to pick up the pieces from the mess you made," she said to her mother.

"I'm sorry you feel that way. I wasn't involved with your father's affairs," said Mrs. Walker.

"I love how you say that and how you pretend you didn't know what was going on," said Abby. "You knew he would do something, and he did."

"Well, I'm truly sorry," Mrs. Walker said.

"Sorry won't bring Walter back," said Abby.

As much as it hurt to admit, her daughter was right. Nothing she could say or do would bring Walter back. She said nothing and watched Abby climb the flight of stairs up to her room.

When Abby opened her bedroom door, she turned on the radio her parents bought her for Christmas the year before and jumped on her bed. "Our boys in Europe are important to us. They are getting hurt every day fighting Hitler and his Nazi army. The United States military is looking for women who are willing to volunteer in the United States Nurses Corps. They are looking for all able women eighteen and older," said the man on the radio.

Hmm, maybe I should become a nurse, Abby thought as she rolled over on the bed.

CHAPTER 11

After eight weeks of basic training, where they were whipped into shape, Randall and Walter signed up for a specialized field. Both of them gravitated toward being a paratrooper. The paratrooper school they went to was in North Carolina. Once they landed in North Carolina, Randall and Walter were assigned to barracks where all the paratroopers were to be housed. The sergeant walked into the solid brick housing unit and yelled, "Welcome, gentlemen! Get to know one another, because for the next four weeks, that's all you'll see. This is not an *I* unit, but a *team* unit. We work as a team around here."

Some poor soldier happened to be whispering under his breath when the sergeant was talking. "You, boy, drop down and give me twenty push-ups," said the sergeant. "Don't ever be talking when I'm speaking. You'll thank me someday." The soldier looked scared and crawled on the floor to complete his push-ups. "We don't screw around here. We give you guidance that will help you survive. This is not a game. This is war! If you want to return home, then you damn well better listen."

The sergeant left the building shortly after his speech. He told the men to report to the mess hall at 1800 hours. As he left, the soldiers started mingling and getting to know one another.

"Gentlemen, my name is Christian Caris, and I'm from Chevy Chase, Maryland. Where are you gentlemen from?" asked Christian Caris.

"Columbus," said Randall.

"Columbus, Georgia?" asked Christian.

"No. Columbus, Ohio. The state capital. Have you ever heard of it?" said Walter.

Christian laughed at the joke, but both Walter and Randall weren't convinced he found it funny.

"So how was growing up in Chevy Chase, huh, sport?" said Randall.

"My name is Christian, not sport. But with the nickname aside, it was very pleasant. My father worked in the government for many years. After working for the government, he decided to start his own practice of law and has been doing that ever since. I want to follow in his footsteps and join him at his practice. I'll be going to Georgetown Law School once this war is over."

"It sounds like you've got everything figured out. I wish I knew what I would be doing after my stint here. How did you end up in the Army? Did you get drafted, or did you enlist?" asked Walter.

"No. I enlisted. My father served in the Great War, and I feel like there is no greater honor than to serve my country," said Christian.

Christian Caris walked away from the two boys from Ohio, and in a hurry. It seemed like he was going to miss that 5:00 p.m. train to return home from work. "What was that guy's deal?" said Walter as he looked at his friend.

"I know right, sport? That doesn't offend you, does it?" said Randall. "Do all East Coast people lack a sense of humor? That guy isn't going to make any friends here. I couldn't stand to be around him for another minute!"

Walter patted Randall on the back and said, "Those people are from everywhere, even in Ohio. Just keep your head down. I wouldn't take it too personally," said Walter.

When the two men arrived at the mess hall. They found a table with a few guys sitting around it. "Mind if we sit here?" asked Walter.

"Y'all can sit here. I'm Bobby Hawkins," said the soldier. Bobby was a young man from Panama City, Florida. He came from a wealthy family. Bobby's father was an entrepreneur who owned a bunch of businesses in Panama City. They live in a big house near the ocean.

Randall and Walter accepted Bobby's invitation of sitting at their table. The two other young men sitting with Bobby Hawkins were Mathew Farr and Luke Feter. Mathew hailed from Toledo, Ohio. Both of his parents were teachers, so he came from a middle-class background. As for Luke Feter, he was from Boston, Massachusetts. His father worked as a janitor at a local high school. Luke was a bright young man. He had been offered a full scholarship to every school in the Ivy.

The five of them ate their dinner and chatted. "So Toledo, huh?" asked Walter.

"Yes. Toledo is a great place. Some of the best young people in the country live in Toledo," Mathew said.

Toledo, Ohio, was located off the banks of the Maumee River in Northwest Ohio. With the city's proximity to Detroit, the auto industry boomed in Toledo during the 1930s and a lot of automobile companies call the city home. The glass industry is also a big part of Toledo, and it became known as the Glass City. Owens-Illinois, Owens Corning, and Libbey-Owens-Ford all originated from Toledo.

"Oh, I know. My father is actually from T-Town, as I like to call it. He grew up in Ottawa Hills," said Walter. "I'm glad he moved to Columbus."

"No way! Why would you ever want live in Columbus instead of Toledo?" Mathew exclaimed.

"Because it's just better." Walter laughed.

"Toledo is better. Would you like to know why?" asked Mathew.

"Sure," responded Walter.

"The economy is doing well, but do you know what beats Columbus any day of the week and twice on Sundays?" asked Mathew.

Walter looked at him and said he didn't know. "The proximity to the Michigan Lakes. We're only a short drive to the Michigan

Lakes, so many people in Toledo have lake houses. It's too far away for any Columbus person to own a lake house," said Mathew.

Walter tapped him on the shoulder and said, "You're right on that point. My grandmother has a cottage on Diamond Lake, which is close to South Bend, Indiana. The drive takes forever when we go up there."

The time spent at the mess hall was short-lived. Soldiers were only allowed a few minutes to eat their dinner. The rationale behind the limited time to eat was that in combat, men only had a few minutes. When the dinner ended, the five guys walked back to the barracks. When in the barracks, Mathew held up a baseball and said, "How about a little ball?"

The other soldiers were enthusiastic about playing baseball, so they walked outside and started playing catch. Walter went to his bag, pulled out a glove and baseball. Walter looked at his glove and baseball, and it took him back to the time he spent with his brother.

* * *

Before Billy's death, the Wilson brothers spent hours in the front yard playing catch. After supper, during the cool evenings of the summer, they would throw the baseball back and forth until it became dark. "Time to come in, boys! It's getting dark," Allison Wilson would say nightly.

"Oh, come on, Mama, just a few more minutes," Walter said every time.

"We promise, just a few more throws, Mom," Billy would say.

"Oh, all right. But just a few more minutes."

A few more minutes always turned into almost an hour. Allison Wilson would "forget" to return after her five-minute warning. Both Billy and Walter knew deep down inside she didn't forget but rather allowed them to have fun for another hour, which they appreciated. They showed their appreciation by never arguing with her a second time.

After they marched inside the house, Billy and Walter brushed their teeth and got ready for bed. They then treaded to the room they shared with twin beds adjacent to each other. Five minutes after Billy and Walter tucked themselves into the sheets, Allison Wilson walked into the room. She kissed them both good night and revealed how much she loved them.

"I love you, boys. Sleep tight," she always said as she turned off the light and closed the door.

On most nights, Billy and Walter loved going to bed. They talked about baseball for hours until they fell asleep.

"Billy, what baseball team was the greatest ever?" Walter would ask.

"Ah, 1927 Yankees," Billy repeated over and over.

"Really?" asked Walter.

"Yes, really. What, 110 wins, Babe Ruth, Lou Gehrig, Earle Combs. That's an easy question, pal."

"That's really good," said Walter. "Wow, 110 wins."

Billy climbed out of bed and turned on the light. "Billy, Mama will get mad. Turn it off," Walter said.

"I'll turn it off in a second. I just have to show you something, bud." Billy pulled out a baseball and tossed it to his brother.

Walter looked at the ball and noticed there were a bunch of signatures. "Who signed this?" asked Walter.

"The greatest team to ever play," said Billy.

"The '27 Yankees?" Walter screamed and became afraid his parents would wake up. "How did you get it?"

"When you were too young to attend ball games, Dad and I went up to Cleveland to watch the Indians play the Yankees. Dad caught a foul ball and gave it to me. After the game, the Yankees were on the field. I went down and asked them to sign it. They couldn't say no to a five-year-old," said Billy.

"You're so lucky!" said Walter.

Billy turned off the light so his parents wouldn't wake up. He climbed back into bed and slid underneath the covers. He looked over at his brother and tossed the baseball at him. "Now you're lucky. It's yours," said Billy.

"No, Billy. I can't have this."

"You can. You love baseball more than any person I know, pal. You just have to make me a promise," said Billy.

"Anything."

"You must work really hard at baseball. You must work really hard at everything you do. If you want to play for the Yankees someday, you need to work your hardest. And that doesn't end with baseball. You need to work the hardest in every aspect of life."

"I will, Billy. You are the best big brother," said Walter as he went to sleep.

Not more than a week later, Billy died while playing baseball with Walter. After that tragic accident, Walter never picked up a baseball. However, he did listen to his brother's advice and never stopped working. He worked his butt off and became one of the most feared tennis players. His hard work paid off in the classroom, as he received excellent grades. And now, more than ever, he needed to work hard to become a good soldier. Being a well-equipped soldier benefited the United States, and Abby; he would help achieve an American victory and return home to his sweetheart.

* * *

"Walter, next one's coming to you!" said Mathew.

Walter was caught off guard while thinking about his brother. "Give me the heat," said Walter.

Mathew threw the ball to Walter, and everyone could hear a *smack* as the ball found a way into the glove. "Good catch, sport," Randall said.

"Truly, well done," said Luke. "Walter, throw it my way."

Walter swayed, cocked his arm back, and fired the baseball toward Luke. Unlike Walter's smacking sound, the ball hoped off Luke's glove and hit a tree. *Clank* was the sound the soldiers heard. "Great catch, Luke. You're a real natural," said Bobby Hawkins.

"This is my first time playing, Mr. Hawkins," Luke said.

"You can call me Bobby," Bobby Hawkins said. "Y'all want to go inside now. It's starting to get dark."

All of them agreed, and the soldiers began walking into the barracks. However, Walter waved his hand in the air and halted them. "Hold up, boys! I have to show you something."

Dusk was almost over, and the darkness of night was upon them. They wanted to settle in for the night, but they gathered by the door because of Walter. Once everyone was in a circle, Walter pulled a baseball from his pocket. He tossed it to Luke, who, he knew, would find it particularly amusing because he was from Boston. "This can't be real," Luke said while his eyes were glowing at the ball.

"It's real, all right," Walter said.

Luke then passed the ball to everyone. "Walter, how did you get this ball? It's signed by the 1927 Yankees, the greatest baseball team of all time," Mathew said. He appreciated the ball the most because he was a baseball coach.

"My brother gave it to me. Let's go inside now. I just wanted to show you boys. No one has seen it before, not even Randall," said Walter.

"How come?" Luke asked.

"It's a long story, so let's just go inside," Walter replied.

The soldiers proceeded to walk into the barracks. Bobby pulled out a deck of cards that had an American flag on the back of them. "Y'all want to play some cards?" said Bobby. The American men grabbed wooden stools and placed them around a light wooden chest.

"So, gentlemen, what will training be like?" asked Luke.

"We're in for a treat. There's a lot of conditioning involved. And we jump out of planes almost every day. It'll be intense, but I'm ready," said Bobby Hawkins.

Mathew laughed. "I heard it's a little more strenuous than jumping out of airplanes and conditioning. My cousin graduated from paratrooper school a few months ago. The four weeks are broken up into four one-week segments: stage A, B, C, and D. Stage A is considered to be the hardest, and they attempt to wash out the weak. It's all about physical activity, and running is all you do. You never walk, and you're always running. We will also be doing a lot of push-ups, sit-ups, and rope climbing. There's a fitness test at the end of the week, and if you don't complete it, you're out."

"Damn, sounds like fun!" said Randall. "What are the other stages like?"

"Well, stage B is the ground training stage. We learn how the chute works, how to jump out of a plane, and how to land on our feet without getting hurt. And in stage C, we continue the ground training. We learn how to prepare our chute. We will be practice-jumping from this thirty-foot tower. It's all fun stuff," said Mathew.

"I wonder what happens in the final stage," said Luke Feter, the young man from Boston.

"The final week consists of jumping out of planes, both during the day and at night. If you complete that week successfully, you will be given your paratrooper patch and you will join an elite fighting group," said Mathew, who was smiling at the thought of becoming a paratrooper.

Mathew's smiling was contagious, and the other boys began grinning. They continued playing poker, and the five guys talked into the night. None of them had any real money, so they played with whatever they had, which were cigarettes and cigars. As they played, the soldiers talked about their lives back home. They chatted about the girls they left behind. "My gal is back home in Florida," said Bobby. "We've been together for a couple of years now. I asked her to marry me before I left for the war."

All the boys said their congratulations to Bobby Hawkins on the engagement. "Any of y'all boys have gals back home?" asked Bobby.

Mathew shook his head no, and Mathew and Bobby looked at Randall, Luke, and Walter.

Bobby looked over in the direction of Luke, and Luke began speaking. "I don't have a sweetheart at home waiting for me, but I do, indeed, have a girl waiting for me," Luke said.

"Go on bud, explain," Mathew said without hesitation.

"I have a baby sister at home. She's eight years old. She was kicking and screaming when I left," said Luke.

Walter put his arm around Luke Feter's shoulder and said, "I bet it was hard on her. I have a sister, who is seventeen, and it was difficult. I'm sure you're her hero."

With a sad look on his face, he said, "It was hard on the both of us. I made her a promise, though, and I intend to keep it. I promised her I would be coming home."

The men were all touched by Luke's story about the bond between him and his sister. Randall couldn't wait to tell the men about Mallie. "My sweetheart is actually his sister," Randall said while chuckling a bit.

"Are you serious, Randall?" said Luke.

"Yeah, boys. It just happened," said Randall.

"I almost had to kill him," said Walter.

The men were astonished and had no idea of what to say. It didn't seem appropriate giving Randall a hard time about her, because it was Walter's sister.

After a few games of cards, the men asked Walter if he was seeing anyone back home. "I am," said Walter.

"Go on," said Mathew. "We all shared our war stories. No pun intended."

Without hesitation, Walter said, "I met a girl over the summer, and she is almost perfect. She is the most thoughtful and caring person I have ever met. We fell for each other, and fast. I didn't intend for it to happen, but it did. It's going to be hard for me not to see her every day, but I'm glad to be serving my country."

"Amen to that," said Bobby.

They began talking about their friends, parents, and what they missed most about home. Even though they all missed home, they all agreed on one principle point, that Hitler needed to be stopped, and the cause was important enough to be away from their loved ones.

When the soldiers dispersed for the night, Walter decided to write a note to Abby.

> *Dear Abby,*
>
> *I hope you're doing well. I miss you every day, but I know there is a reason for me being here. When tyranny and oppression rise up, people need to bring it down, whatever the cost may be. I am proud to risk my life to protect the American way*

of life. I know the cost is to be away from you, but sometimes you need to sacrifice being away from the ones you love when the cause is so great. I think of you every day, and I intend to come back to you and be all yours.

Love,
Walter

After he was done writing, he climbed into bed. By his bedside was a picture of Abby and the note she wrote him the day he left for boot camp. He took it out and read it, as he did every night.

Dear Walter,
    Well, this is the day I've been dreading since you told me about the draft notice. You already know this, but I want to tell you again. I love you, and we have the most amazing times together. What we have is special, and no one can take it from us. I may have trouble sleeping while you're gone, but every time I do, I'll look up at the stars and pretend that I'm lying next to you. I'm proud that you are so brave about serving our country. I'll be waiting for you to return, but I'll admit, I won't be patient. How could I, when I want to spend every day with you? Anyway, stay safe, and I'll miss you every day.

Love,
Abby

The next day, Walter and the rest of the wannabe paratroopers woke up to trumpet sounds. "Rise and shine, ladies! It's time to get up. We have a long day of training," said the sergeant.

Everyone seemed slow to get out of the beds and were even slower to get dressed. Once they put on their green Army uniform, they marched outside. Outside the barracks, the soldiers lined up and were given orders of that day's assignment. The assignment was to march all day. They were to march a five-mile trail and back. It was designed for endurance, and as the sergeant put it, "In case you gents wind up in the middle of Europe, Africa, Italy, or wherever the hell we are fighting, you will have the endurance to survive. This exercise is all about survival."

It took about four or five hours to complete the exercise. The hike was very rugged and nothing like the terrain Walter and Randall were accustomed. Ohio was flat, and it wasn't very high above sea level. North Carolina, on the other hand, was higher above sea level and had more hills and mountains. In particular, the mountain that they would run up and down was full of trees, rocks, plants, and anything else found in a forest. Running up that mountain was difficult, and the men were exhausted at the end of it.

When the hike was completed, the men went to their barracks to relax before dinner. Walter was lying on his bed when the mail courier dropped off letters. He jumped out of his bed and was hoping there would be a letter from Abby. "I have a couple of letters for Walter Wilson," said the mailman.

"I'm Walter Wilson," Walter said as he grabbed the two letters from the mail courier's hand.

Walter traveled back to his bed, where Randall met him. "Letters from Abby, huh, sport?" said Randall. "I received some from your sister a few days ago. She wanted to make sure I was keeping an eye on you."

Without further ado, Walter opened the letters and read them loud enough for everyone to hear:

> Dearest Walter,
>
> I hope you are doing well. I can't stand being without you. I miss you so much and think of you every day. I found out my dad pulled some strings to get you drafted. He figured that since you would be joining the military anyway, there was no harm getting you drafted a few months earlier. I'm so sorry. I feel awful about the whole thing. I'm starting to

regret having met you, because you would never have been in this predicament. Keep on fighting and know I'll be here, waiting for you. So come back to me.

Love,
Abby

Both Walter and Randall couldn't believe what they had just read. Had Abby's father really pulled strings to have him drafted? There were many emotions that ran through Walter, from anger to misery. "I can't believe it," Walter said toward Randall.

"What a jerk! We both would have been back at home if not for him. Now I'm angry. I'm spitting angry!" Randall said.

Walter thought Randall's head was about to explode. "Well, we can't look at it that way. I'm just as mad as you are. But we're here now, and we're here to serve our country. We are fighting for a cause, and we need to see it through," said Walter.

"You're right, Walter. We do need to see this through. I won't think about it from now on. I will continue to think about how I can be a better soldier," said Randall.

The second letter was lying dormant in his hand, and Walter was contemplating if he should open it. He really couldn't handle this new letter bringing worse than the previous one. On one hand, things couldn't get as bad as Walter being sent to the war by Mr. Walker, but on the other hand, maybe Abby felt so guilty that she wanted to end things with him. Regardless of the outcome, he decided to open the letter.

Dearest Walter,
I have decided to move out and join the military. I want to serve, just like you. I realize that I cannot be in combat, so I'll be treating young men who are wounded. I pray that I do not have to treat

you, but I do hope we cross paths. If not, we will see
each other after the war.

Love,
Abby

The next letter from young Abigail shocked Walter. His shoulders shrugged, and his eyebrows rose in the air. "She's joining the military! Are you kidding me?"

He turned to Randall and told him the news. Randall was just as surprised as Walter and said, "Abby joining the military, huh? I would have given pigs a better chance of flying." Randall and Walter couldn't believe she had decided to become a nurse, especially because she was such a spoiled brat.

"Do you remember when we had to run back to her house just because she spilled ketchup on her shirt?" said Walter.

"You bet, and she blamed your slow driving as the reason we were late to the movie," said Randall.

"Good times," said Walter. "God, I miss her."

"Me too. I'm not even dating her, and I think she's a fun girl. I miss us all hanging out," admitted Randall.

Randall and Walter were talking about the possibility of seeing her in action. Bobby Hawkins heard the conversation. "Your gal is enlisting to become a nurse? That's brave. Samantha would never do that. Samantha will be a Seminole next year. She will be attending Florida State," said Bobby. "Good for Abby. I think it's awesome."

"I'm going to be worried about her, but we're all here for the same reason," said Walter.

There was no doubt Walter was impressed with her courage, but there was a small part of him that didn't want her to serve as a nurse. He didn't want to be worried about her.

After Walter was done talking to his fellow soldiers about the letters he received, he grabbed a pen and sat down to write Abby. He wondered where to send the letter but figured, if she signed up to be a nurse, the Army would figure out where to send it.

Dear Abby,

I'm glad to hear that you joined the war as a nurse. I was telling the guys about it, and they were jealous of me. They were jealous that I was with a great girl who is very courageous and who wants to serve her country. And about your father, don't worry about it. Even though he may have had me sent here, I'm glad to be serving my country. I'm doing my part to stop tyranny, and it's a great honor. I want to wish you luck being a nurse, and hopefully, our paths meet. If not, we will see each other after this conflict. Keep writing. It gives me more motivation.

Love,
Walter

Shortly after Walter wrote to Abby, it was time for dinner. Walter and his fellow soldiers walked to the center of the base for chow. Even though his experience wasn't supposed to be enjoyable because the US was at war, Walter enjoyed getting to know these young men. His bond with these men felt as if he were back home with his tennis team. Only instead of battling on the tennis court, he would be battling in Europe. And as luck would have it, Randall Moore, Bobby Hawkins, Mathew Farr, and Luke Feter were assigned to the same platoon as him, a regiment in the 82nd Airborne Division. Walter was promoted with the rank of private first class. Walter felt honored to be in the same unit as them, and he was honored to sacrifice his life with or for them.

During the four weeks of training, there were close friendships that evolved, and Walter felt especially close to Bobby. Often, they would spend long nights talking about their girls back home. Walter loved how Bobby would refer to his girl and Walter's as gal. It was just a Southern thing, Walter thought to himself. They would talk about their past and future. In particular, Walter shared his summer story with Bobby and how it was one of the best summers of his life. Bobby also shared his stories with Walter. He met Samantha at school, and they were prom king and queen together. They were the definition of high school sweethearts. Bobby was the quarterback of the football team, and Samantha was the head cheerleader. Once Walter and the other men discovered he was a quarterback, they gave him the nickname QB.

They would talk about the times together with their girls, but they would also imagine the future with them. Both of them wanted big families, with a dog and a white picket fence. It sounded like a textbook American dream and a fairy tale of sorts. If Bobby couldn't live out his dream, he wanted Walter to be the one to tell Samantha. "If anything happens to me, can you be the one to tell Samantha?" said Bobby.

"QB, don't talk like that. But I would be honored, if something should happen," said Walter. Walter really hoped that day would never come. Bobby was a great man, and he didn't want to be the one to tell Samantha that Bobby wasn't coming home.

Not counting Randall, Walter was closest with Bobby, but he was able to get to know Mathew and Luke quite well. Mathew was tall and athletic and was quite quirky. One time he accepted a dare to shove his whole entire fist in his mouth. Mathew Farr was the comedian of the group, and he always made people laugh. The young man from Toledo, Ohio, helped lighten the stress level. Farr was a few years older than the rest of them, as he was a recent college graduate, and had just accepted a teaching job in Maumee, Ohio. Maumee was a town just south of Toledo. At Maumee, he would have been a freshman science teacher and the head baseball coach. He always had a positive attitude and would say, "Those jobs will be waiting for me when I return. Hell, I'm fighting for my job back in Ohio, because if we fail, who knows what will happen?"

The other member of his group of friends was Luke Feter. Luke was relatively short, and his ancestors hailed from Ireland. His heritage from Ireland showed, as he had fire-red hair and millions of freckles. Luke's father was a janitor, so his family didn't have much money while Luke was growing up. But even though Luke's family didn't have much wealth, Luke acted like a proper gentleman. With hard work, Luke was able to attain a full scholarship to any school in the Ivy he wished to attend. Luke was such an honorable kid that he put his education on hold. After he turned eighteen years old, Feter enlisted in the military. He believed it was his duty to defend freedom for not just Americans but all people around the world as well.

As Walter and Randall became closer to their fellow paratroopers, the rest of training went by fast. The men became experts at jumping out of airplanes, landing safely, survival, stealth, and marksmanship. In a few days, the soldiers would ship out to Europe. Even though they were headed to the front lines of the war, they were ready. Equally, they were excited to begin fighting for the cause. All the men had mixed emotions, whether it was nervousness or excitement, but they were ready.

CHAPTER 12

Months had passed since Abby had left her parents' home in Arlington Heights, Ohio. Her first stop as a member of the United States Nursing Corps was a base just outside Washington, DC. This base was used for a number of things but only had two purposes involving nurses. First, this base was a training center for young women aspiring to help in the medical field. Second, Washington, DC, was one of the first stops for all soldiers wounded in the war.

Coming from a small town in the Midwest, Abby loved her adventure in Washington, DC. It was a big city, with lots of people, and she felt like she was at the center of the universe. She explored the city on most weekends. She admired all the monuments and museums, but she most admired Capitol Hill. On one Saturday that she didn't have an assignment, she went on a tour of the white capitol building that has been a symbol of American democracy for many years. While inside the Capitol, she walked through the same halls of politicians making crucial decisions. She saw the old Supreme Court, which was where the former slave Dred Scott appeared to sue for his freedom. Abby walked through the old Senate and House chambers, where the likes of Abraham Lincoln, John C. Calhoun, and John Quincy Adams worked.

Even though she enjoyed living in DC, she didn't come for pleasure or vacation. She came to do her part in the war efforts. She learned that becoming a nurse in the Army was no easy task. Young Abby Walker was required to understand some of the basic practices of medicine: anesthesia, surgery, blood, removing bullets, and psychiatric care. Not only did she have to understand medical knowledge; she also trained for endurance. In combat, military nurses could walk several miles in one day, so the Army prepared the young girls. These women ran twice a week to ensure they were physically prepared for tending to young men in combat.

Another task she learned to complete was an eye exam. A soldier would stand about twenty feet away and repeat the letters on the triangular chart. It seemed simple, but some of the men couldn't complete this exercise. Some military specialties or sectors did not require perfect vision. One of the few crafts that required twenty-twenty visions was aviation, and Abby dreaded giving pilots eye exams. It was heartbreaking for her if she denied a pilot the chance to fly in the skies.

One occasion, Abby was proctoring an eye exam to a very handsome young man. She felt a small amount of guilt because she passed this pilot who failed his test. Once he failed, he begged her to pass him. His excuse was that he had the flu that day and couldn't concentrate. "Please, ma'am, don't take my wings away," he said. "I'm a great pilot. The best. No one can beat me once I'm in the air. That's where I belong."

This soldier reminded her a lot of Walter. He was tall, dark, and handsome, and if Walter weren't in her life, she would have wanted to get to know him. She touched his forehead, and he did seem to be running a fever. Before thinking twice, she grabbed her passing stamp.

"Thank you so much, ma'am. You won't regret this. You did a great service to your country," the young pilot said.

She smiled at him and said, "Don't you think you're being cocky?"

"No, ma'am, just confident. I just feel that I'm the best pilot in the Marines."

As he was walking away, she asked for his name, just in case he became a hero. If he became a hero, she would smile and take some of the credit. "Street. Jim Street," he said.

The final part of training was on a Friday, and it was a seminar lectured by a nurse who had served on the front lines, and she would prepare these young nurses about the realities of war. The seminar took place in a small classroom with green carpet and wooden desks. It reminded Abby of her high school back in Columbus, Ohio, especially because only girls were present in the classroom. Abby went into the room and sat next to a girl that could be on the cover of a fashion magazine.

"Hi. I'm Abby Walker. What's your name?" asked Abby.

"My name is Gracelyn Turner," the girl said.

Abby nodded and asked, "Where do you call home?"

"I'm from Carlisle, Pennsylvania. It's one of those small towns where there's one of everything. I wanted to get out so bad that I decided to become a nurse," said Gracelyn.

Gracelyn asked Abby about her story. "Well, I wanted to get away too. I've been in Ohio for all my life, and I wanted to see the world. The man I want to spend the rest of my life with is out fighting somewhere, and I felt like I had an obligation to serve. I can't fight, so I did the next best thing."

After a while of sitting in an uncomfortable chair in the small classroom, the speaker finally appeared through the door. "Sorry I'm late," she said to all the nurses. "I want to congratulate all of you in completing the training. It's something to be proud of." She proceeded to start lecturing about the realities of war. This woman told her story about serving in North Africa and how she had the privilege of treating young men on the battlefield. She kept emphasizing to Abby and her fellow nurses, "It could be dangerous work, but it is rewarding work."

This heroic nurse told her story for about an hour. Once she was done with her lecture, a high-ranking nurse walked through the doorway. "I hope you all feel more prepared for the journey to Europe. Monday morning, you ladies will report to room 101 of the nursing wing. Some of you fine ladies will be serving in Europe, while others will be assigned to important work stateside. Dismissed."

Gracelyn turned to Abby and asked her what she was doing this weekend.

"I'm not sure. I'm probably going to stay in and write Walter a few letters," she said.

"You're josh'n me, right?" said Gracelyn.

"Not at all," Abby said.

"That's no fun, Abby. Come out with me tonight. You have the rest of your life to spend with Walter. This could be our last weekend in DC. Come on, what do ya say?" said Gracelyn.

"Fine. I'll come, but we have to do something fun."

"Oh, we will. There will be nurses and soldiers at this party. I'll come to your room at about 1900 hours." As they were about to go their separate ways, Abby agreed and said she was staying in barracks 40.

Abby went to the mess hall to grab dinner before her night out with Gracelyn. The dinner was green bean casserole, baked beans, and bread, and it tasted as delicious as it looked. After she was done eating, she returned to her barracks. She sat on her bed weighing the pros and cons of being a nurse in the United States compared to Europe. If she was chosen to work in the United States, the only danger would be that of everyday life. The patient care would also be less stressful than it would be at the front. However, if she was selected to serve in Europe, her role would be more vital, but more dangerous as well.

Even though Walter would not read her letter and send a response before Monday, Abby felt like writing him.

> *Dear Walter,*
>
> *Today, we officially became nurses. I'm pretty excited that I will finally be able to help people. They have yet to tell me where I'll be working, whether it is in the States or Europe. I have the weekend off duty, and the Nursing Corps will hand us our assignments on Monday. For some reason, I'm not*

sure which one I'd prefer. I know it may be more of a risk on the front, but it would certainly be more meaningful. I know I'll be able to handle the stress of it. Maybe I'll be joining you across the Atlantic very soon, and I pray that I will not be forced to care for you. I hope you're doing well, and stay safe.

Love,
Abby

Gracelyn walked into her barracks as Abby was finishing her letter. "Are you ready?" asked Gracelyn.

Abby said yes and walked out of her barracks with Gracelyn. They left the base and never looked back. The destination was a few miles from the base in a section of Washington, DC, known as Eastern Market. Eastern Market was a place with small town houses that resembled homes built in New Orleans. And there was a market in the middle where farmers sold cheeses, fruit, and meats. The house where the party was located happened to be owned by a soldier's brother who worked on Capitol Hill. He worked for a congressman from Mississippi.

The girls arrived at the blue house on the corner of South Carolina and Eleventh Street. Once they walked up the steps, they knocked on the door. A young man who looked to have reached his quarter-century crisis answered the door.

"Come on in," the man said.

Everyone was sitting in the living room, directly to the right of the door, so Abby and Gracelyn joined them. "What do y'all do?" one of the boys said to them.

"We're nurses in the Army," said Gracelyn.

"Oh, really? Well, I really appreciate what y'all do for us. Y'all seem very helpful," the gentleman said.

Abby and Gracelyn said thank you and sat down in two wooden chairs that were in the middle of the living room. "Can I get you ladies a drink?" one of the men asked. Both Abby and Gracelyn nodded, so he grabbed a couple of beers from the refrigerator.

"I'm Wesley Callahan. Some people call me Wes, so whichever you prefer. What are your names?" the man said.

"I'm Gracelyn, and this is Abby."

Wesley Callahan was from a small town just outside Lexington, Kentucky. Wes was a pilot in the Marines and held the rank of captain. The young man from Kentucky was in law school at Vanderbilt when President Roosevelt declared war over Japan. Many of his friends believed Wesley was smart and ambitious enough to become a senator one day.

It was clear from the way Gracelyn interacted with Wesley that she really enjoyed his company. Gracelyn focused all her attention on Wesley, so Abby had two choices: sip her beer while amusing herself or join the conversation with three soldiers.

"Do you like blondes or brunettes better?" said a young man to his friend.

With that comment, Abby decided to sip her beer in silence. She didn't care too much for the conversation. Plus, with having dark hair, she was of course biased.

"I like blondes. They seem to be easier to sleep with," the friend said.

"No, the broads with darker hair are easier to get into the sack," said the other man.

"Oh, is that so?" said Abby to the soldier.

"Umm," said the soldier, unable to speak.

"At least that's what I've found," said the young man sitting on the couch.

"You disgust me," said Abby.

Abby was ready to jet off like an airplane. Abby gave Gracelyn a stern look and put on her coat as a hint, but Gracelyn didn't understand the subtle movement. She was done trying to be subtle and just walked right beside Abby and Wes.

"Do y'all want to get out of here? I'm supposed to meet my friend for dinner. I would love it if you girls came with," Wes said before Abby could request an exit strategy.

"Sure," Abby said. *Anything is better than this party,* she thought.

The three of them traveled to an upscale restaurant a few blocks away from the house. The restaurant was called Red 72. The white-clothed tables were stationed in the front of the restaurant, and the bar was set up in the rear with a dance floor. Red 72 was located in Barracks Row, which was a strip of restaurants and bars located across the street from the Marine barracks. As they walked in, they noticed that it was a very popular place since many people were sitting down and ordering food. Wesley saw his friend sitting at one of the tables, and the three of them walked over to the table.

When Abby reached the table, she noticed a familiar figure. She recognized him from somewhere but couldn't put her finger on it. He was tall with dark hair and beautiful blue eyes. She sat down, and the man said, "Well, look who it is. If it isn't the nurse that saved my career!" said Jim Street.

"Jim, you know this girl?" said Wesley.

"You bet I do. She passed me when I failed my eye exam. I will always be in her debt," said Jim. "First round's on me."

Jim Street picked up the first round, but that didn't stop the rapid flow of alcoholic beverages. Time was flying by at a fast rate, and everyone was having fun. They were ordering drink after drink and talking about their experiences in the military. "So how do you like working as a nurse?" asked Jim.

"It's been great. We're able to help people, which is such a rewarding feeling," said Abby.

Gracelyn then took a sip of her gin and tonic, saying, "It's definitely growing on me. I accepted the job because I wanted to leave my hometown. I'm just really glad I get to work with my fellow nurses and help our wounded boys."

"You don't have to be politicians around us," said Jim Street.

Both Jim and Wesley nodded and agreed that nurses were important to the war. "Maybe one of you will save my life one day," said Jim.

While smiling, Abby said, "I already saved your career. What else do you want from me?"

"A dance will suffice," said Jim Street.

Gracelyn grabbed Abby and said she needed to freshen up. As they walked in the bathroom, Gracelyn told Abby that she could tell Jim really liked her. "He can't stop staring at you, Abby. You should talk to him more."

"What are you talking about? I'm with Walter, and we'll be together after the war, and—"

"You're living in a dream world Abby. The chances of Walter coming home aren't good. Plus, you're eighteen years old. You're too young to make decisions like that. Go talk to him," said Gracelyn. "I'm not telling you to marry him, just go over and talk."

When the two of them were walking out of the bathroom, Abby was trying to think. That seemed nearly impossible at the time, because she was intoxicated like it was her prom night. "I drank too much of the devil's nectar," she said under her breath. Gracelyn did have a point. Walter might not be coming back, and she was very young. What if she was too young to make such a decision? Was it a crime just to talk to him?

She was nearing the rectangular table, and Abby had about ten seconds to make a decision. She decided that she would talk to the young man since it wasn't a sin to have a conversation. Once she sat down, Wesley and Gracelyn stood up and walked over to the dance floor. "They may be having a little too much fun," said Jim.

"Yes, but they seem happy together. How do you know Wesley? He never told us what he did in the military," said Abby.

"We're pilots together. I've known Wes my whole life. We grew up together in Kentucky."

"Why did you become pilots?" asked Abby.

"It's a long story," said Jim Street.

"I have all night."

"Well, my father was a crop duster, and we were around my father a lot growing up. We've always loved to fly. When we were kids, we used to dream about becoming pilots and fighting in air battles. It's awesome now because we get to live out our dream," said Jim.

Jim and Abby talked while Gracelyn and Wesley continued to dance. Without hesitation, Jim asked Abby if she wanted to dance.

Contrary to Gracelyn not hesitating, Abby did hesitate but finally relented. When she agreed to the dance, they walked over to the dance floor and joined Gracelyn and Wesley. Abby's mind turned to a memory with Walter.

* * *

Several weeks before Abby watched Walter disappear into the military base, she took him to her cousin's wedding. It was a beautiful outdoor summer wedding in her grandfather's backyard; roses and flowers were everywhere. It was everything Abigail dreamed of when she was a little girl, with the exception that she was not the bride standing at the altar.

Abby was only seventeen years old on the wedding date, so her parents almost refused to let her bring Walter. But she was an only child, and she kicked and screamed until they let Walter come.

Walter was wearing his dad's old black tuxedo when he arrived at Abby's grandfather's house. Abby's grandfather, James Millener, was waiting for him by the door. As he knocked on the door, an elderly man with a white mustache who looked like the Monopoly man opened it. "Young man, you must be Walter," said the older gentleman.

"Yes, sir," said Walter, extending his arm for a handshake.

The man grabbed Walter's hand and introduced himself. "I am James Millener, Abby's granddad. I've heard quite a deal about you, young man."

"I hope it was all good," said Walter.

"It was indeed good. My granddaughter is inside. She's been waiting for you all afternoon."

When Walter walked inside, Abby was there to greet him, wearing a gray dress with a white trim. "You look beautiful," Walter said.

"Thank you. You don't look half bad yourself."

"Thank you for the compliment. It means so much to me," Walter said. "Can I escort you to the wedding?" he said in a more serious tone.

"I couldn't think of anything better," Abby said.

The two young adults proceeded to walk into the backyard. There were five rows of white chairs, with ten chairs in each row, and there was a gazebo where the wedding party was standing. It was a small wedding. Many people didn't make it because of the war.

Just as Walter and Abby took their seats, the wedding commenced. It was a long ceremony, and after about an hour, the bride and groom finally said their "I dos." When that happened, Abby grabbed Walter's hand and smiled at him.

The Millener backyard turned into the reception at the conclusion of the ceremony. Circular tables were brought in, and the bar was set up on a big rectangular table. The white plastic chairs were replaced with fancy wooden ones. Abby and Walter sat down at their assigned clothed table and were joined by Mr. and Mrs. Walker.

"Walter, it's a pleasure to see you. Are you enjoying the wedding?" asked Mr. Walker.

"It's good to see you, Mr. Walker. I'm having a good time," said Walter. "Thank you for inviting me."

"Well, young man, we had an intuition not to send an invitation, but Abby insisted," Mr. Walker said with a sly grin. "In our family, you must be eighteen to receive a plus one. Abby demanded that we bend the rules just this once."

While Mr. Walker and Walter were talking, Mrs. Walker was conversing with her daughter. "I can't believe I'm at my brother's daughter's wedding. It's hard to believe she's only two years older than you, dear," said Ann Walker.

"I can't wait for my wedding day. Hopefully, I'll be her age," said Abby.

"That's two years away. You'll be nineteen," said Mrs. Walker.

"And...?"

"Well, you probably haven't met the right man yet," Mrs. Walker said to her daughter.

"Yes, I have," said Abby. "He's sitting right next to me."

"Well, just keep an open mind," said Mrs. Walker.

The server came out at the perfect time to halt a potential argument. Lobster, asparagus, and mashed potatoes were the saving grace.

"Young man, have you ever had lobster before?" asked Mr. Walker while he looked at Walter.

"No, sir. This will be my first time," said Walter.

"You certainly have missed out. Lobster is one of my favorite dinners. My family spent the summers in Maine, and we had lots of lobster. Abby's grandfather flew the lobster in fresh," said Mr. Walker.

"I'm sure it will be delicious, then," Walter said.

It was as delicious as Mr. Walker described. Both Abby and Walter finished their dinner, but everyone else took their time eating, especially the bride and groom. The bride and groom visited every table. When they reached Abby and Walter, Abby introduced them to Walter. "Walter, this is my cousin Courtney, and her new husband, Timothy," said Abby.

"Pleased to meet you," Timothy said, shaking Walter's hand. Timothy was rather dull, but apparently, his money made up for it. He came from a wealthy family that lived in Cleveland, Ohio. His father owned a big steel mill. Timothy and Courtney met at the Ohio State University.

"Likewise. Thank you for inviting me to your wedding," Walter said.

Courtney stopped talking to her cousin and began talking to Walter. "We've heard so many wonderful things about you. We had to meet you, and it seemed like the perfect opportunity," Courtney said while smiling over at Abby.

"Abby has told me so much about you as well. Congratulations on the wedding!" Walter said.

The eight-instrument band began playing, and Courtney and Timothy were obliged to convene on the dance floor. After they participated in the first dance, Abby grabbed Walter by the hand and dragged him to the dance floor. They began to dance, and Abby was impressed by Walter's dancing.

"Who taught you how to dance?" asked Abby.

"My mom used to be a dance teacher. I learned all my moves from her," Walter said as he pulled Abby closer.

"I will be sure to thank your mom. I guess now I'll have to take you to all my social events. My other boyfriends will be pretty upset."

"I always love a friendly competition," said Walter. "What did you tell your cousin about me?"

Abby leaned in and kissed Walter on the cheek. "I told her that you are the sweetest, most amazing man. And that I was happy."

"How happy!" Walter said.

Abby had a big smile on her face. Her eyes were glowing like a Christmas tree. "So happy."

"It's too bad that my dad isn't as thrilled with us as Courtney. It's too bad he's not half as thrilled," Abby said.

"Honestly, I don't really care what your dad, mom, or even grandfather thinks. I'm happy, and you're happy. That's all I really care about," Walter said as he proceeded to kiss Abby on the lips.

Abby smiled at Walter. She realized that her father's feelings toward her relationship didn't matter. Mr. Walker cared about Abby's future financial security, but she couldn't care less. It didn't matter what kind of house or car she possessed, as long as she was happy. They danced all night.

* * *

Abby's mind wandered back to the Red 72 dance floor. Finally, Jim asked, "So who's the lucky guy?"

Startled, Abby asked Jim to repeat the question.

"I said, who's the lucky man in your life?"

Abby couldn't understand how he figured out that she was thinking of Walter. "Just some guy from back home," she said. "How did you know?"

"It's quite apparent something has been on your mind the whole night. No one is usually this quiet around me," said Jim. "He's more than just a guy, isn't he?"

Abby then nodded. "You're just as cocky away from the cockpit," said Abby, smiling. "I met him last summer, and he means the world to me. He was drafted. It's just been a long few months."

They kept on dancing with each other. Abby realized that she never asked Jim about his life back in Kentucky. "So are there loved ones waiting for you in Kentucky?" asked Abby.

"There's too many people to count," said Jim. "My mom, dad, and two brothers are living in Kentucky."

"No girlfriend?" asked Abby. "A confident man like you must have girls lining up back home."

"I was with someone for a while, and she ended things before I enlisted," Jim said.

Abby could tell he was upset, because of his low tone of voice. "I'm so sorry, Jim," Abby said as she gave him a hug.

"It just wasn't meant to be, I guess. She told me that it would be too hard on her, me going to war and all. That was the last time I saw her," Jim said.

"Jim, you tried fighting for her, right?" said Abby.

Jim looked around the room for a minute to collect his thoughts. He didn't really understand the question. She broke it off; how could he fight for her? "What do you mean?" he asked.

"Did you try to go after her? Persuade her to change her mind? Or tell her how you felt?" asked Abby.

"No. Why would I? I didn't think that was a good idea. Her mind was made up. I thought there was nothing I could do," said Jim.

"Sometimes we just have to be pushed, and we change our minds all the time. We are girls! Maybe she thought, by breaking up with you, it would be easier for you to focus on staying alive," Abby voiced. "Walter told me that thinking of me would motivate him to stay alive."

Abby looked at Gracelyn and Wes dancing. Gracelyn had her arms around Wes's neck, and Wes's hand was just south of her waist. The two looked really happy and were all over each other like a couple of high school kids at the Sadie Hawkins dance.

"Are you going back to the base?" asked Abby to Wesley and Jim, as the restaurant was about to close for the night.

"No. My cousin booked me a hotel suite. Do you girls want to come back with Jim and me?" asked Wesley. Abby and Gracelyn both nodded, so they hailed a cab, which took them to the hotel.

After they walked out of the cab, they entered the Marriott at DuPont Circle. All four of them were happy to be in a warm lobby because of the cold, brisk night. Wesley walked up to the front desk and gave them his name. The woman working at the desk was a large African American lady with the name Rhonda. She handed him the key to the room, which was on the fourth floor. The room had two bedrooms, a bathroom, and a living room in the middle. "I've never seen anything so nice," said Gracelyn.

"I'm glad you said that. My cousin booked it for the whole weekend," said Wesley. Abby was excited too. She had never stayed at such a nice hotel.

The four of them popped a bottle of champagne and talked all night. They talked about life before and after the war. The girls were really interested in hearing tales of Kentucky. Abby always envisioned people working the land they owned during the day and drinking bourbon at night.

"I didn't expect guys like you to be from Kentucky," said Abby.

"What did ya think? We would be wearing overalls and a plaid shirt?" said Jim Street.

"And have beer bellies while carrying around a beer?" said Wesley. "There are some normal people in Kentucky, believe it or not. My daddy has his own business. He is clueless when it comes to doing anything with his hands."

"Do you think both of you will go back to Kentucky after the war?" asked Gracelyn.

"Hell yes!" both of them said.

Wesley and Gracelyn wanted to spend the night in the same room. They had been all over each other since they had met, and with the war, time was short. People had to get to know each other and as fast as possible.

Abby had the privilege of sharing a room with Jim, which seemed, on paper, like a bad idea. In reality, Abby was comfortable sleeping in the same room with Jim Street because of her time on the dance floor. He respected her relationship with Walter, and she respected Jim for it. He even offered to sleep on the floor, which she accepted without any hesitation.

Abby would have never imagined that the last weekend before she was potentially sent to Europe would be spent with two boys, venturing around the nation's capital. It was a nice change of pace from spending every day inside the base. The four of them visited museums and art galleries during the weekend off. Gracelyn and Wesley became quite close and even decided to stay connected throughout the war.

The fun was over before they could blink an eye, however. Monday morning rolled around, and the real world was upon them. Abby and Gracelyn said goodbye to Jim and Wesley. Abby vowed to stay in contact with them, and Gracelyn said she would write Wesley almost every day.

Once they said their goodbyes to the boys, they were off to their Monday-morning meeting. Abby was ready to learn her fate of where she would be serving in the war. Both Abby and Gracelyn walked into the room, trembling from anxiousness.

"Do you want to serve in Europe?" asked Gracelyn.

"Yes."

"Me too."

Abby received her wish, and so did Gracelyn. Both nurses were selected to serve in Europe, and both of them were excited. They were eager to be an instrumental part in the Allied war effort. It would be no walk in the park, but they embraced the challenge.

CHAPTER 13

Almost a year had passed since Walter joined the military. It was late May 1944, and the Allies were gaining momentum in the war efforts. People back home were talking about an Allied invasion of France. And about a week before the invasion, Walter and his platoon mates were given confirmation that the attack would take place in the coming week. After the Allies penetrated France, they would have their sights set on Berlin. These were the first steps to ending the war in Europe. It wouldn't be easy. It would be far from easy. Hitler and the German military had been building an Atlantic Wall for several months, and they had put the most competent German in command, Erwin Rommel. With Field Marshal Rommel at the helm, the Germans were confident the Allies couldn't break through the wall or the stout defense of the German soldiers.

In preparation for this attack, Walter and all the paratroopers had been training in England. They practiced jumping out of airplanes in the day and night. The command believed strongly that nighttime jumping was far different from daytime jumping. With the emphasis on jumping in the dark, Walter believed that there could be an important attack at night. The invasion plan was a little above his pay grade and rank, so Walter and Randall could only speculate.

One night after training, the platoon had dinner at the mess hall together. Bobby, Mathew, Luke, Randall, and Walter all gossiped about the upcoming invasion. "Y'all, if I had to guess, they'll send us in after the initial attack," said Bobby.

"You have no knowledge to even make a prediction like that," said Randall.

Walter took a sip of his water and said, "I think it's pretty dumb to be guessing at all. We should just be ready. We could be the first or the last ones. Let's just focus on what we know and what's in our control."

Everyone agreed with Walter and started talking about things other than the war. "So how's Mallie doing, Randall?" asked Bobby.

"Great. I received a letter from her yesterday. She just graduated high school and is planning on going to the Ohio State University next year."

"So your gal will be a buckeye, huh?" said Bobby Hawkins. "Y'all have to be careful about those buckeyes."

With a grin on his face, Luke said, "I wonder whom Mallie talks to more, Randall or Walter."

"I guess you will just have to ask her when we return to the States," said Randall.

The five of them continued their meal talking about women and home. "Do you gentlemen like English women or American ladies better?" asked Luke.

"Being from the South, I love my Southern belles. They are gorgeous and have class. No one makes better sweet tea," said Bobby Hawkins.

"I love those British accents, boys. I wish we could import English ladies to the States. Nothing like pretty English girls talking dirty to you in bed," Mathew said.

"Are you bloody joking?" Randall said in a British accent. "Our American girls are much prettier than the Brits."

"I agree with you, Randall. The English mouths are deal breakers for me. They have mouths like Albanian mountain goats," said Walter.

Everyone at the table laughed and continued to eat their dinner. Just as the platoon was about finished, an officer in an all-white uniform marched toward their table. "Gentlemen, you have orders to report to Major Hopper at 0800 hours tomorrow," said the officer.

"What's this regarding?" asked Walter.

"I'm not at liberty to discuss it with you. Just report to Major Hopper tomorrow," said the officer.

After the officer left, Walter and the platoon followed suit. They went back to their barracks. "I wonder what Major Hopper will say tomorrow," said Mathew.

"There's no need to speculate or worry. We'll find out tomorrow morning. Anyway, Luke, have you heard from your sister?" said Walter.

"I received a letter from her a few days ago. Apparently, she just graduated from third grade. They had a ceremony and everything. I'm sad that I missed it," said Luke.

Walter put his arm around Luke and told him there would be plenty of events throughout the girl's life. "Plus, we are fighting to preserve a better life for her."

Luke told him he was right, and all the men started talking about people from back home. None of them dared to speculate about the meeting. Tomorrow, they would find out their role in ending German occupation in France.

The next morning, the platoon showed up at Major Hopper's meeting room before 0800 hours. Major Hopper wasn't at the meeting yet, so Walter and his fellow soldiers looked around his tiny office. There was a picture of a beautiful girl on his desk. Walter figured that the woman in the photograph was his wife.

"Damn. What I wouldn't do to get with her," said Mathew.

"Admiring my wife, I see," said the major as he walked into the room.

All of them held up a salute faster than the blink of an eye. The soldiers didn't know what to say, especially Mathew. He was caught red-handed. They decided to be extra-attentive with the major.

"Good morning, gentlemen. Thanks for coming. Now I'm going to get right to the point," said Major Hopper. "In a matter of days, Operation Overlord will be a go, and your platoon will be an important instrument of this operation."

After hearing those words, the men smiled at one another. They had waited six months for this opportunity. "What will our duties be on this mission?" asked Walter.

"Your platoon will be some of the first men on French soil since Dunkirk. Operation Overlord will be the largest amphibious assault in the history of mankind. Your job will be to parachute down to France in the middle of the night. You will be responsible for destroying bridges, railroads, and roads so that reinforcements cannot bail out the German armies at the beaches," said Major Hopper. "Gentlemen, are you ready to serve your country in the most important battle of the war?"

"Sir, yes, sir!" said the men.

"Captain Hanks will lead your outfit. And your radio operator will be Private Banks. Several other soldiers will be under the command of Captain Hanks. Is that understood?"

"Sir, yes, sir," said the soldiers yet again.

The rest of the meeting consisted of discussing the details of the assault. During the night, the platoon would land in northern France. Gliders would follow them, and they would be filled with jeeps, bazookas, explosives, and other weapons. Once in France, the platoon would find their weapons and get to work destroying bridges to prevent German Panzer divisions from reaching the beaches. German panzers would strive to complete their mission at all cost. The Germans were taught never to retreat. As a result, the mission would be very costly, and many young men would pay the ultimate price.

As the meeting adjourned, the boys were walking out of the meeting room. However, Major Hopper called them back into the room. "I almost forgot. I do bring some good news. You lads will get a few days off before this operation. I assume you will behave yourself if you choose to spend it in London. Dismissed," said Major Hopper. "I'll be sure to tell my wife you boys said hello."

The meeting was over. The soldiers walked back to their barracks and talked among themselves while sitting on bunk beds. "Well, this is what we've been waiting for, boys," said Randall.

"Hopefully, I'll make the folks back in Boston proud," said Luke.

"I feel the same way, y'all. I want to bring honor back to Florida," said Bobby.

The next few days saw very broad training of all paratrooper platoons. Platoons trained for everything they would be sure to encounter. They trained in preparation of jumping out of planes, taking offensive positions, taking defensive positions, and destroying railroads. It was nothing the platoons hadn't seen before, but the military wanted to make sure that every soldier was more than prepared. This could very well be the most important battle of the war, and there was no such thing as overpreparing.

After a hard week of training, the soldiers hopped the train headed toward London. "All aboard!" said the train conductor. Walter and his fellow platoon mates played cards and talked among themselves in one of the crowded train cars. "I heard there's a women's baseball league back home," said Randall.

"I'm sure it's not as entertaining as the men's league," said Luke.

"Y'all, it's gotta be more entertaining. Gals in skirts playing baseball! I would pay to see that game," Bobby said while laughing.

Mathew put his arm around Luke's shoulder. "I wonder if the New York team is better than the Boston team, just like in the men's league," said Mathew.

"I have no idea. But don't worry, Mathew. I predict that the Red Sox will be back soon. We'll win a few championships before 1950."

"I don't think so, bud. The Red Sox haven't won anything since they traded Babe Ruth. They are cursed," said Mathew.

"Aren't you too old to believe in curses?" said Luke. "That's a bunch of hogwash."

One of the guys asked Walter something that had been on his mind since Major Hopper told them they would be forced to undergo physicals. "Do you think Abby will be in London?" asked Bobby. "I heard there are some nurses stationed up there?"

"I'm not sure, QB. It's hard to keep track of where she's located. They were going to send her to North Africa, but that campaign ended last summer," said Walter. Walter sure hoped that she was in

London, giving physicals. Walter would do anything to hold her for one night before the war ended.

"Speaking of North Africa, I still can't believe we beat the Nazis," said Randall.

"General Montgomery sure did rally the troops in El Alamein. I never thought that German general—what's his name?" stated Luke.

"Erwin Rommel," Bobby said.

"Yeah. I can't believe we took down Rommel. He's one of their best commanders," said Luke.

"Well, we get a chance to take him down a second time. Rommel is the commander for the defense of France. He won't know what hit him," said Walter.

"I can't wait to make that happen," said Randall.

After about a two-hour ride, the train arrived in London. The gentlemen jumped off the train and got on a long red-and-white bus. This bus shuttled them from the train station to the base, where they would be staying the night. Once they were at the base, a young man from Britain showed them to their lodging arrangements. It wasn't London's finest lodging; it consisted of two large rooms with five or six bunk beds.

As they put their stuff down on the bed, the soldier was about ready to leave. Walter shouted at him to wait. "Where is the medical wing of this base?" asked Walter.

"It's not far. I'll walk you there," said the British soldier.

While they were walking, Walter asked the soldier how long he had been serving England. "A couple of years. I decided to enlist after my brother was killed in the Battle of Britain. He flew one of those Hurricanes and was shot down protecting London."

"I'm sorry for your loss. I've heard stories about the bravery and courage of the pilots," said Walter.

If not for the bravery of the men in the British Royal Air Force, England would have fallen before the Americans joined the war. The German Air Force was weeks away from defeating the Royal Air Force in the Battle of Britain. If that happened, there was talk by Hitler that he planned to invade Britain. However, no invasion took place, as the British pilots were able to win the battle in the skies, and Germany was forced to turn their attention elsewhere.

Once they were at the medical wing, Walter looked everywhere for Abby. He was like a hawk searching for his prey. But instead of prey being what he was trying to find, it was the love of his life.

He looked everywhere and couldn't find Abby. As he walked toward the exit of the medical wing, he froze and was as still as a statue. His blue eyes saw the girl he had been thinking about night and day for the past several months. There she was, standing next to a soldier, giving an eye exam. He couldn't believe it. Abby was standing in front of him for the first time in months. Walter shouted, "Abby!"

Abby turned around and had a huge smile on her face. She wanted to sprint to him, but she had to wait until the eye exam was over.

It felt like eternity until the eye exam ended. Right after it ended, Abby ran over to Walter and jumped into his arms. She wrapped her arms around him and couldn't stop kissing him. "I can't believe it's really you," said Abby. "This just feels too good to be true!"

Walter soaked in the moment. He told her how much he missed her and how much he thought about her. "I think about you every day."

"I miss you so much. I can't believe you're holding me in your arms," Abby said. Both of them felt like they were in a good dream while in the middle of a horrible nightmare.

Abby wanted nothing more than to take him by the hand and disappear for the day. She had longed to be with Walter since he left on that July morning. However, that wasn't possible because she was needed for more medical exams. Walter didn't ship out until the next day, so they made plans to see each other.

"I'm staying on the west side of the base. Come find me when you're done," said Walter.

The young nurse returned to work. She wasn't sure how she could focus on administering medical exams. Abby was anxious to see Walter, and oddly enough, it felt like a Friday afternoon back at Oakhaven School for Girls. She was ready for the weekend to begin but had to get through a couple of more boring classes.

Walter was just as anxious, but he had the luxury of waiting in his room. While he was waiting for Abby, the other men left the base to spend the night out in London. The other soldiers had been gone for an hour when there was a knock on the door. Abby was waiting in the hall. Walter grabbed her and pulled her inside. No words were exchanged, and they started kissing each other like they were at the high school prom. While they were kissing, they slowly made their way to one of the beds. Both of them managed to take off their clothes. Abby climbed on top of Walter, and they made love for the first time since Walter joined the Army.

When they were done making love, words and sentences began flowing out of their mouths like the current of the Ohio River. "How have you been?" asked Abby.

"I've been good. They haven't had me out in any combat yet. Only training. Training is tough, though. It may be tougher than combat," said Walter. "What about you? How are your parents? How's being a nurse?"

She took a big sigh. "I haven't talked to them since the day I told them about joining the Nursing Corps. I love being a nurse. I've made a lot of new friends. It also makes me feel closer to you," said Abby.

Walter sat up on his bed. He felt bad that Abby hadn't talked to her parents. "I think you should write your parents. I've forgiven them, and I think you should too," said Walter.

"Maybe I will. I just feel guilty about the whole thing," said Abby.

"Don't," said Walter. "I'm glad it happened. Like I said in my letters, it's an honor serving my country."

"Well, even though I'm worried sick about you every day, I'm happy that you're happy," said Abby, kissing him on the check.

"And this is the happiest I've been since I can remember," said Walter.

"Me too," said Abby.

"Are you sure about that?" Walter said, his face drawing closer to Abby's.

"Yes," Abby said.

Abby was able to get those words out of her mouth just before Walter began attacking her lips like a piranha. He missed kissing her for the last several months, so there was no time to waste. Walter was a man on a mission, and in more ways than one.

After a while, the boys came back from London. Mathew, Bobby, Luke, and Randall bolted through the door. "Abby! It's so good to see you," said Randall.

"Boys, this is Abby," said Walter, his big bear paw around Abby.

"We've heard a lot about you. Walter talks about you every day," said Bobby. "I'm Bobby, this is Luke, and that's Mathew," he added while pointing to Luke and Mathew.

"It's nice to meet you too. I'll see if my friends can come over," said Abby.

While Abby was walking back to her barracks to fetch her friends, the boys told Walter how beautiful Abby looked. "You're one lucky man," said Bobby. "It makes me miss my gal even more now."

Walter tapped his shoulder and said, "QB, I'm sorry, then. I know how it feels."

"Don't be. It gives me even more motivation to make it back to her."

Abby was gone for almost thirty minutes. *Are her barracks in Switzerland?* Walter joked to himself. Abby and her friends waltzed through the door shortly after his amusing thought. "Welcome back," Walter said.

"It's good to be back," Abby said as she kissed him on the lips. "This is Gracelyn, and Susie," Abby said to Walter and the rest of his platoon mates.

Susie was short and had dark-red hair. Abby and Susie had met while serving together in London. Susie was from San Jose, California. She was literally halfway across the world.

"I'm Gracelyn," said Gracelyn. "And I'm Susie. It's nice to meet you, boys."

Luke, Randall, Walter, Mathew, and Bobby then introduced themselves. Before the boys finished their introductions, Gracelyn grabbed Abby.

"Wesley proposed," said Gracelyn with excitement. "I guess he's on base somewhere in England and called over to London. They patched me through to him. Can you believe it?"

"I'm so happy for you!" said Abby, giving her friend a hug.

"I'm getting married!"

Everyone told Gracelyn their congratulations, and they seemed to be happy for her. There wasn't much to celebrate during war, but an engagement was one of them. "So did Wesley tell you if he has any big assignment coming up?" asked Abby.

"Yes, he did. Apparently, he has a mission that's big. He couldn't really get into detail about it, though," said Gracelyn.

"I wonder what he's doing. I hope it's not too dangerous," said Abby.

"What's his unit?" Walter asked, listening to the girls' conversation.

"Wes is a pilot. He's a fighter pilot, but on occasion he does fly those big bomber jets," said Gracelyn. "Do you know what his mission could be, Walter?"

Walter's guess would be that Wes would be flying in Operation Overlord, but it was on a need-to-know basis. Quite frankly, Walter didn't know Gracelyn well enough to share that kind of information. So he told her he didn't have knowledge of the type of assignments pilots received.

The nurses and paratroopers drank all night. Everyone had a good time, and no one wanted it to be over. For one night, they could pretend to not be at war. They could pretend that millions and millions of people weren't perishing. They could pretend that the most evil tyrant in the history of mankind wasn't still in power. And they could all forget the dangers that came with serving their country.

After a while, Walter wanted some alone time with Abby, so they stood up and walked into the other room.

"Where do you think you're going?" asked Randall.

"It's top secret. I'd tell you, but I'd have to kill you," Walter said while walking into the other room.

"I really don't want this night to end," said Abby as she climbed into the bed that Walter occupied for his stay in London.

"Me neither. I missed you so much. I do need to tell you something," Walter said.

"What is it?" Abby said while placing her arm around Walter's shoulder.

"I know you will be aware of the situation soon. It's just a matter of time," said Walter. "I just wanted to let you know that I could be in danger the next couple of weeks."

"What do you mean?" asked Abby.

"There's a plan in place to liberate France. It's supposed to be the biggest battle of the war. They want us on the front lines," said Walter.

Abby was terrified. When she heard *front lines* and *soldier* in the same sentence, it was synonymous with *death*. In her head, she pictured traditional warfare, the warfare where two armies would stand in rows and fire back and forth. "What do you mean front line?"

Walter put his arm around Abby and said, "We'll land in France before an amphibious assault. Our primary job will be to destroy bridges and roads so that reinforcements can't get to the beaches, where the assault will take place," said Walter.

Abby didn't know what to say; she just looked at Walter in silence. Her fear of losing him was not reassured. From her body language of keeping her head down and her eyes astray, Walter saw that he needed to comfort her. "It will be fine. I promise. I'll come back alive."

"Don't make promises you can't keep," said Abby as she was trying to hold back tears.

"I promised you a house with a pink door, a white picket fence, and a golden retriever. I'm going to keep my promises," said Walter.

Abby wasn't convinced but didn't want to argue. "Okay. I believe you. Just be careful."

"You know I will. Every step I take is one step closer to being with you forever," Walter said.

"I know," said Abby. "I'm just worried."

"Just worry about something more important," said Walter, cracking a smile. "Worry about how big our house is going to be. Worry about how many times a day we're going to have sex. Worry about where our first vacation will be."

Abby smiled. "I always wanted to go to Europe. But right now, I'd prefer my second option of Florida."

"Normandy doesn't sound awesome right now." Walter laughed.

They cuddled up next to each other and held on tight. Both of them didn't want to let go. However, as tight as they could grab, both of them knew it wasn't any use. Walter would be shipping out the next day.

The next morning, they woke up to a gray and cloudy morning. The weather told a story of how they felt: the sadness of separating from each other. "What a night," Walter said.

Abby turned toward him and kissed him on the forehead. "I didn't want it to end. If that was the last night I spent with you…," Abby said.

"Don't talk like that. I'm coming home after this war."

Abby and Walter climbed out of bed, and they had to return to their respective places in the war. Walter and his platoon were scheduled to ship out at 1200 hours, and Abby was supposed to report to work at 1000 hours. It was almost 1000 hours, so Walter escorted Abby back to her barracks. "Well, this may be the last time we'll see each other until after the war."

Both of them didn't want to part ways. Walter knew his sacrifice would benefit not only people in America but also people all over the world. If he had to be away from Abby to make a better place for the world, then he was willing to make that sacrifice.

"Well, I guess this is goodbye," Walter said while hugging Abby in front of her barracks.

"It's not goodbye, it's see ya later," Abby said while trying not to sob. "You better come back to me."

Walter looked at her and said. "I told you before that I'm coming back to you. Every step I take, I know that it's a step closer to you."

Abby seemed content enough with that answer, so they said their goodbyes. At the conclusion of a long hug, Abby walked into the barracks. Walter headed back to where his platoon mates were located. In his heart, Walter knew that he would eventually be able to hold Abby again; he just didn't know when.

CHAPTER 14

Abby's supervisor called her and the nurses into an office. It was the size of a small room and had pictures of the supervisor's family. Since Walter told her about Operation Overlord and the assault into France, Abby knew what to expect. "Good morning, ladies. You may have heard rumors about the big assault taking place in a matter of days. I'm here to tell you that those rumors are 100 percent true. Soon the Allied forces will make an amphibious assault on the shores of France. Consequently, and unfortunately, the casualties will be high. We need to be prepared. Thousands of wounded soldiers will be brought back to London for treatment. We need to be ready," said the supervisor. "Any questions?"

One of the nurses raised her hand and asked, "Could this end the war?"

"I can't answer that question. I don't have enough knowledge. But I do know it could be a turning point in the war. Any more questions?" she asked. No hands were raised. "Dismissed," the supervisor said.

Abby and Gracelyn left the room together. When they walked outside, it wasn't a typical English day. The sun was beating down in full force, and there were no clouds to hide under. Abby tried shielding the light by putting her hand above her eyes. "It's really hot out today, huh, Gracelyn?" Abby said.

Gracelyn looked at Abby with a confused face. She couldn't understand why Abby could be so calm and collected just after they were told about the assault. How could she ask about the weather when Walter and Wes could be heading into the heart of the lion's den? "How could you be talking about weather at a time like this?"

"Because it's really hot today. And it heated up while we were inside, getting briefed," said Abby, laughing.

"How can you be laughing at a time like this?" said Gracelyn.

"It helps me relieve stress. I'm sorry if it offends you," said Abby.

"I'm just worried, that's all. I think Wes was talking about this assault when we talked the other day. Now I'm really scared for him. Tell me he's going to be okay."

"He'll be fine. He's one of the best pilots in the Marines. At least he won't be going in the boats or he won't be on the ground. Walter may be in danger."

"What do you mean?" said Gracelyn.

"When Walter was in London, he told me he would be on the front lines," said Abby.

"He told you about the assault?" asked Gracelyn.

"He did. He didn't tell me about Wes's job in the operation, which is why I didn't mention it. He told me it was confidential," said Abby.

"What will Walter be doing during this operation?" asked Gracelyn.

"He will be securing the beaches. He's landing in France during the night, and the amphibious assault will be in the morning," said Abby.

"What if the assault doesn't work? Will Walter be stranded?" asked Gracelyn.

It never crossed Abby's mind that the amphibious assault might fail. If it did fail, there would be no rescue mission, and Walter would be stranded behind enemy lines. That thought terrified her.

"It better work," Abby said to herself.

When Abby and Gracelyn returned to their rooms, they began planning a trip to the city. The nurses were given the night off, and downtown London was only a few miles away from the base. They wanted to grab dinner and see a theater production.

Around 5:00 p.m., Abby, Gracelyn, and a few of the other nurses hopped on a bus and left for London. The itinerary for the evening was to eat in Trafalgar Square and watch a showing at the Western Theater of *Me and My Girl*, a story of a poor girl that inherits a title of nobility. Abby was hopeful that a night of entertainment would help alleviate her fears of Walter and the other soldiers who would be venturing into France.

Trafalgar Square was at the heart of London and was home to many wonderful restaurants. However, many people chose not to eat out due to the ongoing war. So Abby and her friends were able to eat at one of the best pubs in London, which was the Old Shade Pub. As they entered the traditional English pub, the hostess said, "Right this way."

She seated them at the corner booth in the back of the restaurant. As the hostess left, the ladies talked among themselves about the menu. "The chicken alfredo looks pretty good," said Abby.

"We're not in Italy, Abby. And I don't think you should order an Italian dish when we are at war against them," said Gracelyn.

"Then what should I get?" asked Abby.

"You have to get the chicken burrito. That's what England's famous for," said Amy, a fellow nurse.

"Are you kidding me, Amy? Chicken burritos are from Mexico," said Gracelyn. "If you want something the British are famous for, try the fish and chips."

When Gracelyn was finished with her history lesson, the server walked over and took the ladies' order. None of the girls were persuaded by Gracelyn's lecture, as she was the only one who ordered fish and chips.

After dinner, the ladies walked into the dark, but warm night of London. They walked out of the restaurant and searched for a British patron for directions to the theater. Not many people were walking the streets during wartime Britain, but they did manage to find an elderly couple walking their Yorkie. "Hello, sir, would you mind pointing us in the direction of the Western Theater?" asked Abby.

The couple heard Abby and stopped in front of the nurses. "I do apologize, dear, but the Western Theater has been closed for some time now," said the elderly wife.

"That's too bad. Would you suggest something else?" asked Gracelyn. "We have the night off."

"The cinema is still open. That would be my best suggestion, young lady," the elderly man said. The nurses indicated that they wanted to see a flick, so the man pointed them in the right direction. "If you walk up Strand Street and take a right on Bedford Street, the theater will be on your left."

The ladies thanked the couple for their suggestion and directions and walked the few blocks to the cinema. Once they arrived, they walked up to the ticket booth and asked about what movie was playing. "What flick is playing tonight?" asked Amy.

"*Pinocchio*," said the young girl at the ticket booth. "But we're sold out."

"How could that be?" Abby asked.

"We just are. Come back another time"

That answer wasn't good enough for Abby and her fellow nurses. They knew damn well that the show wasn't sold out. Abby couldn't understand why the employee was lashing out at her customers.

"Can we talk with the manager?" said Gracelyn in a stern voice.

Just as the girl was shaking her head no, an older gentleman walked inside the ticket booth. "May I help you girls with something?" he asked.

"Yes. We really want to see the movie tonight, but your employee said it's sold out," said Gracelyn.

He looked at her with a puzzled face. "Sold out? We are barely at 25 percent capacity. You have some explaining to do."

The girl ran out of the ticket office in tears. "I'm sorry, ladies. Her sister was a nurse for the British military and was killed during a German bombing raid. She has never gotten over it," the manager said.

The nurses had no hard feelings and certainly understood. They handed the older gentleman some money and grabbed a ticket.

Pinocchio was in theater 3, which was the last theater at the end of the hall.

Before the film, Winston Churchill came on-screen and spoke his famous line, "Keep calm and carry on." Other commercials appeared that were filled with propaganda. When the propaganda was over, the movie began. Abby was able to dangle her feet on the seat in front of her, sit back, and enjoy the Walt Disney movie.

During the scene of Pinocchio's nose growing in length from his lies, loud sirens sounded off from outside the theater. Everyone heard the bombs exploding.

"What's going on?" said Gracelyn.

"The Germans must be dropping bombs over London!" said Abby.

The nurses then turned to a citizen who was just as frantic as them and asked, "What do we do when the sirens are going off?"

"We should sit tight. Most venues have bomb shelters," said the British citizen.

After a few minutes of wondering about the proper course of action, a man stood in front of the theater and started shouting directions. He was an older man who wasn't very tall but was round in the waist. "Everyone, remain calm. There is an underground bunker under this theater. If you all follow me, I'll lead you to safety. I won't let anything bad happen to anyone. I promise," said the man. Abby, the nurses, and everyone else followed the man down to the basement. He seemed to calm everyone down, and maybe that was because he resembled Winston Churchill.

As the nurses wandered down to the basement, they didn't glance outside. They didn't want to see London getting bombarded, and they didn't want to see people lying in the streets. The nurses reached the bottom of the steps. "We'll be safe here until the sirens turn off. We just need to wait it out," said the chubby man in the bow tie and a top hat.

Abby sat down in the basement and looked around. The basement, or de facto bomb shelter, was a big room with a small ceiling. The walls were white; it was a terrifying room. There were so many people, young and old, who were just as scared as the nurses were.

145

Since Abby was a nurse in the United States Army, she believed it was her job and duty to keep people calm. In the corner of her eye, she saw a little boy crying. He appeared to be about six years old. He was sitting down on the ground by himself, and she didn't see his parents. She walked over to the boy to keep him company.

"What's your name," she said into the boy's ear.

"Eli," the boy said.

"Where are your parents?" asked Abby.

"I don't know. Mama and I went to *Pinocchio*, and she went outside to meet my dad," the boy said while shivering in fear.

He could barely speak. He was alone, and it was probably the most terrifying time of his young life. Abby walked closer to him and held him in her arms. "Everything will be fine. I promise," she said to him.

While Abby was consoling the young boy, Gracelyn was talking to other fearful citizens in the basement. "When will this stop?" said an older British woman.

"Soon, I hope. The Allies are close to turning the tide of the war," said Gracelyn.

"I sure hope so. So many of our people have perished. This has become a normal routine for us," said the woman.

"I'm sorry. I know the boys are doing everything they can to end this war," said Gracelyn.

"They certainly are. My son was killed in this war. He served in the Royal Air Force. He flew one of those Spitfires. His plane crashed while he was protecting London," she said while shedding a few tears.

"I'm really sorry to hear that. He sounds like a great young man," said Gracelyn.

"He was a good boy. Do you have any relatives in the war?" said the old woman.

"The man I plan on marrying is in the war. He actually asked me to marry him a few days ago. He's also a pilot. I worry about him every day," said Gracelyn.

"Well, congratulations. I know the feeling. My husband was in the Great War." The woman paused for a moment, then asked, "Why are you in London?"

"I'm a nurse in the US Army. It was our night off," said Gracelyn.

"That turned out to be a poor decision, didn't it? It will be fine. I'm sure we will be out of here by morning," said the woman in a thick British accent. Gracelyn was hoping it would be safe come morning, because the nurses needed to return to the base.

After the conversation with the British woman, Gracelyn walked over to see Abby. As she moved closer, she noticed a young boy sitting in Abby's lap. "Who's your friend?" Gracelyn asked.

"This is Eli. He's keeping me company until he finds his parents," said Abby.

"I'm glad he's sitting with you, keeping you safe. He's such a brave young boy," Gracelyn said, trying to raise the boy's morale.

The man next to them pulled out a radio. No one knew where he got it from, as he was like a magician pulling a rabbit out of his hat. Right when he turned it on, Winston Churchill was on the radio. "Citizens of London and all of Great Britain, this is a tough time. The Germans keep bombing our city, and they can do damage to building, streets, and factories. But they will do no damage to the great nation of England. Keep calm and carry on."

There was something in Winston's voice and demeanor that provided tranquility to so many concerned citizens. The mood changed, and there was a certain level of comfort. The sirens stopped shortly after his radio speech. Maybe the Germans were scared of Winston Churchill.

As the sirens stopped, the Winston imitator spoke and said, "All right, everyone. The sirens have stopped. We can all leave this basement. It's safe to go outside."

The nurses stepped outside to sky filled with darkness. People were lying in the streets, dead and wounded. They could see rubble all around them. Abby feared that Eli's parents were at least one of the perished citizens lying in the street. "Eli, let's try to see if your mom is around here," said Abby.

The boy grabbed her hand, and they looked for his mom. He ran over to a woman lying in the street. He started sobbing. When Abby stood next to him, the young boy jumped in her arms and continued crying. She didn't need to ask the identity of the woman.

Abby felt sick to her stomach, but there was little she could do about the situation. All she could do was hold the young boy and tell him everything would be fine. "Let's try to find your father," said Gracelyn, who was only a few feet away.

The boy agreed, and Abby and Gracelyn found a policeman walking in the street. He was standing next to a pile of what used to be a building. "Sir, we are looking for this boy's father. Could you be of any help?" asked Abby.

"What's the gentleman's name?" asked the police officer.

"George Merlin," said the boy.

"I'll radio in the name and see if anyone knows his location," said the police officer. "You can wait at the park across the street while I try to find your father."

Gracelyn, Abby, and Eli walked to the park. They waited for the policeman to discover the whereabouts of the boy's father. Gracelyn and Abby glanced around and saw bodies of people everywhere. They wanted to help but knew that they needed to stay with this young boy. He needed them.

The police officer came strolling to the park half an hour later. He looked at the two ladies and young boy with a disappointed look in his eyes. "Son, I have some bad news. Your dad was taken to the hospital. He's in critical condition."

The boy started to cry again. Abby put her arm around him and held him close to her. While she was consoling Eli, Gracelyn asked the officer what hospital Eli's father was taken to. The police officer looked Gracelyn in the eye and said, "St. Thomas. They took him there about an hour ago."

Abby and Gracelyn thanked the police officer and headed straight to the hospital. They rushed as fast as they could to see Eli's father. As they walked inside, they saw masses of people sitting and standing in the lobby. Abby felt a need to help, but her most important task was to make sure this boy was safe. When they arrived at the help desk, Abby said to the nurse, "Hi. I'm looking to find the status of George Merlin."

The nurse looked at some files and replied, "How do you know Mr. Merlin?"

"This is his son."

With glossy eyes, she looked at the young boy and said, "I'm so sorry for your loss. Your father passed away an hour ago."

The boy collapsed into Abby's arms. He was devastated. Both of his parents died on the same day, within an hour of each other. He was now an orphan.

Abby, Gracelyn, and Eli walked out of the hospital. It was still a dark and gloomy day, which accurately reflected the mood of the three people leaving the hospital. "What are we going to do about Eli?" Gracelyn said.

Abby hesitated for a few moments to think about the circumstance. She didn't know anything about Britain children services, but if they were anything like the United States children services, she didn't want to send him there. Orphanages and group home were overcrowded during wartime. She answered Gracelyn's question and said, "I don't know. Let's take him back to the base. And then we'll figure something out. I don't want to leave him alone, and I think he will be safest with us."

After they left the hospital, they hopped on a bus back to the base. Abby asked Eli if he had any relatives. "Do you have any grandparents, aunts, or uncles?" Eli shrugged and said no. Abby then wondered what would happen to him. With him having no place to go, she felt terrible for him. Hopefully he could stay with her at the barracks for the time being.

When Abby, Gracelyn, and Eli arrived at the base, they headed straight to the barracks. "Abby, what are you going to do about Eli?" asked Gracelyn.

"I'm not sure. I think I'll go talk to Mary Safford. I'll explain the situation," said Abby. "Can you watch Eli while I'm talking to Mary?"

Mary Safford was a high-ranking officer in the US Army Nurses Corps and was the rank of major. Her husband was not in the military, so it was surprising when Mary joined. Mary and her husband didn't have any kids but had been trying for quite some time.

Gracelyn nodded and agreed to Abby's request. Abby then looked at Eli, saying, "Eli, you are going to hang out with Gracelyn for a while. I'll be back soon." She proceeded to walk out of the room and walked toward the nursing center, where Mary's office was located.

Feeling a little nervous, Abby walked into Mary's office. "Can I help you?" asked Mary.

"I'm in a dilemma," said Abby.

"What's the dilemma?"

"Well, we went to London yesterday, and the Germans bombed the city. We had to take shelter in the basement of a theater," said Abby.

"Are you okay? Is everyone all right?"

Abby nodded and said yes, then went on to elaborate. "The problem is that we met a little boy. His name is Eli. His parents were killed in the bombings. I'm sure the Army will be furious with me, but I brought him back to the base with us," said Abby.

"You what?"

"He was all alone. He didn't have any relatives, so he came back with us. What should I do with him?"

Mary didn't respond, because she didn't know how to respond. The two women sat in silence until Mary figured out a solution to the problem. In fairness to Mary, the Army had never had a situation quite like the one Abby was involved in. "Well, why don't you just keep him in the barracks with you for right now? We will figure something out after this operation in France. We don't have time to worry about where this boy will go right now," said Mary.

"I'll drop him off with my Military Police friend before my shift tomorrow. I don't want him to be alone at the barracks," said Abby.

"That works for me. You were very kind for taking this boy in. We will find him a home after the war," said Mary.

Abby walked back to the barracks. Eli came up to her and put his arms around her. "What did Mary say?" asked Gracelyn.

"Eli is going to stay with us until the war is over. We will find him a home after the war," said Abby.

Abby, Gracelyn, and Eli sat around, playing cards, for the rest of the night. Both Gracelyn and Abby were confident that a young boy wouldn't understand the game rummy, so they played an easier game.

Ironically, they played the game war. In war, all the players put down a card and the highest card wins the hand and takes the other players' cards. They all had fun playing, but Eli had the most fun. He won every single round of war. "We better take him to Vegas someday," Abby said, chuckling.

As it became late, Abby was ready to call it a night. "Gracelyn, we should probably go to bed. We're going to have a long day tomorrow," said Abby. "Eli, while I'm working tomorrow, you're going to spend time with my friend Bethany. She is really nice. You will really like her."

Eli nodded, indicating that he understood. Abby turned off the lights, and they all climbed into bed. As Abby lay in bed, she thought of Walter. In a matter of hours, Walter would parachute into enemy territory. She was nervous but excited for him at the same time. She was excited that he was part of the mission to turn the biggest tide of the war. Yet she was nervous for him. He was walking into the heart of the lion's den.

CHAPTER 15

The mess hall was more quiet than normal. Walter and the rest of the soldiers could hear the metal scratching the plates. It was the evening of June 5, 1944. In several hours, approximately thirteen thousand soldiers would be flown across enemy lines and dropped into a territory that had been occupied by the Germans for the last five years.

As some of the members of Walter's platoon walked back to the barracks after their meal, they saw fellow soldiers standing around, talking among themselves. In the group of soldiers, there was an all-too-familiar face. He was wearing his green military outfit and had four stars painted on his collar. (He would get nominated for his fifth later that year.) It was Dwight Eisenhower, the supreme commander of the Allied forces. General Eisenhower was attempting to lift his men's morale and discover the soldiers' mental state before the big invasion.

While Walter and Randall were walking by, General Eisenhower stopped talking to the group of soldiers he'd been speaking with and turned toward Walter and Randall. When they noticed he had turned in their direction, Walter and Randall saluted him faster than the snap of fingers.

"Gentlemen, are you ready for a big fight?" asked General Eisenhower.

"We are ready, sir," said Walter.

"Yes, sir," said Randall.

"Well, gentlemen, this will not be an easy fight. Our opponent is not scared, nor will they go down easily," said the general.

"We know that, sir. We are well equipped for this invasion. You have trained us well. We're ready to do our part to ensure a victory," said Walter.

"I have full confidence in you. You men are brave, some of the bravest men I've ever commanded. The tide will turn after this invasion, and the free men of the world will rise up. We will get this victory, and we will accept nothing less than a total victory. Good luck and Godspeed," said General Eisenhower.

Randall and Walter saluted General Eisenhower and walked to the barracks. When they reached their barracks, the sun was starting to set over England, and most of the men didn't want the sun to go down. The darkness signified the start of the invasion, and the soldiers only had a few more hours until they boarded C-47s and made the jump into France. Every man had different ways to prepare mentally for battle: talking, reading, writing, playing cards. Walter braced for the dangerous task by lying in his cot and thinking about the loved ones back home.

Of course, the first person that entered his mind was Abby Walker. On most occasions, while lying on his bed, he thought about the summer he spent with her. They spent every waking minute together, whether it was swimming, playing tennis, walking around Millener Farm, kissing, and so much more. Walter began to ponder the future with Abby. He imagined a day in the life they had planned together.

In this day, he would wake up bright and early for work as a lawyer. Abby would still be sleeping and curled up under the covers. He wouldn't want to wake her, so he would kiss her on the forehead before he left for his corner office. During the day, he would work hard, just as his brother had taught him so many years ago. Once he was done with work, he would rush home to see Abby. When Walter walked through that pink front door that he promised her the night before he left for the war, his total attention would be on Abby. They would enjoy dinner together and talk about each other's day. After dinner, and if it was a cool summer night, they would sit on the back porch, sipping red wine and talking about the world, politics, and sports. When both were exhausted, they would stroll upstairs. On the days they weren't too exhausted, they would make love. He would kiss her good night, and the process would start all over.

The idea of spending his life with Abby was a dream, and a dream worth preserving. When he would be fighting in France, he would be fighting for two causes. Walter would be fighting to uphold freedom throughout the world and destroy tyranny over the oppressed people in France. Second, and just as important, he would keep the aspiration of holding Abby for many years to come by staying alive.

Abby wasn't the only person whom he thought of before the big mission. Walter's family entered his thoughts as well. He knew he needed to return for his sister, father, and mother. His sister looked up to him, and he had always been there to protect her, through both good and bad times. As for his father, Bill Wilson had always supported him. Walter had always appreciated his father's support, and one day, Walter wanted to return the favor. Even though his mother had turned into a witch for so many years, he wanted to return for her, just as much as his other family members. Although Walter's mother had stopped drinking, turned her life around, and apologized to Walter many, many times, he never really forgave her. Walter thought he never would be able to accept Allison Wilson's apology, but with everything he had seen throughout the war, he had a different perspective. He desired to put his arms around his mom and say, "I forgive you."

Walter fell asleep after his visions of people back home and was awakened by a sergeant yelling about the time.

"Fellas, you have one hour to be at your assignment hangar for departure. Departure is at 0100 hours," said the sergeant.

Walter woke up and rose to his feet. He climbed out of bed and began preparing for his journey. Walter stepped into his camouflage pants and buttoned up his camouflage shirt. He proceeded to tighten his belt and attach his water canteen, rifle, first aid kit. He was ready.

When the time came, the soldiers stepped out into the humid night and walked toward the hangar. As they reached the hangar, all the men boarded the big transport airplanes. Every soldier aboard the aircraft sat in silence until the plane took off from the runway. And for the most part, the silence continued while they were in the air. They were mentally preparing, and some were even placing war paint on their faces.

"Gentlemen, in a few minutes, you will be in France. We will drop you off, and this will be the first time in the war that the Allies will be behind German lines. This mission will come with a price. It may be the most dangerous mission of the entire war. Are you ready?" said a colonel on the plane.

"Sir, yes, sir," said the other soldiers.

"Good, gentlemen. When the green light comes on, that signals the jump. The hatch will open, and you boys will jump silently into the night. Godspeed."

It was game time, Walter thought to himself. It was minutes before battle, and Walter seemed ready to storm into France. Every muscle in his body was tingling. He wasn't nervous, but ready. Beside him were his brothers, Randall, Luke, Mathew, and Bobby, and Walter was honored to be sitting next to them. Randall nudged him and said, "Walter, if anything happens to me, can you tell your sister that I love her and that I'm sorry I didn't make it?"

Walter slapped him across the face. "Randall, listen to me. You're going to tell her yourself. I won't let anything happen to you."

Randall shook his head and said, "I hope not."

Walter then put his arm around his best friend's shoulder, saying, "I know so. I can envision us living near each other. Let's fight like hell, force the Germans to their knees, and go home heroes!"

One of the officers waved his arms, and the green light appeared. Captain Hanks, the leader of the outfit, was the first soldier to jump off the plane. In the dark of night, the men dropped into the French sky one by one.

Walter was able to land safely in a wooded area, so he unhooked his parachute and started looking for the rest of the men. He wasn't able to yell, or he would risk being discovered. And he wouldn't want

Nazis crawling out of the woodwork. As Walter looked to the right of him, he saw Randall crawling out of a bush.

"Thank God!" said Walter. "Randall, over here."

Randall walked over to Walter's position and asked, "Have you located any of the other boys?"

Walter shook his head, saying, "Negative. Let's search the surroundings and try to find them."

Walter and Randall searched nearby. They saw some men who were not able to safely land. One of these soldiers was Captain Hanks. He was their leader, but they would move on without him. All the soldiers were briefed on the possibility of confusion and loss during the jump. The plan was to gather the soldiers nearby who were alive and formulate a plan.

A few minutes after they found Captain Hanks dead, Walter and Randall located Mathew, Luke, and Bobby behind a few trees. They all landed safely, and everyone gathered around Walter.

"Boys, Captain Hanks didn't make it. In the next hour, we'll locate every Allied soldier nearby and devise a strategy," said Walter.

The men followed the order and began searching the area for other soldiers. Walter and his platoon mates were able to find nine Americans alive and ready to fight. Eight of the nine were privates, just like Walter, Randall, Mathew, Bobby, and Luke, but one of them was a captain. His name was Captain Jimmy Cameron, and he hailed from Des Moines, Iowa. Captain Cameron and his ancestors came from Ireland. He was the first of his family to be born in the United States, and his family was proud of his decision to join the United States Army.

"Captain Cameron, pleasure to meet you. I'm Walter Wilson," Walter said as he saluted the officer.

"Walter, call me Jimmy," said Jimmy Cameron. "What's the status of your men?"

"Well, sir, our commander didn't survive the jump. So I guess that makes you the leader of this outfit now," said Walter.

"It certainly does. We all missed our drop zone by almost a mile. We are two miles west of La Fiere Bridge, which is our target. Every soldier is working hard, but damn, those C-47 pilots are just inexperienced," said Jimmy.

Jimmy Cameron began directing orders. "Boys, we are two miles away from the intended target of La Fiere Bridge. We need to begin our trek, but we must be careful. The German soldiers are aware that we are in France. Let's move out, but quietly."

Soldiers under the command of Jimmy Cameron began marching. They traveled through trees, bushes, and fields while encountering no enemy activity. Walter and Bobby Hawkins were the point men. "QB, we must be careful. The Germans could be lurching anywhere. This platoon depends on us," said Walter.

"I'm aware of that slick. What do ya think about France," said Bobby in his Southern accent.

"It's a pleasant country. I wish I could see it under better circumstances. Maybe after the war is over, we'll all return," said Walter, reaching for his belt and grabbing his canteen.

Luke Fetter chimed into the conversation, saying, "Gentlemen, nothing would sound more ideal. I've studied French for the last four years. I'm somewhat upset our mission won't take us to Paris. It would be historical if we liberated the people of Paris."

"Parlez-vous Francais, huh, Luke?" Mathew said. "The only language I speak is English. It's the only language I need to know."

"And you don't even know it very well," said Randall.

"When we need to speak with some of the locals here, being fluent in French will certainly be helpful," said Luke.

Bobby and Walter halted at the edge of the large field, which kept the soldiers hidden. In front of them was a small and curvy dirt road. "Jimmy, we've reached this dirt road. You make the call on the next decision," said Walter.

Jimmy pondered the strategy for a few moments. He then proceeded to discuss the matter with Walter. Jimmy Cameron was a West Point graduate who believed in order and discipline to his core. Although he thought the best results came from collaboration. "Walter, what do you think we should do? I see a house a few hundred yards in the distance that sits on this road. I'm thinking we see if there's a light on and possibly speak with the owner of the house," said jimmy.

"Sounds like a solid plan to me," said Walter.

The men began walking on the dirt road. They had walked almost twenty yards when gunshots were coming directly behind them. The soldiers turned and spotted three German soldiers. Without thinking, the men from the 82nd Airborne Division turned and fired. The German soldiers fell to the ground. Unfortunately, the platoon had a casualty. One of the privates was shot and collapsed on the dirt road.

They said a quick goodbye to the fallen friend before moving on with the mission. Walter and Bobby continued to walk near the front. When they marched closer to the house, Walter noticed there was a light on. He alerted Jimmy about the light, and Jimmy ordered them to stay on course.

When they reached the house, a few of the soldiers knocked on the door. After hearing the bang on his door, a Frenchman came to the door. This man had a scar across his forehead, which looked to be caused by a knife. "Bonjour," said the man.

"Bonjour, parlez-vous Anglais?" said Luke Feter, the only person in the company that was fluent in French.

"Yes. Just a little," said the Frenchman. "Come in, come in."

Jimmy decided to trust the man and ordered his men to enter the house. The Frenchman ushered the soldiers to the kitchen table, which had enough room for four people to sit down. The rest of the soldiers were standing around the kitchen walls.

"My wife is sleeping," said the man. "My name is Jean Claude. I'm part of the French Resistance."

"Well, thank you, sir, for your support. We appreciate the intelligence everyone has gathered," said Jimmy Cameron.

"No, thank you. Thank you for attempting to liberate our people. It's been a hard few years. Everyone in my country has suffered," said Jean Claude.

Jean Claude and his wife, Margeax, had struggled ever since the Germans had occupied France, which began in 1940. Germany established a military state in northern and western France. Due to the tough reparations following the First Great War that France placed on them, Germany wanted to return the favor and gave them a taste of their own medicine. They even forced France to sign a treaty in the same train car that the Treaty of Versailles was signed.

Due to the surrender, the French Armed Forces became non-existent. But the citizens suffered just as much as the Army. There was a shortage of food. Farmers were forced to provide a substantial percentage of their crop to the German soldiers. To make matters worse, there was also a shortage of oil and fuel. Without an adequate amount of oil, many farmers were unable to fertilize most of their crop.

Some French citizens were able to play at least some part in fighting back against the Germans. There was a small pocket of people that were part of the French Resistance movement. Jean Claude happened to be one of those brave souls. Jean Claude was able to gather information of troop movements and send them via radio transmission to London.

"Can I help you boys with anything?" asked Jean Claude.

Before Jimmy could answer the question, Jean Claude's wife came down the steps in her nightgown. Jean Claude said something to his wife in French, then introduced her to the soldiers. "This is my wife, Margeax," said Jean Claude.

Margeax just waved her hand to all the soldiers because she didn't know English. After she was done moving her hand in the air, Jimmy Cameron asked directions to the La Fiere Bridge. Just as Jean Claude was about to answer the question, there was a knock on the door, and German voices were shouting in the background. Jean Claude had locked the door after the American soldiers walked into his home, which was fortunate for everyone inside the house.

Jean Claude ordered his wife to hide the Americans under the trapdoor in the dining room. They walked over to the dining room, which was the room adjacent to the kitchen. Before Walter climbed down the steps, he was able to notice the nice wooden floors, vintage glass tables, and leather couches in the dining room.

The soldiers were in the hidden room when they heard Jean Claude opening the door. The German soldiers were shouting in both French and German.

"What do you think they're saying?" asked Walter.

"They're probably inquiring about our possible whereabouts. We did kill three German soldiers not too far away from here," said Luke Feter.

"Do any of y'all speak German?" asked Bobby Hawkins.

"I don't, QB," said Walter.

"No one speaks German here," said Randall.

"Let's just remain silent until the Germans leave," said Captain Jimmy Cameron.

The platoon sat in the fifteen-square-foot trap room in silence and in darkness. No one dared to speak, as the soldiers' lives depended on it. They continued not to talk until Jean Claude and Margeax opened the hatch door. "It's safe. Come on out," said Jean Claude.

Every soldier in the hiding place climbed the ladder back to the first floor. They all gathered in the kitchen and asked what the Germans wanted. "They wanted to know if we were hiding any American soldiers," said Jean Claude.

"Did they discover the three dead Germans?" said Walter, looking Jean Claude in the eye.

Jean Claude proceeded to squat down at his round kitchen table. "I presume so. But they never mentioned it," said Jean Claude. "Can I be of any service to you boys?"

"As a matter of fact, you can. Can you point us in the direction of the La Fiere Bridge?" asked Jimmy Cameron.

Jean Claude stood up from his chair. He looked out the kitchen window and pointed west. "Walk straight west. It's a straight shot from here."

Jimmy Cameron thanked the man for his help. The soldiers filled up their canteens with water in the sink and walked out the door. Just as the last soldier had left the house, Jean Claude sprinted after them. "Don't forget, be careful around the hedgerows. Germans have been known to hide in them."

Jean Claude was referring to agricultural bushes known as hedgerows. Hedgerows were enclosed bushes used to control cattle and mark boundaries. It was like a hidden tunnel constructed from bushes, which could be used as a good hiding place.

As they left the French couple's house, Jimmy Cameron and the rest of the American soldiers proceeded to walk west toward the bridge. It was their duty to secure the bridge so the German panzer division couldn't reach the beaches. The sun would soon rise above Normandy, and the American soldiers knew they couldn't waste any time. D-Day was about ready to begin.

CHAPTER 16

Sunrise. It was the morning of June 6, 1944, and Abby had a feeling of nervousness when she crawled out of her bed. She wasn't nervous for herself, but rather for Walter. By the time she woke up, Walter had been in France for several hours. Abby hoped that he was alive and well.

Abby and her fellow nurses were scheduled to report for duty at 1100 hours. Her alarm clock went off, and she looked at the cot next to her. Eli was sleeping. "Time to wake up, kiddo," Abby said to him.

Eli woke up, but with difficulty. The previous day had been long and strenuous, so he was exhausted. As he was lifting his head above the pillow, Abby said, "Good morning, sunshine. How are you feeling?"

"Good. I slept good. Good morning," Eli said.

Eli and Abby were both wide-awake by nine. They looked over in the direction of Gracelyn and noticed she was in a deep sleep. Abby felt like it was time to wake her up, so she knelt down to ear level of young Eli. "Eli, go jump on Gracelyn. It's time for her to wake up."

Eli followed through on Abby's request and jumped on Gracelyn. Gracelyn practically jumped out of her bed. "I'm awake, I'm awake. Eli is sure heavier than he looks," said Gracelyn while she was climbing out of bed.

When Gracelyn was up and at it, the three of them walked outside to the mess hall. As they strolled to breakfast, the sun was shining. Abby took that as a good sign.

The three of them reached the mess hall at half an hour past nine. Eli, Abby, and Gracelyn could all smell the scent of bacon, eggs, and orange juice. Both Abby and Gracelyn liked the smell of the cafeteria because it was a pleasant change from the scent of blood and piss, which was the odor of the medical ward.

During breakfast, both Gracelyn and Abby vented to each other about their fears of D-Day, where Walter and Wesley were currently participants. "I do hope Wesley was able to fly safely through France," said Gracelyn.

"I'm sure he did. Like I said, he's a great pilot. He'll be fine," Abby said as she was drinking her orange juice. "I was up late last night, worried about Walter. He's in France somewhere."

It was Gracelyn's turn to reassure Abby. "Don't worry so much, Abby. He will return home, I promise."

"These eggs are super good," Eli said.

Abby and Gracelyn were thankful he spoke, because it allowed the subject to change from worrying about the men in their lives.

"I'm glad you like them, because they'll turn you into a strong young man someday," Abby said, patting the young boy on the back.

"She is right, Eli. I bet every soldier in this war has eaten over a thousand eggs during his lifetime," said Gracelyn as she took a bite of eggs.

"Really?" asked Eli. "How do you know?"

"I just know," said Gracelyn.

Eli smiled at Gracelyn and Abby, and the girls smiled back at him. Eli missed his parents, but he was thankful to be with these two young nurses. And these two nurses were equally happy he was on base with them. War was a tough time, and young Eli was a joy to be around.

After breakfast, Abby and Gracelyn dropped Eli off with her friend Bethany and walked over to the nursing headquarters. When they walked in, everyone was sitting down in front of a supervisor. Once the clock struck 1100 hours, Mary, one of the head nurses, spoke to everyone. "This morning, just a few hours ago, I received confirmation that the Allies have invaded Normandy. From everything that I've gathered, it's been successful in the beginning stages. There will be many casualties, and in the next few days, we will get many young men who are severely wounded. Make sure you help the doctors in whatever they need. And sometimes you will need to make decisions, and they will be important decisions. You ladies have been trained well. I have no doubt you will do a fantastic job."

Once Major Mary Safford was finished with her speech, the nurses continued with their daily routine. Abby had been helping a soldier relearn how to walk after a bullet had crippled his leg. His name was Doug Martin, and he was a first lieutenant in the Army.

"Hi, Doug," said Abby, walking into the rehabilitation center.

"Hello, ma'am. How are you today?" said Doug Martin.

"I'm doing just fine. Are you ready to begin today?"

"Yes, ma'am," said the lieutenant.

Abby and Doug Martin began with their rehab session. First, Doug would sit on chair and move his leg up and down. Then, he would proceed to move his leg from side to side. After his leg was nice and loose, Doug would attempt to walk in a straight line with a cane propping him up on one side of his body. Lieutenant Martin was successful in walking with a cane and was almost ready to walk without any assistance.

Just as Abby's rehab session ended with First Lieutenant Martin, Abby walked back to the nursing office, which was located in the back of the emergency room. While in the room, she saw Gracelyn waiting for assignment. "Have you been in this room since the day began?" asked Abby.

"Yes. I feel like they've called everyone's name but mine," said Gracelyn.

"Well, I just helped with Doug and his rehab," Abby said.

Abby and Gracelyn sat in the nursing office for a few minutes until one of the supervisors called them out to the emergency room. "It's about to get really busy in here. Why don't you ladies come out to the ER and help out?" asked the supervisor. The young girls followed her order and marched out to the emergency room.

Many young men in stretchers were coming through the hospital door. One by one they filed into the room. Just about every table or bed was occupied by a wounded soldier. There were not enough doctors to operate on wounded soldiers. As a result, Abby and some of the other nurses were forced to work on wounded men without the assistance of doctors. "Ms. Walker, attend to the soldier on table 13. You're going to have to plug his artery. It won't stop bleeding," said one of the supervisors.

Abby rushed to the man on table 13. By his uniform, Abby could tell that he was a colonel in the Army. Other than that, she knew nothing and didn't want to ask him about his life or injury, because he was in excruciating pain. "I'm Abby. I'm going to try to plug that artery of yours. I'll grab you some morphine," said Abby.

"Stick me with it, damnit! It hurts so much," said the soldier.

Abby hurried with the medicine and injected him.

"Thank you, ma'am. Hopefully, that will ease the pain some," said the colonel.

Abby was holding the artery together for almost an hour, as she was desperately trying to stop the bleeding. It was the hardest assignment she had been given, because she wasn't sure if this man would live or die. She tried talking to him, to not only calm him down, but to calm herself down as well. "Sir, where are you from?" she asked.

"I'm from a small town just outside of Wilmington, Delaware. It's called Newark," said the man.

"Are you married?" said Abby, asking another question.

"I have a wife and a little girl. I have another on the way," said the colonel. "Hopefully, you can fix me up so I can return to them."

"We will do the best we can. I'm sure you will be able to hold your girls again."

"I appreciate it," said the colonel. "What about you? Is there someone in your life? I'm guessing you don't have kids, because you're way too young."

"My man was drafted. He's part of this D-Day invasion," said Abby. The colonel nodded at her and kept screaming in pain.

Abby was able to stop the bleeding. Once the bleeding stopped, she was able to stich the soldier back up. "Well done, Abby," she said to herself. Abby was ready to tell the colonel the good news, but he was unconscious. She checked if his heart was beating, and she could feel it. She came to the conclusion that he passed out from the amount of blood loss.

After six hours of working in the rehab center and the emergency room, Abby and Gracelyn had their shift over. They went into the nurse's office to receive permission for the shift's dismissal. "Are we fine to leave?" asked Abby.

"Not yet. We have an assignment for both of you. Just wait in here for a few minutes, and Major Safford will be with you," said one of the nurses on staff.

Abby and Gracelyn waited for a few minutes, just as they had been told. "What do you think about this assignment? Any guesses as to what it could be?" asked Gracelyn.

"I have no idea. But we will find out in a few minutes," said Abby as she sat down in one of the chairs.

Mary Safford came into the room where Abby and Gracelyn were sitting. "Sorry to keep you ladies waiting," said Mary. "You two are some of our bravest and brightest nurses stationed here in London."

"Thank you very much," said Abby. Gracelyn also turned to Mary and said, "Yes, thank you for the compliment. We try our best."

Mary turned to the ladies, saying, "Listen, this assignment we want to give you will put you in harm's way. Will you be okay with that?"

Gracelyn looked at Abby, and Abby looked at Gracelyn. The girls weren't sure what to think and wanted to gather more information before accepting the assignment. "Can you go further into detail regarding this job?" asked Abby.

"In a couple of days' time, the Army wants to set up mobile hospitals in Normandy. If you choose to accept, you ladies will be shipping out to the front. There will be many of our wounded men that will need immediate medical attention and won't have time to be transported across the English Channel," said Mary.

Gracelyn and Abby both nodded at each other, and Gracelyn told Mary, "You can count on us."

Mary was pleased with their decision and said, "Affirmative. You will be transported to the base near the English Channel soon. Dismissed."

The girls were walking out of the nursing room when Abby realized that a young boy was in her care. She turned around and walked toward Mary. "I totally forgot. Do you remember Eli is staying with me? What shall I do with him?"

"Oh, yes. That's right. He can stay with me until you get back," said Mary.

Abby walked out of Mary's office feeling relieved that Eli could stay with someone. Abby didn't want to leave him, but she didn't have much of a choice. Abby's duty was to serve in Normandy and save as many young men as possible.

Gracelyn was waiting for Abby outside the office, and when she saw Abby appear from the door, she asked, "What did Mary say about Eli?"

"She told me that Eli could stay with her."

As the girls were done with their shift, they walked over to where Bethany was assigned and picked up Eli. When Eli saw Abby, he ran over to her and gave Abby a big hug. "I missed you too," Abby told Eli. "Are you hungry? Let's grab some dinner."

Gracelyn wasn't hungry, so she just went back to the room. It was just Abby and Eli eating dinner. There were hundreds of nurses and soldiers eating food at the round tables. "How was your day, Eli?" asked Abby.

After taking a bite of his chicken, Eli said, "It was good. Bethany is nice."

Abby took a sip of water and looked at Eli. She wasn't ready to tell him that he would be staying with Mary for a few days. Quite frankly, she was scared of his reaction. He had just lost his parents, and now she was going to the front lines. She didn't want to leave him, but it was her duty. "She's great. You had a better day than me, that's for sure. I was busy helping people. What did you and Bethany do?" asked Abby.

"We played board games and hide-and-seek. It was really fun," said Eli with a smile on his face. "Can you play with me tomorrow?"

"Actually, Eli, there's something I've been meaning to tell you. I've been assigned to travel to France. I've talked to my supervisor, and she said that you could stay with her when I'm gone. I'll be back before you know it."

After Abby told him the news, Eli had a sad look on his face, but he understood. "I understand," he said.

Abby felt sorry for him and wanted to treat him like a prince tonight. "How about we play hide-and-seek when we get back to the room?" said Abby.

When they arrived at the barracks, Gracelyn was there to greet them. "How was dinner?" Gracelyn asked.

"It was really good. They served mashed potatoes, broccoli, and chicken. It was yummy," said Abby. "Gracelyn, did you get anything to eat?"

Gracelyn took a sip of her water and said, "Yes. I grabbed a sandwich on the way."

Abby then tapped her on the shoulder, saying, "Good. You'll be playing hide-and-seek with Eli and me."

Eli heard Abby and said, "Yay! I'll hide first." Eli disappeared to hide, and it marked the beginning of the game.

The three of them played hide-and-seek for a long time. Each of them took turns hiding. It didn't take too long for the seekers to find the hider, because the room was so small; there were only tables, beds, and dressers to hide behind. Nonetheless, Eli was amused. After Abby found Eli for the seventh or eighth time, she told Eli, "All right, Eli, let's get ready for bed. We all have a long day tomorrow."

Eli complied with her request; he brushed his teeth and hopped into bed.

As he fell asleep, Abby decided to write Walter. "Gracelyn, I'm going to write Walter in case anything happens to me. You should do the same. You should write Wesley." Abby pulled out her pen and began to write:

> *Dear Walter,*
> *I just wanted to let you know that I've been*
> *assigned to serve in Normandy. Our supervisor told*

Gracelyn and me that we are the bravest and brightest nurses in London. I know I won't see you until after this invasion, but I hope you're doing well, wherever you are. Anyway, I could be in danger, and if anything happens to me, I just want you to know that I'm sorry and that I love you. Hopefully, that won't happen, but you know me. I always need to be prepared. I miss you, and I can't wait to see you.

Love,
Abby

Once Abby was done writing the letter, she went to bed. While she was lying in bed, she was wondering where Walter was in France, and she hoped he was okay. She really wished that he would not be one of the young men she treated in France.

CHAPTER 17

T he sun had begun to rise above French soil. It had been a few hours since Walter and his fellow platoon members had left the house owned by the French couple. Allied boats were en route to France through the English Channel, and young men would soon be storming the beaches of Normandy. Some of the men who were part of the 82nd Airborne Division were almost to their destination point, the La Fiere Bridge. In order for the invasion to be successful, the Allied troops needed to secure the bridge to prevent German reinforcements.

"Are we almost there?" asked Mathew while they were walking through another French farm.

"ETA is about thirty minutes if we keep the pace," said Captain Cameron.

Walter and Bobby were ordered to lead the platoon from the front, and Jimmy Cameron marched in the back of the pack. Walter didn't mind that he had the most dangerous job in the platoon. He enjoyed the challenge of leading the group and enjoyed conversing with Bobby Hawkins.

"Walter, ya think the boys will be successful stormin' the beach?" said Bobby as he looked at Walter.

"I sure hope so, QB. The last time the Allies were on French soil, it didn't turn out too well for us," said Walter.

Walter was referring to the Battle of Dunkirk, or the evacuation of Dunkirk. Early in the conflict, French and British soldiers retreated to the beaches of Dunkirk. For some reason, the Germans halted their advance, which allowed the British to rescue more than three hundred thousand troops through the English Channel. Rescuing so many troops was a small victory in a large defeat for the Allied powers.

"No kidding, but we weren't in the war when the Allies retreated to Dunkirk, ya know," said Bobby, who then grabbed his water canteen from his belt and took a sip.

"I think you're right. It helps when we join the fight. We don't lose, and we won't lose. I think we'll be fine, but for us, we have to first get to this damn bridge and, second, secure it," said Walter.

"Yeah, soon we'll win this war," said Randall.

The sun was shining down on the boys. They were about a quarter of a mile away from the bridge, but first, they had to pass through another property that consisted of multiple buildings. This property was about two hundred yards in the distance from their current location.

"All right, gentlemen, we will rest a few minutes at the beginning of this marsh," commanded Captain Cameron as he saw a marsh that was located between their position and the property.

It didn't take the men long to reach the marsh. And when they did, every man stood as still as a statue, with their eyes wide open. Some of them even took off their heavy green helmets. Their eyes gazed into the marsh that took the life of many young American soldiers. All these soldiers drowned.

"Oh my god," said Randall as he took his helmet off and cradled it like a baby.

Walter patted his friend's shoulder, saying, "That's the saddest sight I've ever seen." It was hard seeing fallen soldiers. He wondered what these men were thinking during their last breaths. Did they think about their family? Did they think about their friends? Or did they even think about the war? Maybe it was a combination.

"It looks like the Germans intentionally flooded this marsh. Our intelligence just missed it. They didn't have a chance with all the gear attached to them. It must have weighed them down. Rest in peace, fellas," said Jimmy Cameron, waving a cross near his chest and head.

Once everyone was done resting and paying their respects to the fallen men, the soldiers continued to march toward the La Fiere Bridge. Walter and Bobby were in front, and everyone was following them from behind. Since the marsh was flooded, they were forced to walk around it. As they walked around the marsh, the soldiers came to a little dirt road that led to property just before the bridge. Walter halted his movement.

"Jimmy, what's the call? There's that farm fifty yards from our current position. It looks like the property consists of a mansion, a couple of barns, and a woodshed. What do you want us to do, sir?" asked Walter.

"Proceed to the French property. But it's vital that you keep a lookout. I have a feeling that Germans will be lurking around," said Jimmy.

Walter obeyed the order and proceeded to walk down the dirt road. He took a glimpse of the house, which was no more than twenty-five yards out. There was a stone wall separating the buildings from the hedgerow. *Hedgerow!* he thought to himself.

It didn't take him long to let his discovery be known to Captain Cameron. "Captain, I've discovered a hedgerow that is west of the farm. There could be Germans hiding in them," said Walter.

"Men, let's slowly make our way behind that stone wall over there," said Jimmy Cameron, pointing to the wall made of rocks.

Not more than five seconds after Jimmy Cameron yelled the order, the Germans began firing from the hedgerow. Bullets were flying everywhere, and the American men ran for cover behind that wall. They were under fire for the first time since the Normandy Campaign had begun.

When Walter jumped over the stonewall, he noticed that not every soldier had made it. Mathew was missing. He must have been hit with one of the spraying bullets. Walter was devastated that his friend didn't make it to the wall, but he couldn't afford to think about it. If it was a fatal shot and Mathew was killed, he would mourn his loss, but at the appropriate time.

"Y'all, what do we do now?" said Bobby Hawkins.

"Listen up, gentlemen. It's obvious the shots are coming from the hedgerow. And in my estimation, the Germans are also occupying the barn. But we must take care of the enemy in the hedgerow before we turn our attention elsewhere," said Captain Cameron.

The platoon followed the captain's orders. All of them loaded their M1 rifle and began firing at the hedgerow. It was like shooting at an invisible target, because none of the American men could see the German soldiers in the bushes. They could only shoot in the direction of the proximity to where the bullets were originating. Without seeing the enemy, it was frustrating.

"We aren't doing any damage to them," said Walter.

"I hear you, Walter. It's the same as shooting blindfolded. We need to change our strategy," said Luke.

Jimmy Cameron pondered Luke's suggestion, but he didn't know what to do differently. He asked for Walter's opinion. "Have any ideas, Walter?" asked Jimmy Cameron.

Walter hesitated a moment. "Why don't we throw some grenades and see if we can flush them out?"

"Let's execute it." Jimmy paused and took a deep breath before giving orders to his men. "It's clear that we aren't causing as much damage as we would like just shooting at them. Let's launch grenades in their direction, and hopefully, we can flush them out. On my count, we will throw grenades into the hedgerow," said Jimmy. "One...two...three..."

The soldiers began throwing the grenades in the hedgerow like water balloons. The result was exactly what the American soldiers had planned. Germans leaped like frogs out of the agricultural bushes. As a result, they were exposed in the open field, and it gave the Allied troops an opportunity to fire upon the German soldiers. The Germans fell one by one, and the Allies put a dent into the German lines.

It was just that, though, a dent. German soldiers were not totally defeated. They kept firing at the Americans with a depleted force. Far fewer bullets were fired in the direction of the American troops.

Several minutes passed, and the platoon was still firing into the hedgerow from behind a wall that gave them protection. "Walter, sport, do we have a new plan? This isn't working anymore. We're not hitting anything," said Randall as he lowered his rifle.

"It's not my call. Why don't we ask Captain Cameron?" said Walter.

Jimmy Cameron overheard Randall and Walter's conversation. "Why don't we surprise them by entering the hedgerows? That will eliminate them for good."

"Not a bad idea," Walter said as a bullet came ever so close to his face. He ducked even farther under the wall.

They all looked at Jimmy Cameron for guidance and leadership, but he had a look of confusion on his face. He wasn't in love with the strategy to send men into the hedgerow. If the Germans discovered them attempting to reach the hedgerows, they could be sitting ducks. "Gentlemen, let's give them a taste of their own medicine. We'll surprise them in the hedgerows. And we'll take them out," said Captain Cameron. "Randall and Walter."

"Yes, sir," each of them said.

"You two will be the ones to enter the hedgerow. And you'll know what to do when you're there," said Jimmy Cameron.

"Sir, how will we get there and not get blasted by bullets?" asked Walter.

"Slowly walk to the end of the wall. You will be far enough away that they probably won't see you when you enter the hedgerow. The rest of us will fire at them, and you will make your move," said Jimmy Cameron.

"And what's the plan when we're inside the hedgerow?" asked Randall.

"You're on your own then. You men will be the best judge of what to do. Good luck and Godspeed."

Walter and Randall proceeded to walk to the end of the wall, which was thirty yards away from the rest of the troops. The sun was now beating down hard on their faces, and they had been awake for almost twenty-four hours, so the two friends from Ohio were exhausted. But the adrenaline kept their motors running, and they were functioning quite well, like a fine-tuned automobile.

"How do you feel?" asked Walter just as they were almost to the edge of the wall.

"Focused," responded Randall.

"Good. Let's keep it that way. Time to get it done," Walter said.

As they reached the edge of the stone wall, Walter gave Jimmy a thumbs-up sign, which signified the attack. Shortly after Walter's thumb went up in the air, the rest of the platoon began firing. Within seconds, Walter and Randall dashed to the hedgerow. They ran as fast as they could, hoping the Germans wouldn't notice, and indeed, they did not spot the running Americans.

Once they were inside the agricultural bush, they walked toward the Germans. When they were about twenty yards away from the enemy, Randall and Walter observed five German soldiers pointing their weapons toward the rest of the platoon. Without a thought, Walter ripped the pin off his grenade and launched it in the direction of the Nazis. *Boom!* The grenade resulted in all five of the Germans falling to the ground. "Got 'em!" said Randall with a big smile across his face.

Randall and Walter stepped out of the hedgerows and walked toward the stone wall to join their team. They walked with a pair of smiles on their faces, just as if they had landed the prettiest girl in school. When they reached the wall, Jimmy Cameron told them that they did good, real good.

"That was fine work, gentlemen," said Jimmy Cameron while looking at Randall and Walter. "All right, everyone, gather around!"

As they gathered around their leader, waiting for their next assignment, Luke Feter's eyes wandered. It didn't take him much time to realize his friend and fellow soldier was missing. With the small skirmish that broke out, the men forgot about Mathew Farr. "Boys, Mathew, we need to find him," said Luke.

"Damn, you're right. Hawkins, you and Luke go look for him," said Captain Cameron.

Luke and Bobby jumped over the wall and into the open field. Mathew was the only American soldier lying motionless in the green grass. As Bobby and Luke walked closer to their friend, they noticed he had a bullet wound through his chest. Even though Luke wasn't a medic, he learned how to check pulse during his high school days in Boston. Luke Feter knelt down and put his finger on Mathew's neck. Mathew had no pulse.

"I'm afraid he's dead," said Bobby Hawkins as they walked back and rejoined the others. "Y'all, let's have a moment of silence for our fallen friend."

The American soldiers who were still alive bowed their heads and said a prayer. For Walter, it was the first friend he saw die in the war, and it was the second person he cared about who died right in front of him. It was sad and heartbreaking to lose a friend, but the best way to honor him was to continue fighting. If the Americans lost the war, Mathew and the rest of men who died would have died in vain. Walter couldn't let that happen.

As the prayer came to a conclusion, Jimmy barked the next order. His order was to eliminate the rest of the German soldiers on the French property. It was clear that the last of the Germans were hiding in the gray barn on the other side of the farm. "Gentlemen, the barn is on the other side of the farm. Why don't we meander over to the other side of this here property and reassess the situation?" said Captain Cameron.

Captain Cameron proceeded to lead his men to the other side of the property. They had to pass a big red mansion with a wrap-around front porch that stood at the center of the land. Presumably, the family that resided on this property had left, but that assumption was in question when the American soldiers saw the upstairs light on. "Private Wilson, Private Hawkins," said Jimmy Cameron in a silent voice but bold tone.

"Yes, sir," said Bobby Hawkins.

"Yes, Captain," said Walter.

"Go inside the house and see if there is anyone inside. It may be nothing, or it could be something. There could be a French family inside, but there could also be Germans. Be careful," said Jimmy Cameron.

Bobby and Walter proceeded to walk up the steps of the mansion. They pushed the door open and went inside. Together, the two American soldiers swept through the first floor. No human life was in the kitchen, dining room, or study. "One floor down, one to go," said Bobby Hawkins.

They walked up the winding staircase and did so without a peep. The only sound coming out of the American men were the small breaths each inhaled and exhaled; they were as quiet as church mice. When they reached the top of the stairs, both soldiers could hear French voices coming from one of the bedrooms. Walter walked toward the bedroom, and Bobby Hawkins followed behind.

"I'm going to open the door on the count of three. One... two...three!" said Walter.

Once Walter reached three, he shoved open the door with his M1 rifle in front, ready to fire. He saw a family holding one another on the floor. The family consisted of a young couple with two small children.

"We are American soldiers. Do y'all speak English?" Bobby Hawkins asked as he followed Walter into the bedroom.

"Very little," said the French man.

"Fair enough. Where are the German soldiers?" asked Walter.

"In the barn," the French man said with his thick French accent.

The French man let go of his family, managed to get off the ground, and stood on his own two feet. He walked over to the only window in the bedroom and pointed his finger in a specific direction. Bobby and Walter walked over to the window and observed the French citizen pointing to his barn. They looked down and saw their platoon. Only a few seconds passed until a firefight broke out between the Americans and the German soldiers in the barn.

When Bobby and Walter's platoon began firing, they rushed out of the bedroom and sprinted down the stairs. They treaded carefully to the woodshed directly in front of the barn. The men were hiding behind the shed. Every soldier noticed there wasn't as many rifles firing compared to the bullets flying from the hedgerow.

"I believe we have them outnumbered. From my estimation, there're only three or four remaining," Jimmy Cameron said. "If I'm not mistaken, there's an entrance on the other side of the barn. I want to send two soldiers to the other side. We'll surprise them," said Captain Cameron, trying to speak louder than the gunfire. "Randall, you and Luke go. The rest of us will stay here, firing in their direction!"

Randall and Luke carefully walked to the other side of the barn. The German soldiers hardly realized it, as they were ducking from the bullets coming from the other Americans. Luke and Randall made it to the other side of the gray barn.

Meanwhile, the rest of the platoon continued to fire in the direction of the German soldiers. They fired, and fired, and fired. No damage had been done because the Germans kept firing, but they kept firing less and less, until the bullets ceased. Walter peeked behind the woodshed, and they noticed a white pillowcase hanging from the barn window. It appeared as if the Germans were surrendering. "That can't be," Walter said under his breath, knowing that the Germans were not allowed to surrender.

A few minutes later, Walter heard a shot from the other side of the barn. After this shot, the Germans continued to fire in the direction of the woodshed the Americans were behind. The American soldiers picked up their rifles again and fired back.

They had been firing only for a few minutes when there were several gunshots coming from the barn. And then the bullets coming from the enemy's direction ceased once again. "Randall and Luke must have been successful," said Walter to the other soldiers.

Walter was right, as Randall and Luke came strolling out in their green American uniforms with their heads held high. Their body language trickled down to the rest of the platoon, and each of them lifted his head a little higher. Everyone was pleased with the victory, but they weren't content, not even close. They probably wouldn't be content until they reached total victory in France.

"All right, gentlemen, we are ever so close to the La Fiere Bridge. Should we rest for a few minutes or keep moving ahead?" asked Jimmy Cameron to the men he was leading.

Everyone was exhausted, but they wanted to forge onward. "Y'all, let's keep pounding the pavement," said Bobby Hawkins.

The men looked at one another and agreed. No rest was needed. They might have been craving rest, but they had a greater itching to arrive at the La Fiere Bridge. The platoon, which was a part of the 82nd Airborne Division, began marching toward the bridge. They would stop German panzer divisions from reaching the beaches of Normandy.

CHAPTER 18

A few days after the initial attack, Abby and Gracelyn were on a boat sailing across the English Channel. This ship was carrying soldiers, medics, equipment, and nurses. The nurses were sent to a separate part of the ship because the military didn't want the soldiers knowing nurses were on board.

Abby and Gracelyn were sitting on chairs in their small room, which was located three decks below the surface. They tried to keep their mind off the constant sound of bombs near their location. Multiple times, the Germans came ever so close to direct contact. Neither Gracelyn nor Abby ever imagined they would be serving so close to the front.

In order to take her mind off the war, Abby began talking about Eli. "Eli, is the sweetest boy, isn't he?" Abby said while she was looking at Gracelyn.

"Yes. He is a very nice boy," said Gracelyn.

"What do you think...about...me...maybe adopting Eli?" Abby asked, pausing in intervals from fear of Gracelyn's opinion.

Gracelyn wasn't expecting that question from her friend. "I don't know, Abby. On one hand, he seems to be attached to you, but on the other hand, do you think it's a good idea to take the boy away from the only world he knows?"

"You're right. But it's a world that has brought him sadness."

"That's true. Let's talk about it later. There are a lot of pros and cons, but let's figure that out later," said Gracelyn.

Gracelyn was right about making a decision later. Abby was gearing up for the most dangerous situation she would ever face throughout her life, and she needed to be sharp.

The ship came to a standstill. Abby and Gracelyn, along with the other nurses, hopped up from beds, cots, and chairs and walked to the surface of the ship. When they were at the surface, they gazed toward the French shore. It was the closest any of them had ever been to France.

An hour after the ship came to the edge of the English Channel, the nurses were standing on the beach, awaiting their orders. "Welcome to France!" said an Army officer, who appeared to be the rank of colonel. As the wind was blowing in his face, he continued by saying, "I'm Colonel Redford. Our objective is to establish mobile hospitals. Half of you will help me set up a hospital one-half mile south of here, and the rest will establish one three miles southeast from here."

The soldiers, medics, and nurses were split up after Colonel Redford's speech. Abby and Gracelyn were assigned to the same unit. They were assigned to establish a mobile hospital half a mile south of the beach.

While Gracelyn and Abby were awaiting their orders, they looked around the beach and saw bodies and blood everywhere. Men were lying everywhere, and some men were where the water met the sand. These men had been killed storming the beaches of Normandy. It was the most horrific sight any of the nurses had ever seen. Many honorable men lost their lives on the beach, where the nurses' feet were planted on the ground. Abby wanted to cry, but she knew that she couldn't. She was an Army nurse and had to be strong.

Abby and the other nurses weren't forced to stare at death in every direction for too long, because they marched toward the location where Colonel Redford wanted to establish a military hospital. They walked very cautiously—soldiers in front, and the nurses in the rear. She didn't know about the other nurses, but Abby felt safe that the brave soldiers led the way into France.

They arrived at the specified location just after dusk, but it was too dark to set up the hospital, so the medical staff would be forced to wait until morning. "Get some sleep. We wake at dawn," said Colonel Redford.

"Where are we going to sleep?" asked one of the other nurses.

"Well, just to be safe, I want everyone to dig foxholes and sleep there tonight," said Colonel Redford.

Both Abby and Gracelyn went to work building a deep foxhole. It took them almost an hour to build a big-enough foxhole for both of them to sleep in. Once it was completed, they slowly crouched down into it. The two American women sat across from each other and put cloth up against the dirt to place their head. "I feel like a real soldier," said Abby with an upbeat tone in her voice.

"I don't think I have ever slept on the ground before," said Gracelyn.

Abby had. "The last time I slept on the ground, I lost my virginity."

* * *

It was a few nights before the previous Fourth of July, which seemed just like yesterday. Walter and Abby had spent the entire day together. The day was winding down, and Walter was driving Abby home for the night. "Can we stop and get ice cream on the way home? Papa's Famous Cream is still open? Pleeeassee?" asked Abby.

She was looking at him with those beautiful blue eyes and cute smile. How could he say no? "Sure, but we can't stay too long. I don't want to get in trouble with your father."

They pulled into the ice cream place a few minutes before it closed. Abby ordered the raspberry chip, and Walter picked the chocolate chip. Walter handed the cashier a dollar, and they walked outside with their ice cream to sit on the outdoor benches.

The two young adults took a seat next to each other at the red picnic table and began licking their ice cream off the waffle cone. "Hmm, this raspberry chip is yummy," said Abby.

"I can't let you be the only judge. Can I try it, sweetheart?" asked Walter.

Abby smiled. "You can, under one condition."

"And what is this condition?" Walter asked.

"If you kiss me."

Walter didn't waste a minute before he leaned in with his lips to kiss Abby. One hand was holding his cone, and the other was wrapped around the back of Abby's neck. They kissed for a few minutes, and Walter forgot about the ice cream.

When Abby pulled away from him, she offered him the raspberry chip. She held the ice cream cone in front of his mouth. "That was the easiest condition I've ever had to do to get what I wanted," Walter said right before he tasted the raspberry chip.

It didn't take long for Abby and Walter to finish their ice cream. And once their ice cream was gone, it was time for Walter to drive Abby to her house. They hopped in the black Ford Coupe and drove toward the Walker house.

Walter's car pulled into Abby's driveway just before her curfew. He swung his door open and hurried around to the other side of the car to open the door for Abby. After she climbed out, Walter walked Abby to her door while holding her hand. Before she turned the handle of the door, she asked Walter to come back in a couple of hours.

"Excuse me?" said Walter.

"Mom and Dad went to some party tonight. They probably got drunk and will be passed out in a couple of hours, and I want to spend the night with you," Abby said, kissing Walter on the cheek.

"I'm not sure I want to sneak into your house. Who knows what your father would do if he caught me?" said Walter.

"Good point. Meet me by the tennis courts. Meet me there at midnight," said Abby as she walked into her house.

Walter returned to the Walker house at midnight, and the adrenaline was running through his veins. He was a rule follower, but tonight, he would be a ruler breaker. He was nervous and excited, a combination he thought was exhilarating.

Abby was waiting for him on the grass by the tennis court. She had been lying on the blanket that she carried out of the house for the last hour, ever since her parents collapsed in bed together. When she saw him in sight, Abby sprinted to him and leaped into his arms with her legs wrapped around his backside.

"You made it," said Abby.

"Of course, anything for my princess," he said as he carried her back to the blanket.

"Anything, anything," said Abby.

"Well, maybe not *anything*," said Walter. "Within reason."

"I'll keep that in mind," said Abby, smiling and winking at him.

They both proceeded to lie on the blanket together and wasted no time before kissing each other. Abby and Walter kissed each other for several minutes, until things intensified—they both began stripping off their clothes. Walter started cupping Abby's breast as they both lay there naked. They kissed for a few more minutes while cuddling on the blanket. However, they soon stopped, as Walter came inside Abby for the first time.

When they finished, both of them were exhausted. Abby and Walter took a few deep breaths and pulled the blanket around them.

"You make me so happy," Abby said to Walter, snuggling against his shoulder.

"That makes two of us. I knew the moment I laid eyes on you that I loved you," Walter said.

The two soon fell asleep together under the stars. Abby and Walter lost their virginity to each other on a warm summer night. They could hear the crickets chirping and could feel cool breeze against their bodies. The night was so peaceful and so full of tranquility.

* * *

The night in Normandy couldn't be more opposite than it was on the night Abby lost her virginity. With the sound of gunfire around them, it was violent instead of tranquil, and hostile instead of peaceful. And the biggest difference was the absence of Walter. He wasn't there to protect her.

When the sun had risen, nurses, doctors, soldiers, and medics woke up to prepare the hospital for the wounded. They set up multiple hospital tents—emergency room, operating room, and preoperating room. It didn't take long for the field hospital to be up and running, and it was an operating field hospital by nightfall.

When it became an operating hospital, Colonel Redford addressed the medical staff. The medical staff huddled around one of the tents and were gazing at the commanding officer. Abby couldn't stop staring at his mustache. It reminded her of Sherlock Holmes. "We are officially ready to operate. We will get many young men coming here to be treated. It is vital that we make them feel comfortable and treat them adequately. Let's do a good job."

Colonel Redford was a medical doctor who went to medical school at the University of Southern California. He joined the Army upon graduation and had risen through the ranks to colonel. He was professional in the way he operated his unit; he was organized and disciplined. However, he had sarcasm and humor in his arsenal to lighten the mood, which sometimes was needed at a medical hospital in the middle of a war zone.

As troops rushed in for treatment, Abby was assigned to anesthesia. In most cases, she would inject morphine into the men and place a mask over the soldier's face. Nitrous oxide would funnel through the mask and into the soldier's airways. It would put the soldier into an unconscious state. While he was in an unconscious state, the doctor or surgeon would begin treating the patient.

In some particular cases, Abby was required to use a different method. In particular, this method happened when a soldier was injured in the face. During this scenario, she was forced to use endotracheal anesthesia. This called for gases to be delivered into the trachea by an endotracheal tube.

The first encounter Abby had with endotracheal anesthesia was with an injured private by the name of Christopher Roberson. He was a young man from Birmingham, Alabama, and had been in the Army for nearly two years. A German mortar hit Private Roberson, and it caused gruesome injuries to his left jaw, nose, and cheekbone.

The private's jaw was bobbing down, his cheekbone was caved in, and part of his nose had been blown off. It was not a pretty sight.

When Abby strolled to his bed, she told him that she was a nurse in the Army Nurses Corps and explained the procedure that needed to be done. "I'm Abby. I'm a nurse with the Army. I will be injecting you with morphine, and then I'll be placing a tube down to your trachea, and that will put you to sleep," said Abby.

"Thank you, ma'am," said the soldier in a thick Southern accent.

With the acknowledgment of the wounded soldier, Abby began the procedure. She grabbed the morphine from the medical supplies and injected the patient. After the soldier was numb from the morphine, Abby inserted the endotracheal tube in the proper place. It didn't take very long for the soldier to fall into a deep sleep.

Shortly after Private Roberson fell into an unconscious state, the doctor arrived to perform facial reconstruction on his face.

"I see that the patient is under anesthesia. Good work, Nurse Walker," said the surgeon.

While Abby was giving anesthesia, Gracelyn was in the preoperation tent. It was full of soldiers who were waiting in agony to see the doctor. Her responsibility was to clean soldiers' wounds and remove bullets before surgery.

The first soldier Gracelyn treated was a man who had multiple bullet wounds, one through the arm, and the other through the upper chest. Gracelyn reflected on how lucky this man was that neither bullet pierced through any organs. "Hi, sir. I'm Gracelyn. I'll be cleaning you up before surgery," said Gracelyn, looking down at the soldier lying in a bed.

"Do what you gotta do," said the man. "It's ridiculous. I've been in pain for some time, and this is the first you've seen me."

"I'm sorry, sir," said Gracelyn, who was in her white nursing uniform. She began cleaning his wound with alcohol and attempted to dislodge the bullet. The bullet was buried deep in his arm, and it was a tall task for Gracelyn's first assignment in a combat area. After a few minutes, she was able to hold the bullet in her hands.

"You can keep this as a souvenir," Gracelyn said while she placed the bullet by the soldier's body.

He looked at the bullet and was amazed that something so small could cause so much pain. "Thank you. It's Gracelyn, right?"

"Yes."

"Sorry about earlier. I was in a lot of pain, but I had no right to take it out on you. You're just trying to help, and I appreciate it," said the soldier.

"It's quite okay, sir. I understand," said Gracelyn.

"You can call me Skip," said the soldier. "Has anyone ever told you how beautiful you are?"

"My fiancé does every time I talk to him," said Gracelyn while she was putting the alcohol back in a drawer.

"He is one lucky man. Is he back in the States? Or is he serving somewhere?" asked Skip.

Gracelyn took a moment to answer the soldier's question. She pondered what Wesley could be doing at that very moment, and she hoped he was safe. "He's a pilot. I think he flew over Normandy. Maybe he's flying right now," said Gracelyn.

"What's his name?" asked Skip.

"What's it matter?"

"I'm just wondering. I used to be a gunner in the aircraft, but I made the switch to infantry not too long ago," said Skip, who had begun to clutch his arm in pain.

"Wesley. Wesley Callahan," said Gracelyn.

Skip's jaw dropped in awe. He had met Wesley Callahan about a month ago while he was serving with him, and he thought highly of the young pilot from Kentucky. Wesley was brave and ambitious, and it didn't surprise him in the least that he was engaged to someone so beautiful and talented.

"I served with Wesley. He's a good man. The only thing he talked about was you. You must have worked some magic on him, because he was head over heels for you."

Gracelyn smiled, and smiled big. It was a nice dose of kindness during the Normandy Campaign. "Really?" she said, her eyes sparkling like diamonds in the sun.

"Oh, yes. He talked about you all the time. I can now see why," said Skip.

"Do you know where he is right now? Do you think he is okay?" asked Gracelyn. Her tone and body language changed from that of joy to worry.

"I don't know where he is, but I know he's fine. He's the most resilient man I have ever met. He'll be just fine," Skip said with a wink.

Just after Skip reassured Gracelyn, the doctor called him in for surgery. He was able to stand on his two feet, so he limped gingerly to the surgery tent. As the young man disappeared from her sight, she felt a sense of comfort. Gracelyn hoped that she was able to comfort Skip half the amount he comforted her.

After a couple of hours working on patients in the field hospital, Colonel Redford summoned Gracelyn and Abby to his office. Colonel Redford was sitting on a chair, smoking a cigar and looking at paperwork. The smoke of the cigar traveled near where the girls were standing, and Abby began coughing. Colonel Redford pretended not to notice.

"When your supervisor, Major Safford, sent you to France, she told me that you two were some of the bravest nurses she worked with."

Abby and Gracelyn both looked at the colonel and said, "Thank you very much, sir."

The colonel took another puff of his cigar. He took the cigar out of his mouth and said, "We never intended for you ladies to just be injecting morphine all day and removing bullets. We want you to help bring injured soldiers to this medical center."

"Let me get this straight. You want us to go into unsecured France?" asked Abby.

"Correct. My men will protect you. The areas that I will be sending you to are not hot spots. I believe Major Safford explained that you could be in harm's way. I'll understand if you don't want to carry on this mission, but we wanted to ask our most reliable nurses."

As soon as she heard the colonel's response, Gracelyn asked Colonel Redford if she could confer with Abby before their decision. "Take a few minutes outside my tent to talk among yourselves."

"What do you think, Abby?" Gracelyn said, standing outside the colonel's tent.

"I think we should do it. It would be a great honor to serve our country like this. Our boys are behind enemy territory, and now it's our turn. We're the best, and we should go," said Abby. "It's our duty."

Gracelyn nodded, saying, "Let's go, then. We'll walk back in and tell the colonel that we accept the assignment."

Gracelyn and Abby strolled into the colonel's tent and told him of their decision.

"Good. You will be assigned to this farm a few clicks away. There was a battle there, and many of our soldiers were wounded. Our men have secured the area. You will rendezvous with Captain Stahl. He will give you orders," said Colonel Redford.

Gracelyn asked Colonel Redford if they would be traveling alone. "Yes, of course. We'll give you a couple of machine guns, a couple of grenades, and a couple of rocket launchers," said Colonel Redford.

"Really?" said Gracelyn.

Abby then looked at Gracelyn, saying, "He is being facetious, Gracelyn."

Colonel Redford chuckled and said, "I need some sense of humor during this war. It helps me keep my sanity. Abby is correct. I am kidding. I will have two soldiers travel with you via jeep. You will travel to the specified area and treat the soldiers. If the area is secure, you will radio in to me and I will send a convoy to pick up the wounded."

Abby and Gracelyn nodded, and Colonel Redford took that as an understanding of the mission.

"You ladies will rendezvous with Private Smith and Private Miller in exactly one hour behind the medical center. Dismissed."

The girls met the two privates an hour after they had left the colonel still smoking his cigar. The girls saw the two privates standing by the jeep. They looked to be in their early twenties and were striking young men. As they were walking toward the men, Gracelyn said to Abby, "They're pretty cute."

Abby laughed, saying, "I'll take the one on the left."

"That's fine with me. I like guys with dark hair, anyway," said Gracelyn.

Once they were closer to the two privates, they introduced themselves. "You must be Private Miller and Private Smith," said Abby.

"Yes, ma'am. That's us. I'm Private Miller, and that's Private Smith," said the man with beach-blond hair. He then turned to Gracelyn, asking, "What are your names?"

"I'm Gracelyn Turner, and that's Abby Walker."

"Now that we have introduced ourselves, let's get a move on. There are a lot of injured soldiers who are counting on us," said Private Smith.

Private Smith seemed like the opposite of Private Miller. He had dark hair and was a few inches shorter. The biggest difference Abby and Gracelyn noticed was that he was much more serious. But who wouldn't be serious during a time of war?

In their camouflage uniforms, the two privates loaded up the jeep. Private Smith and Miller climbed in front, while Gracelyn and Abby hopped in the back. A few minutes into the drive, Private Miller leaned back and asked Abby if they'd grabbed all the medical supplies. "Everything is in the back," said Abby.

"Excellent. We wouldn't want to return to the medical center and listen to Colonel Redford's poor attempt at sarcasm," said Private Miller.

"It's so bad that some people don't get it," Abby said while nudging Gracelyn.

While the privates focused on the road, Gracelyn and Abby talked in the back seat. "I've never been in a jeep before. These things are fun," said Gracelyn.

"I want one. Maybe Walter will get me one when we get back home. He said he would do anything for me," said Abby.

The ladies' eyes began wandering to the French countryside. There was green grass and trees everywhere. "France is beautiful. Maybe someday we should come back and visit France," Gracelyn said.

"I would really like that. We'll come back with the boys some-time after the war," said Abby.

Private Miller leaned back again and said, "We're almost there. Just a few more minutes."

"Thank you for the update," said Gracelyn.

Private Miller wasn't done talking to the girls, and he asked them if they had ever been in a jeep. "We we're just talking about this a few minutes ago. We think it's fun," said Abby as the wind was blowing in her face.

"I'm hoping the general public someday gets to use these vehicles," said Private Miller.

The girls started laughing. They hadn't laughed so much since the war first began. "I couldn't imagine anything more impossible. And maybe we will get to the moon someday. See, I can be sarcastic, just like Colonel Redford," said Gracelyn.

"I'm with ya, Gracelyn. I couldn't imagine anyone in a suburb like my hometown driving jeeps. Better yet, driving yellow jeeps," said Abby.

Private Miller was taken aback by the girls' attitudes. "You'll be wrong. One day, jeeps will be the most popular brand in America. Just you wait," said Private Miller.

As the military personnel reached the farm, Private Smith parked the car and all four of them hopped out of the jeep. They looked around and witnessed Americans and Germans lying in the field. Abby covered her mouth with her hand and whispered under her breath, "Oh my god."

Privates Smith and Miller asked the girls if they were all right with seeing so much blood. "We'll be fine. We saw what happened on the beaches," said Abby. "Let's find our boys who are alive that we can save."

"What about Captain Stahl? Aren't we supposed to get our orders from him?" asked Abby.

"Ahh, yes," said Private Miller. "We will try to find him as we look for injured soldiers."

The four of them separated so they could find injured soldiers at a faster rate. As they split up, Abby began walking toward one of the barns. This particular barn was big and red, and it appeared to have housed horses. When she was about twenty yards away from the barn, she heard a voice. "Help me. Please help me. I'm an American," said a wounded soldier.

She rushed over to him as soon as she could locate the man. Once she laid her eyes on the soldier, she could tell that he had been shot in one of his legs and one of his arms. "I'm a nurse in the United States Army. We're here to help you," said Abby.

"I thought I was going to die here alone," said the soldier, who was lying in the grass.

"You're not alone. What's your name?" said Abby.

The soldier lifted his head up and said, "The name is William Dennis."

"I'm Abby," said Abby. "Where is Captain Stahl?"

"He's dead," said William Dennis.

Abby yelled over to get the others' attention, and it took a few minutes for everyone to arrive at Abby's location. Once they did, Gracelyn asked, "What's the status of this soldier?"

Abby turned to Gracelyn, saying, "He's badly wounded. If we can stop the bleeding, I think he has a real shot."

Private Smith looked down at Abby, who was kneeling on the ground next to the injured soldier. "Well, we better get started, then. Private Miller and I will get supplies from the Jeep. What shall we bring back?"

Abby looked up at him and said, "We need bandages and stitching supplies." Private Smith and Private Miller walked to the jeep following Abby's request.

While the men were walking back to the jeep and getting supplies to help this man, Abby and Gracelyn tried to comfort William Dennis. "This is my fellow nurse, Gracelyn," Abby said to William Dennis.

William Dennis fought to raise his head a few inches to see Gracelyn. He succeeded and said, "It's a pleasure to meet you. I'm William." He paused a moment to catch his breath, then he went on to say, "I never thought the Army would send a team to rescue us."

Gracelyn gave him a strange look, because she didn't believe that four people were big enough to call a team or a rescue mission.

"It's our job to help you. Our assignment was to save as many people as possible," said Gracelyn.

"How many soldiers were assigned to protect you?" asked William.

"Two of the finest escorts you could ask for," said Abby. "But we were supposed to get orders from Captain Stahl. We haven't been able to locate him or anyone."

"Captain Stahl is dead," snapped William Dennis.

William was puzzled. He didn't understand why the United States Army would permit two nurses with almost no protection detail to wander off into hostile territory. The Allied troops were forcing the Germans to retreat, but there were still German soldiers roaming around the area. "I hope operations knows what they're doing sending you two into the heartland with only two privates protecting you. It's dangerous. I just hope they know what they're doing," said William.

Abby and Gracelyn looked at each other. Would the United States Army really send two young girls into dangerous territory? Colonel Redford cautioned them, but he also said that the majority of the land surrounding Normandy was under Allied control. Gracelyn opened her mouth and said, "Do you think we're in danger?"

Abby thought about it for a few moments, then said, "I think we're fine. Colonel Redford reassured us that we would be safe. He would have assigned more men to us if we were in danger."

Just as Abby made that statement, a couple of gunshots could be heard. Abby and Gracelyn jumped in fright. "What was that?" said Gracelyn.

"I'm not sure. It sounded like a couple of rifles went off. Hopefully, Private Smith and Private Miller are fine," said Abby as Gracelyn held on to her arm for comfort.

"I don't think those rifles came from our soldiers. You two should go hide in that barn over there."

Abby looked at the injured soldier and didn't think she could leave him. "We can't leave you," said Abby.

"This is not up for a debate. I'm the rank of captain, and I'm ordering you to hide in the barn," said Captain William Dennis.

Abby and Gracelyn followed the captain's orders and sprinted to the barn like a couple of racehorses.

When they were in the barn, the nurses climbed to the top loft, which was surrounded by hay. There were two windows that over-looked the farm, so Abby and Gracelyn could see Captain Dennis. They wanted to keep an eye on Captain Dennis and wanted to know if German soldiers were indeed coming. They waited for almost thirty minutes, and nothing happened.

"What shall we do? Do you think any Nazis will show up?" asked Gracelyn to Abby as they were gazing through the window.

"I don't know. There's a good chance. Something happened to Private Smith and Private Miller. It wouldn't take them this long to get medical supplies," said Abby. "We don't know anything yet. Let's just hope for the best, Gracelyn."

It didn't take too long to prove Abby's theory correct, as three German soldiers walked toward Captain Dennis, who was still lying in front of the barn. "We need to be quiet," said Abby.

Abby was no native German speaker, but she could tell the soldiers were speaking in German. However, they began speaking English. "They must be talking to Captain Dennis," said Abby.

The two nurses attempted to make out what the German sol-diers were saying but had no luck until the German soldiers put a gun up to William Dennis's head. "I will ask you one more time. Are there any soldiers hiding in that barn?" said a German soldier with a strong accent.

"I've already told you. There are no soldiers in that barn. You can check if you want," said William Dennis. The man holding the gun nodded to the other soldiers, and the other German soldiers began walking toward the barn.

Abby and Gracelyn saw them getting closer and closer to the barn. Their hearts began beating faster and faster with every step of the soldiers. "Quick! Let's hide in the hay. Maybe they won't find us," said Abby.

The German soldiers threw open the door as loud as they could. "We know you're in here," said one of soldiers.

"If you come out, we won't kill you," said the other soldier.

Gracelyn might have not caught on to some of Colonel Redford's jokes, but the two nurses were not that gullible. The soldiers saw some of the hay move, so Abby and Gracelyn were discovered. "We see you up there. We're going to give you five seconds to show yourself," said the German soldier. They started counting, and by the time he said two, the girls popped out of the hay.

When the nurses came down from the loft, the Germans were shocked. They expected a couple of men in green uniforms and not a couple of young nurses. The two soldiers weren't sure how to handle the situation. "Should we shoot 'em?" asked one of the German soldiers in broken English.

"Let's see what Captain Tressemann wants to do."

The two nurses and two German soldiers walked out of the barn together. The girls were terrified. They were shaking with fear.

As the nurses and soldiers were standing in front of the German leader, the German commander said to William Dennis, "You lied to me."

William Dennis lifted his head above the ground in an effort to defend himself. "You were looking for soldiers. These ladies aren't soldiers. They're just nurses helping injured men," said the American captain.

"No, they are spies. They are soldiers. And do you know what we do to American soldiers?" said the German captain.

None of the three Americans answered the question. Since no one spoke, the German leader said while looking at William Dennis, "We kill them. And you know what I'm going to do?"

Unlike the last rhetorical question, William Dennis was quick to provide an answer or, for his sake, a comment. "You can't shoot them. In the rules of war, they are not soldiers. These ladies are nurses. Show some humanity and let them go."

"Don't lecture me about the rules of war. I'm considering them American spies. I'm going to shoot them. And I'm going to have you watch."

William Dennis tried pleading his case once more, but the German soldiers weren't listening. The appeal was denied, and the girls were ordered to march in front of the barn. They only had a few minutes left to live. And the one thought that entered Abby's mind was Walter. She wasn't scared of dying, but she was scared of not seeing him again. She dreamed of growing old with Walter and raising kids with him. She at least wanted to spend one last night with him. As she looked at the two German soldiers holding their weapons, it didn't seem like her dreams would come true.

Abby turned toward Gracelyn, saying, "It's been an honor serving with you."

"I wouldn't have had it any other way," Gracelyn managed to say, tears running down her face. "I guess this is the end."

Abby tapped Gracelyn on the shoulder, saying, "Look them in the eye when they shoot. They won't ever forget your face."

The girls were staring at the German shooters, almost daring them to do it. The German soldiers were about to pull the trigger, but out of nowhere, the two young nurses heard gunshots. All three German soldiers fell to the ground. Abby and Gracelyn were stunned. William Dennis was stunned. Both girls started crying from relief.

Abby and Gracelyn were standing by the barn. They looked in the direction of the gunfire and could see a few soldiers in the distance walking toward them. It looked like there were three soldiers, and two of them were carrying a stretcher. As the soldiers drew closer to the girls, they looked to be wearing American uniforms. Once they were standing a few feet away, both Abby and Gracelyn recognized the soldier lying on stretcher. "Do you know that injured soldier? It looks like someone that I know," said Gracelyn.

"He does look familiar to me. We've met so many people during this war people just blend together," said Abby.

When they were standing within talking distance, the soldiers carrying the stretcher placed it on the ground and proceeded to introduce themselves. "We are part of the 82nd Airborne Division. We are on our way to the medical center," said one of the soldiers.

Due to William Dennis's rank of captain, both Abby and Gracelyn let him talk to the soldiers. "Pleased to meet you. I was part of the Normandy invasion. The name is Captain Dennis. Captain William Dennis. Thank you for rescuing us," said Captain Dennis, who was still on the ground, wounded.

One of the other soldiers looked at Abby and Gracelyn and asked William Dennis about the two nurses. "What happened here? Why are there two nurses?"

"Well, they came to rescue me, but the privates escorting them were shot. They were about a minute from getting shot themselves. You saved all our lives," said William Dennis. He pointed in the direction of Abby and Gracelyn and said, "That's Abby and Gracelyn."

Soon after Captain Dennis introduced the two nurses, the soldier on the stretcher waved his arm and motioned them to go to him. "I don't know if you remember me, but I'm Luke Feter. I serve with Walter in the same unit. I met you when we traveled to London a few weeks ago."

Abby placed her hand over her mouth and stared at Luke like he was some sort of ghost. The young nurse from Ohio couldn't believe that she crossed paths with one of Walter's platoon mates in the middle of Normandy. "Oh my god," Abby said. She paused for a few moments. "I wish it were under better circumstances, but it's nice to see you."

When Abby regained her bearings and realized a person from Walter's unit was injured, her mind began racing. How did Luke get injured? Was Walter hurt? Was Walter's unit successful?

"How did you get hurt? How is Walter doing?" Abby asked Luke.

"Walter is a fighter. I was hurt by a German mortar while securing the La Fiere Bridge."

"What happened?" asked Gracelyn.

Luke took a deep breath before he answered the question. "We were successful in securing the bridge. German Panzer divisions kept coming at us, and we proved to hold strong. They came at us with tanks, bazookas, mortars, and whatever else they had. They threw everything but the kitchen sink at us, and they couldn't break through," said Luke. He then glared at Abby and continued talking. "Your boy saved my life. I was hit by a mortar, and he dragged me to safety. I will always be indebted to him."

Abby was very proud of Walter, and she wasn't surprised by his heroics or selflessness. He had always been a generous person, which was why she was so in love with him. Abby hoped his courage wouldn't cost him his life, though, because she wanted him and, quite possibly, needed him.

"Do you think he will be okay?" asked Abby while looking at Luke.

"Oh, most definitely, and he must pull through," said Luke.

"Why do you say that?" Abby said without hesitation.

"When I was lying on the battlefield, wounded, I told him that if anything happens to me, I want him to tell my younger sister that I'm sorry and that I love her. He needs to fulfill that promise if, God forbid, anything happens to me."

"Is that it?" asked Abby.

"The second reason is you. I've never met someone who is more in love with a girl than Walter Wilson." Luke cracked the biggest smile, which was uncommon for someone wounded, lying on a stretcher. "I'll be frank. It was rather annoying. He talked about you all the time. He wouldn't shut his mouth about you. And I'll tell you, it made a lot of the men jealous."

The smile was contagious, like the common cold, as a smile appeared across her face. It gave her great pleasure to know that she was on Walter's mind all the time. She did hope that it didn't interfere with his focus in combat, but it couldn't have. His focus had been achieving victory so he could secure a better life for he and Abby. Walter couldn't have one without the other.

After a while of talking among each other, one of the American soldiers who saved Abby, Gracelyn, and Captain Dennis asked where the medical center was located. Captain Dennis didn't know the answer and asked the nurses.

"It's about three clicks away from here toward Normandy," Abby said. "We can drive the jeep to the medical center."

Captain Dennis shook his head and, with a smile, said, "Just as long as you ladies aren't driving."

Everyone laughed, and they headed to the jeep. Abby and Gracelyn carried Captain Dennis on a stretcher.

When the group of the Americans reached the jeep, Abby noticed the radio was on the front passenger's side. "Look, our radio's on the front seat. I'll call in to Colonel Redford, our commanding officer," Abby said. She proceeded to call the colonel. "Colonel, this is Abby. We're heading back to the base."

"Abby, why is Private Miller not using the radio?" asked the colonel.

Abby hesitated a minute, as she didn't want to reveal the circumstances via radio. However, she relented, "They were ambushed, sir. They didn't make it. We almost didn't make it, but a few American soldiers saved our lives."

It didn't take long for the colonel to respond, and he was very clear with his orders. "Drive the jeep back to the base. The soldiers who need medical help will receive it, and it will allow you to regroup before your next assignment. Be careful, and we will see you soon," said the colonel.

CHAPTER 19

Walter and his platoon had been in France for a couple of weeks. The airborne divisions were told they would only be fighting south of the English Channel for only a few days. However, during war, circumstances can change, and the paratroopers were forced to continue with the invasion of France.

The 82nd Airborne Division had been fighting German troops near farms, hedgerows, dirt roads, and forests. They were exhausted, and the ones who were alive felt fortunate to be exhausted. On some nights the fighting ceased, while other nights the fighting ravaged on.

On one particular night in late June, Walter Wilson, Bobby Hawkins, and Randall Moore were huddled around one another in a foxhole. The fighting had stopped for the day, but they could hear Germans firing artillery in the distance.

"It could be worse. At least it's not raining," said Walter.

"You always see the positive in everything, don't you, sport?" said Randall.

An hour had passed since the last round of gunfire from the Germans, or at least it had ceased in that particular area. Without the sound of gunfire, the American soldiers felt more at ease. Walter felt comfortable enough that he pulled a bottle of Jack Daniel's from his sack.

"I was saving this for a rainy day, so maybe we shouldn't drink it," said Walter.

"Y'all, we can pretend it's raining. Where did you find this?" said Bobby Hawkins.

"I went into an abandoned French home the other day, and Mr. Daniel was having a seat at the table. I couldn't let him sit there by himself, so I took him with me," said Walter. "I thought it was the right thing to do."

"We wouldn't want Mr. Daniel to be lonely," said Randall.

"You were brave to rescue Mr. Daniel, Walter. That boy could have been captured by the Germans if you didn't save him," said Bobby.

"And who knows what those Krauts would have done to him," said Randall.

Walter then proceeded to untwist the cap and placed the bottle on his dry lips. The Jack Daniel's went down smooth as silk. "Damn, that tastes good," said Walter, passing the bottle of whiskey to Randall.

Randall wasted no time taking a swig of whiskey. "Drinking here with you boys makes me feel, ahh, better. I really needed a night like this. It helps me recharge my batteries," said Randall.

It was Bobby Hawkins's turn to take a gulp of Jack Daniel's. He grabbed the bottle from Randall and took a big sip. "I'll tell ya, boys. This reminds me of back home."

"And how is that? We are surrounded by the enemy, in quite possibly the biggest campaign of the war," said Walter, looking at Bobby.

"Y'all, I live in Florida. I have a beach house. So on some nights, my gal, Samantha, and I would sit by the beach and drink. We would drink usually the way we are tonight. Samantha hates whiskey like some Southerners hate you Yankees," Bobby said. "So she would bring her wine, and I would bring my whiskey. We would drink and talk for hours about our future."

"You are one lucky man, because that sounds amazing, chief. We don't have any good bodies of water near us. We have a river and a man-made dam in Columbus," said Randall. "What are your plans for the future with Samantha?"

Bobby slipped a picture of Samantha and glanced at it. Once he was done looking at it, he passed it around to Randall and Walter.

Walter looked at the picture and saw the beauty of Samantha. Samantha had long blond hair, pale skin, and a few freckles under her eyelids. "She is really beautiful," said Walter.

"Thank you," Bobby said to Walter, then looked at Randall. "To answer your question, Randall, I'm excited for our future together. She's my best friend. We want to have a big family and live somewhere by our folks. I plan on joining my pops in business, and she's going to be a teacher. Y'all, it's a dream."

Randall and Walter smiled, enjoying Bobby's plan for after the war. They both had similar plans with their respective girlfriends. "I showed y'all my gal. I want to see Mallie and Abby."

The two friends from Ohio pulled out a picture from his respective pocket. They both glanced at the pictures and handed the picture over to Bobby. Bobby viewed the pictures. "Mallie looks a lot like Walter."

"Well, she is my sister," Walter said, smiling.

"Randall, I don't know how you do it," said Bobby. "Every time I would kiss her, I would think of our boy Walter."

"Shut up," said Randall, giving Bobby a playful punch in the shoulder.

"Y'all, all joking aside, these girls are beautiful. Both of you boys are very lucky men. Looks like we all did very well for ourselves," Bobby Hawkins said. "I talked about my relationship with my gal. Gents, it's your turn to spill the beans."

Randall opened his mouth first. "Just like you, sport, Mallie and I have become really close. I tell her everything, and she tells me everything. I can't wait to be with her again."

Bobby took another sip of whiskey and laughed at Randall's comment. Walter and Randall looked at each other with a confused look on their faces. The confusion was clarified when Bobby explained why he was laughing. "How did Walter find out about this love affair? Randall, I bet he wanted to pound you."

"At first, you bet ya. I was so angry. But then I thought about it. Mallie was so happy, and Randall is a great guy. I want my sister to be with someone like that. So it became easy for me to accept."

Randall put his arm around Walter. "I appreciate it, sport. You know your sister means the world to me, and so do you. I would do anything for you and your sister. Hell, I would take a bullet for you. You're the closest thing I've had to a brother," said Randall.

"You know I would take a bullet for you. Any day of the week and twice on Sundays," said Walter.

"Y'all, what about me? Where is the brotherly love?" said Bobby.

"Sharing foxholes together automatically qualifies you to join us as brothers," said Walter.

"Looks like our wolf pack just grew," said Randall.

"I appreciate it, y'all. I can now take a bullet for you," said Bobby. "Walter, it's your turn to talk about Abby."

Walter grabbed the bottle from Bobby, who was starting to get a little tipsy. "Well, what do you want to know?" asked Walter.

"Everything. We have all night."

"Well, like both of you, she is my best friend. She is more than that. She is my soul mate. I couldn't ask her out at the tennis club, and lucky for me, I saw her at our community fair. We started talking, and from that moment on, we were inseparable," Walter said while possessing a huge smile across his face. "Now, let's share our favorite memory of our girls, or, like our fellow-brother-slash-wolf-pack-member says, gals"

Bobby and Randall really liked the idea. They both shook their heads in a positive direction, so Walter began with his memory. "My favorite memory with Abby? That's a tough one, because there are so many. If I had to choose one, it would be the time I spent with Abby at her lake house. Randall, Abby, her friend Martha, and I all went to Abby's lake house one weekend. We went canoeing, fishing, and swimming. And the last night there was maybe the best time I've ever had," Walter said, then took another sip of Jack Daniel's before passing it to Randall. "On the last night, while her parents were sleeping, we sneaked out on the dock. We lay on some blankets and looked up at the stars for hours. That was when I knew that I wanted to spend the rest of my life with her. God, I can even remember what she was wearing. It was a purple nightgown," Walter said.

"If only her dad caught you," said Randall.

"Samantha's pops would have chased me with a shotgun if I sneaked out with her."

"Except I doubt he would have taken a shot. Abby's dad would have fired," said Walter.

Randall took the whiskey from Walter's hand. He took a chug, then said, "sport, it's hard to believe that was over a year ago. It seems like we were at the Walker lake house just yesterday." Randall proceeded to look at Bobby and asked if he would like to share his story before him.

"Yeah. I'll share my story," said Bobby. But before he became the storyteller, he asked for the bottle of whiskey. Randall passed it to him, and he took a sip. "Hmm, let me think about it, y'all."

"Think about it, QB? Why did you volunteer to go ahead of Randall?" said Walter.

"Good point, but I know what story I'm going to tell," Bobby said. "It was my senior season, and it was the final game of my career. We were down four points, with only seconds remaining in the game. Before the snap, I looked around. I looked at our fans, and they were as silent as church mice. My parents were covering their faces. I then looked over at the cheerleaders, and I saw Samantha looking at me, smiling. She had the utmost confidence in me. It was like she knew I would pull through for the team."

"Well, did you, QB?" Randall asked.

"Hold your horses there, fella. I'm getting to it," Bobby said, then continued with his story. "I snapped the ball. It was the final play of the game. One of the boys up front slipped, so a big guy from the other team came after me. I spun out of his arms and ran to the right of the field. My friend Tony was open downfield. I threw a dart to him in the corner of the end zone. We won the game, and y'all, our fans celebrated with us on the field. I found Samantha near the center of the field. I picked her up, and we kissed in front of everyone."

"That's a good story, but it didn't really involve her," said Walter.

"Save that one for the story basket," said Randall. "There must not be a lot of excitement down South."

"I'm getting there. After the game, she sneaked over to my house and we spent the night on the beach. It was the first time that we made love. And that was when I realized I loved her."

The bottle had been passed around quite a few times during Bobby's story and was resting in Walter's lap. "Great story, QB." Walter looked at Randall. "Your turn. But let's not go in-depth, because quite frankly, I don't want to hear about my sister in that manner."

Randall pondered for a few moments, as he, too, had to think about his favorite moment with Mallie. "My favorite moment was the night before we left for basic training. I know it was the night before we left, but I was much more at peace when you knew of our relationship, sport," Randall said as he looked at Walter. "The four of us grilled hot dogs and drank beer all night. And then Mallie and I parted ways from you and Abby. We talked all night and about a variety of things."

"Is that why you overslept?" Walter asked, referring to when he shook Randall awake before leaving for the base.

"That's right, sport. I really loved how scared she was about me going off to war but yet so confident. We talked about how many children we would have and what holidays would be like. And how she would miss me like crazy during the war, and how I would miss her. She also told me that I better keep an eye for you, sport," Randall said, winking at Walter.

"How many little Randalls and Mallies will be running around?" asked Bobby Hawkins.

"That's one of the few things we cannot agree on. I am an only child, so I want four kids. Two boys and two girls would be ideal. She wants a maximum of three children."

"You're going to have to put your foot down. Show her who's boss," Bobby said while laughing.

"Hey, now! Don't be talking about my sister like that."

It was the first time since June 5, 1944, that they were able to have a smile on their faces. It was also the first time they consumed alcohol. And because of that, they were drunk. Bobby Hawkins was the first to pass out, but it was probably a combination of exhaustion and alcohol.

Randall looked at Bobby peeled over against the French dirt. "I guess some people aren't meant to be soldiers."

"Those who aren't man enough to handle their liquor shouldn't be in the war," said Walter.

Both of them were of course joking. Any man who was brave enough to jump out of a plane in the dark of night and behind enemy lines was no doubt a warrior. And that was exactly who Bobby was, a warrior. Every soldier fighting in Normandy was a fighter.

Even though Bobby had been like a brother to Walter and Randall, they were content that Bobby fell asleep. It felt like the days of their youths, when they would spend late nights talking at summer camp.

"Sport, I just wanted to let you know, I really do appreciate your blessing on my relationship with Mallie. It really does mean a lot to me. You're my brother, and I never wanted to ruin that relationship. I always had a crush on your sister but never acted on it. You see, sport, my feeling toward her intensified during the night of the community fair."

"So once you felt something strong, you just said, 'Screw our brotherhood,'" said Walter, laughing.

"No. I spent a lot of sleepless nights contemplating it. I came to the conclusion that you would understand. And once you were 100 percent on board, you may come to enjoy it. I mean the family holidays, they will be something, huh, sport?" said Randall.

"We probably won't remember half of them," said Walter.

"It may get dangerous," said Randall.

"Oh, there is no doubt they will be a blast. Hell, I can one-up that," said Walter, taking another sip of whiskey. After that swig, he was feeling nice and toasty.

"Sport, how could you one-up how awesome the family holidays will be?" asked Randall.

"Well, both Mallie and Abby want to live in Arlington Heights. I really want to live on Abington Road. You should live a few doors down, and the good times will always be rolling," said Walter.

"God, Mallie and Abby would hate that. We would send the kids over to one of our houses while we would be in the other. We would booze for a while, then walk home," said Randall.

Both Randall and Walter smiled at that idea. "Boy, would it be fun!" Walter said under his breath.

"It certainly would," commented Randall.

Shortly after Randall spoke, he passed out. Randall did drink his fair share, but he was exhausted. War can have that effect. Walter looked at his brothers, who were fast asleep, and decided it was time to get some much-needed rest. He had talked a lot about his future during the night, and he was so excited about it. Walter couldn't wait to spend Christmases and Thanksgivings with Abby, Randall, Mallie, and the rest of his family. It gave him extra motivation to fight even harder in the upcoming days. And he still had a long journey before he exited France, before the Allies achieved a total victory.

Just before he went to sleep, he said under his breath, "I better make it home."

CHAPTER 20

"Welcome back, ladies," said Mary Safford as Abby and Gracelyn were sitting in her office. She was glad they were back and not just because they were two of the best nurses. Mary cared for them on a personal level.

Mary's words were the best sentence Abby had heard since she left for France. "It's good to be back. I appreciate the opportunity to serve near the front. It was a rewarding experience to help the young men on the front lines," said Abby.

"Thank you as well. It was an honor serving in France," Gracelyn said.

Mary was pleased to hear about the ladies' experience. "Well, I'm glad you were able to help those young men. There are many young men that could use your experience here in London," said Mary. Mary looked at the clock and decided, after their long trip, they needed the night off. "I'll expect you to be at the nursing center at 1000 hours. Now, get out of here."

Abby got up from her chair and walked toward the door. As she was about to twist the doorknob, she turned back to Mary Safford.

"Oh, I almost forgot. Where is Eli?" said Abby.

"Sit back down, Abby," said Mary.

Gracelyn looked at Abby and asked her if she should stay too. Abby nodded at her to go ahead. The young girl from Ohio sat in front of her supervisor's desk while her friend walked back to the barracks.

"I have some bad news about Eli," said Mary.

"What is it?" snapped Abby.

"Before I begin, you must know, it wasn't my decision. We had to turn Eli over to the British Social Services. We couldn't have a little boy running around a military base. I'm so sorry," said Mary.

"You could have waited until I came back," said Abby.

"It doesn't work like that," said Major Safford. "I'm truly sorry."

"Sorry doesn't make him come back," said Abby. "I wanted to adopt him."

Mary sighed. She had no idea Abby cared so deeply for the child, but it didn't really matter. Feelings had no factor in the decision. It was no doubt the right decision, but it was still difficult.

"You can see about adopting him after the war. That's the best advice that I can give you," said Mary. "Now, why don't you decompress? You've had a long few days."

Abby trembled back to her room with practically a million different thoughts racing through her mind. She was upset about Eli and wondered if she would be able to adopt him after the war. Would young Eli even remember her? They'd only spent a few day together.

She walked into the barracks, and Gracelyn was lying on the bed, reading *Time* magazine. Bob Hope was on the cover of the magazine. He was a comedian from London but had moved to the US.

"What's wrong?" Gracelyn asked, noticing the negative body language coming from Abby.

"Eli's gone," said Abby.

Gracelyn sat up on her bed. "What do you mean *gone?*"

"British children services took him and placed him in a group home," said Abby, trying to hold back tears.

"I'm so sorry to hear that," said Gracelyn. "I'm not surprised, though. We're trying to win a war. The Army can't be worrying about a little kid."

Abby couldn't disagree. "I understand. I just wish they would have waited until we were back."

Gracelyn tapped Abby on the shoulder. "I know."

The two girls just sat in silence. There was nothing to say about Eli, and there was nothing to say about their service in France. The girls were almost shot by a German officer, and now Eli was gone. They needed to "decompress," just as Mary Safford suggested.

There was suddenly a knock on the door. Abby checked her watch, and she and Gracelyn had been sitting like zombies for a good forty-five minutes. "Come in," said Abby.

Mary Safford entered the room with two soldiers accompanying her. "Abby, can we speak with you in the hall?" asked Mary. Abby looked at Gracelyn for comfort, because Abby was worried something was wrong. She then looked at Mary and agreed, so Mary, the two soldiers, and Abby stepped into the hall.

Major Safford had a disappointed look on her face. Mary put her arm around Abby and said, "Abby, I'm so sorry. It's your mother. She's really sick."

Abby almost fainted. Her mind was traveling in all kinds of directions; she just didn't know what to think. "What happened? Is she okay?" Abby asked while trying to hold back tears.

"All I know is that she is sick and you've been granted permission to fly home," said Mary. Just as Mary finished her statement, Abby broke down in tears. If the military granted her leave, then it must have meant her mother was ill.

As Abby began crying, Gracelyn walked outside to console her. "I'll take care of her tonight," Gracelyn said to Mary.

"You're a good friend. Abby, you're welcome to take the leave of absence if you wish. Think it over tonight and let us know tomorrow," said Mary. Mary then walked away, and the two nurses went inside to their barracks.

While in their room, Abby and Gracelyn sat in silence. Gracelyn didn't know what to say, and she wished there were some magic words to make her feel better, but no words seemed to exist. "I'm really sorry, Abby," said Gracelyn, as those were the only words she could think to say. Abby just kept sobbing.

Abby continued to sit and cry, and she kept thinking about her decision on whether to leave her post. Her work was really important, and sacrifices must be made for the greater good. However, this was her mother, and she was sick. Abby left for the war on bad terms with her mother, and she didn't want her mom's last thought to be of regret. Although maybe her mom would make a full recovery. Abby kept playing the different scenarios in her head.

"I don't know what I should do. I want to return home to see my mom, but my services are needed here. This cause is bigger than just one person," said Abby.

Quite frankly, Gracelyn didn't know how to respond. When she collected her thoughts, Gracelyn told Abby she should return home. "Abby, I really think you need to go home. See your mom. I hate to say this, but this may be your last chance to see her."

Abby still didn't think it was right for her to return. Her work was important. The war was not over, and plenty of young men would be wounded from now until Germany surrendered. "I still don't know. The cause is just too great."

Without hesitation, Gracelyn reiterated her sentiment. "Abby, you really need to go home. I understand the cause, just as much as everyone else, including you. We are here to stand up for humanity," Gracelyn said. "We are fighting for people at home and abroad, so they can live a free life. What are we fighting for if we don't take care of the ones we love?"

There was no denying the fact that Gracelyn was right. Abby needed to return home. "I think you're right. I'll inform Mary of my decision tomorrow," Abby said toward Gracelyn.

"You're making the right decision."

Abby began to pack her things. She folded a few of her nursing outfits and placed them in her brown leather suitcase. As she was walking to her nightstand, she noticed the two toothbrushes, one much smaller than the other.

"What about Eli?" Abby said.

"What about him?" said Gracelyn.

"I told you about wanting to adopt him. How can I leave without him?" said Abby as she sat on her bed.

"You're going to have to. There is nothing you can do. You can figure it out once this war's over," said Gracelyn.

"I don't want to wait," muttered Abby. "But I don't have a choice."

Gracelyn sat next to Abby on her bed. In times of struggle and turmoil, people became close. Abby and Gracelyn were no exception to that rule. They became nurses as complete strangers and transformed into sisters.

"Do me a favor?" asked Gracelyn.

"Anything," responded Abby.

"Eat a nice, juicy burger for me. The English burgers taste like coal," said Gracelyn.

"That's the first thing I'll do." Abby smiled.

Abby woke up the next morning as the sun was rising over the English soil. She grabbed her suitcase and placed it next to the door. Gracelyn was asleep, so she nudged her awake.

"I'm off," said Abby.

Gracelyn rolled over and fought to wake up. "Good luck. I hope your mom is okay. If I don't see you before the war ends, look me up after," said Gracelyn.

Abby gave her a hug. "I will. Stay safe, and thanks for everything."

The young nurse from Ohio proceeded to pick up her suitcase and walk out the door toward the direction of Major Safford's office.

As she walked into Major Safford's office, Mary Safford was sitting at her desk. She was looking at a picture of her husband. By the look on Major Safford's face, Abby could tell she really missed him.

"Judging by the suitcase in your hand, I take it you've decided to go home," said Major Safford.

"Yes, ma'am," replied Abby.

"Very well, then. Your plane leaves for Washington, D.C. in two hours. Good luck, and I hope your mom makes a full recovery."

"Thank you," Abby said as she left Mary's office and walked toward the hangar.

While Abby was sitting on the plane, so many emotions ran through her. She was happy to be returning home but felt guilty about leaving all the soldiers and nurses behind. She was also thinking of Walter and hoping that he would be sitting in a plane one day, returning home. In her heart, Abby knew that he would return, but she just didn't know when that day would come. On the other hand, her brain told her that there was a possibility he would never return home. Obviously, she really hoped that her heart would win. But only time would tell.

CHAPTER 21

Twenty-six days. It had been twenty-six days since Walter had last taken a warm shower. It had been twenty-six days since he had been in France, fighting with his brothers. As the Allies were making headway in their quest for total victory, Walter was hoping to be dismissed from France soon. Just like most of his fellow mates of the 82nd Airborne Division, he wanted to return to England and wait for the next assignment of the war.

Walter's hope was becoming ever so close to reality. In his estimation, it was a matter of days before they left. The Allies were close to capturing the Cotentin Peninsula and the Port of Cherbourg, which was tucked inside the peninsula. The Port of Cherbourg was a deepwater harbor, and it would allow the Allied forces to shuffle supplies and men into France. Once they captured this port, the thought was that the airborne division troops would be no longer needed.

During the morning of July 2, 1944, Walter and his fellow soldiers woke up, and the sun was nowhere to be found. It reminded Walter and Randall of days back in Ohio. They didn't mind, because metaphorically speaking, the sun should never be shining during days of war.

"Hmm, y'all, this is good coffee. It must be freshly brewed from Colombia," said Bobby Hawkins. Bobby Hawkins made this joke on numerous occasions, because the coffee supplied by the Army could never be mistaken for quality Colombian coffee. It tasted like watered-down dirt, but none of the troops complained. They were happy to drink something that resembled coffee, and the caffeine helped them stay alert.

After the cook served the boys a hearty breakfast, which consisted of beans and ham, the commanding colonel, Colonel Jacobs, briefed them on the day's assignment. When the American boys gathered around the colonel, he began speaking. "Gentlemen, today we are tasked with taking the highest point in Normandy. We have given the name Hill 131 to this high point. It is vital that we capture it, and when we do, we will have eyes on the highest point in Normandy," said Colonel Jacobs. He looked up at the foggy sky and continued talking. "Unfortunately, the skies are too foggy for air support, so we will be on our own. Artillery will be behind us the entire way. We will be cutting through the town of La Haye-du-Puits and make our way to the top of the mountain. The German soldiers will not just hand us the hill, so we need to take it, and take it with force. Is this understood?"

"Yes, sir," said the soldiers.

As soon as the meeting adjourned, the soldiers picked up their weapons, put on their heavy green helmet, and marched toward the hill. Right on schedule, the soldiers saw the little medieval town in the distance. It had an array of houses, and dirt roads connected the buildings with one another. "This reminds me of the old South," said Bobby Hawkins.

"And how is that, QB?" asked Walter.

"There were so many towns like this. Maybe not the same style, but a lot of small towns. Your Ohio boy Sherman destroyed many of them," said Bobby. He was referring to General William Tecumseh Sherman. According to many proud Southern people, this Union general burned down many old Southern towns on his march to the sea. "The necessity of this destruction has been debated ever since you Yankees won."

Neither Walter nor Randall wished to engage in an argument with Bobby Hawkins on the Civil War, so they just nodded. Also, Randall, Bobby, and Walter needed to stay sharp, and their ability would be greatly diminished over an argument of a previous war, especially a previous war that pitted brother against brother, cousin against cousin, and American against American. "All right, boys, let's keep our eyes peeled for these damn Germans," said Walter.

When the soldiers first stepped foot in the French town, they saw no Germans in sight. Some of the buildings were destroyed, which, in all likelihood, must be a result of air strikes. "This is like a ghost town," Walter said to himself, as he saw no living person in the town.

Suddenly, Germans began firing from some of the abandoned houses, and the bullets came flying toward the Americans. Some soldiers were hit, while others began fleeing for cover. Randall, Walter, and Bobby were all fortunate to find cover behind a wall. They waited for the artillery to gun down the Germans.

They didn't wait too long, as the American machine guns began firing in the direction of the Germans. The machine gun fire lasted for several minutes. Once the last machine gun shell fell to the ground, the soldiers appeared from hiding.

"That was a close call," said Walter.

"I know, sport. Our boys with those machine guns really saved our asses," said Randall, taking a sip from his canteen of water.

As German gunfire ceased in the town, the American soldiers began progressing toward the daunted hill. When they were past La Haye-du-Puits, they began to see the elevation rise. However, they could not see the top of the hill due to the fog. But if they couldn't see the top of Hill 131, the Germans with machine guns on the hill could not see them either.

The terrain en route to Hill 131 was not ideal for the American soldiers. They were forced to walk through farmland, and this farmland contained numerous hedgerows. There was little doubt that German soldiers would be hiding in the hedgerows and would be looking to surprise the Americans. As a result, the paratroopers had to be careful if they wanted to succeed.

"Y'all, I may be forced to move from Florida," said Bobby Hawkins as they crossed a dirt road by a farm.

"Why would you do that, QB?" asked Walter.

"Because I don't think I can see one more damn farm for the rest of my life. Maybe I'll move to Boston. Luke seems to think Boston is the place to be," said Bobby Hawkins.

"I'm not sure you could ever live in the North. You're a Southern boy through and through, chief. I'm sure when we get out of France, you will get used to farms again," said Randall.

"Maybe you're right, slick. But Samantha doesn't like Florida, so maybe we'll move up to your neck of the woods," said Bobby.

"You would love it," said Walter. "And we would love having you. You should really take your talents to Ohio."

"Y'all, maybe I will. Let's talk about this after the war," said Bobby.

After they crossed the dirt road, the American soldiers were walking by an old barn. It was white, but the white color had faded. In the corner of his eye, Walter noticed a hedgerow to the right of them. He grabbed his rifle from the back of his shoulder, just in case he had to fire in a hurry.

"Walter, that's a good idea," Bobby Hawkins said while pulling out his rifle.

No more than ten seconds after Bobby Hawkins and Walter pulled out their weapons, the Germans began firing from the big green hedgerow. The three American soldiers who were clustered together made an attempt to run behind the barn. However, only two of the three made it. Randall and Walter looked at each other, terrified. "Where is Bobby?" said Walter.

"I thought he was right behind us!" said Randall.

They didn't know what happened to their friend, but they didn't have the luxury of pondering about it, because the Germans continued to fire in their direction. In response, Walter and Randall both took turns firing their rifles and throwing grenades. Because of the distance from the hedgerow, Randall and Walter did little damage. "Where's the artillery? They need to pound this hedgerow," said Randall.

The artillerymen's ears must have been burning, because they began pounding the hedgerow after Randall's comment; the German gunfire ceased to exist. When the Germans stopped firing, Randall,

Walter, and a few other men sprinted into the hedgerow to finish the job. The job didn't need to be finished because all the German soldiers were lying motionless on the ground in pools of blood.

Once the area was secure, Randall and Walter tried locating Bobby Hawkins. Bobby was found where the Germans first began firing at them, and it appeared as if a bullet had pierced through his chest. "Bobby, Bobby, Bobby, can you hear me?" said Walter, kneeling next to his friend. On the surface, he acted calm and confident. Inside, he was scared and terrified that he would lose a good friend and brother.

Bobby was breathing, but barely. His breaths were louder than normal because his body was struggling to take in oxygen and spit out carbon dioxide. "Hey, boys. Looks like they got me pretty good," said Bobby Hawkins. "It looks like y'all will have to carry on without me."

Walter grabbed his hand and told him it would be okay. "You stay strong. The medic will be here in a few moments. You're going to be fine."

Bobby knew that was a lie. He only had a few minutes left on this earth, and he thought about Samantha. Bobby was a man of faith, and he wasn't afraid of dying. But he was terrified of the thought that he would never be able to see Samantha again. As he was lying on foreign soil with a bullet hole through his chest, he realized that life just wasn't fair.

"Can you do something for me?" said Bobby as he looked up at Walter.

"Anything," said Walter.

"Do you still have that letter I gave you?" said Bobby, who was struggling to speak.

"Yes."

"Can you deliver it to Samantha after the war? Hand her the letter and tell her that I'm so sorry. Tell her that I love her and that I hope she finds happiness. Tell her that we'll be together in the next life."

Walter nodded, and Bobby stopped breathing. The boys from Ohio looked at each other with eyes full of sadness. They had just lost a dear friend and brother. However, there would be a time to mourn young Bobby Hawkins's life, but this was not the time or place.

They had one last moment of silence for their friend and began marching toward the top of the hill with the rest of the soldiers. Somehow, they had to get refocused again, but it would be a challenge. As Randall was thinking about how hurt Samantha would be, his next train of thought was how Mallie would feel if he died. She would be devastated, and he realized he could not let that happen. He refocused toward the task at hand, which was capturing the highest point in Normandy.

Walter had more trouble staying alert. He was much closer to Bobby than Randall. Walter didn't know how everyone could go through the rest of the war like nothing happened or pretend that nothing happened. The Army trained him well for battle, but he wasn't prepared to lose a close friend.

Just like Randall, he, too, thought about Abby, his family, and his friends. How would they react if he didn't return home? He played in his head the reactions of everyone. Abby wouldn't leave the house for days, and his mother would be forced to endure the loss of two sons. Would both of these people ever recover? Walter didn't think so, and he didn't want to find out. He focused his attention back on the enemy. Plus, if they failed to capture Hill 131, Bobby Hawkins would have died in vain.

The Allied paratroopers still couldn't see the top of the hill, but they estimated it was about two hundred yards away from their current location. The troops continued to walk through farms, fields, and dirt roads. The soldiers were coming up on yet another hedgerow, which was the sixth or seventh since they had begun walking toward the top of the hill. "Be alert," said a fellow soldier who was beside Randall.

As they walked past the hedgerow without any German fire, almost every soldier breathed a huge sigh of relief. It appeared as if they had just passed the last hedgerow on their way to the top of Hill 131. "It should be smooth sailing from here," Walter said under his breath. In reality, he hadn't the slightest clue. There might not have been any more hedgerows to worry about, but that didn't mean the soldiers were out of danger.

Finally, after hours of walking in the light rain, which covered their shoes in mud, they could see the top of the hill in the distance. They were able to spot German soldiers manning small machine guns. Colonel Jacobs made the decision to pound them with artillery fire. "Gentlemen, we are almost to the top of Hill 131. It's not a question of *if* we will capture this ground but a question of *when*. We'll let the boys with the heavy weapons pound them, and then we'll make our way to the top. If you're not part of the artillery team, sit back and enjoy the show," said Colonel Jacobs to the soldiers participating in the mission.

The boys with the big guns went to work. They set up their machine guns and fired round after round. Continuous machine gun fire lasted for about an hour, and it stopped when Colonel Jacobs gave the order to halt. When the artillery finished firing, silence fell upon that part of the hill. "Let's march to the top and claim the hill ours. There could be German troops who are still alive, so be alert. Good luck, gentlemen, and Godspeed," said Colonel Jacobs.

Both Randall and Walter wasted no time marching to the top of the hill. When they reached the top, the boys from Ohio observed German soldiers lying dead. "Looks like we got 'em pretty good, huh, sport?" said Randall.

"Don't get excited yet. We still have to make sure there are no Germans on the other side of the hill. And you better believe that the Germans will try to recapture it," said Walter.

There weren't any Germans alive at the top of the hill, so the troops began venturing to the other side. Walter and Randall were leading, while others trembled behind them. For the first time since the day began, they were decreasing in altitude. The troops of the 82nd Airborne continued through mud down the other side of the mountain.

They walked about fifty yards when Walter and Randall questioned whether any Germans were on the other side.

"Sport, let's turn back. I think we got 'em all," said Walter.

"Okay, let's—"

Just then, a couple of German soldiers popped out of a foxhole twenty feet from Randall and Walter's position. Walter and Randall quickly pulled out their rifles, but they weren't quick enough. One of the Germans shot Randall in the leg, and Randall fell to the French soil.

The German soldier aimed his rifle in the direction of Randall. Before he thought twice about it, Walter leaped in front of Randall like a bat out of hell and took a bullet in the upper chest. He, too, fell to the ground.

The American soldiers following Randall and Walter were able to shoot the German soldiers. After the German soldiers were dead, the two other paratroopers rushed over to where Randall and Walter were lying on the ground.

"Boys, stay put. I'll run and grab a medic," said one of the soldiers.

The soldier ran to get a medic, while the other stayed with Randall and Walter. Randall's wound was in his leg, so there was little chance it was a fatal. However, the same could not be said of Walter's wound. He was shot in the chest, and when Randall glanced at it, the wound didn't look good.

Randall leaned over to Walter. "Sport, stay strong. You will be fine, I promise."

Walter was hanging on by a thread. He wasn't sure if he would make it, but he would fight like hell to survive. "I'll try," said Walter in a soft voice.

"Why did you do that?" Randall said. "You didn't have to save my life."

Randall felt guilty and ashamed. His best friend had just saved his life, and he wished it were the other way around.

"I didn't want to lose another brother."

CHAPTER 22

Abby's father and grandfather were waiting for her as she hopped off the plane. When she saw them, Abby sprinted over and gave them a hug. Her father was standing there, confident as always, and her grandfather had the same swagger about him. James Millener even had a tobacco pipe in his mouth. "I've missed both of you so much," said Abby. Abby hadn't seen her father since leaving for the war, and she didn't know when was the last time she was able to spend time with her grandfather.

"How was your flight?" asked James Millener, who grabbed Abby's bags.

"Long. We stopped in Greenland for fuel," said Abby.

"Is Greenland green?" asked Abby's grandfather, giving a slight smile.

"Greenest place I've ever seen," joked Abby.

The three of them began walking toward James Millener's new Cadillac. Mr. Millener opened the door for his granddaughter and threw Abby's bags in the trunk. He then walked toward the driver's side, opened the door, and started the engine.

As they drove up to the Walker house, Abby couldn't have been more excited to be home. "It sure does feel nice to be home. I didn't think I would ever miss this place, but I was wrong," said Abby, standing in front of the big Victorian house.

Abby's excitement turned to anguish. Even though she was happy to be home, there was one glaring thing missing: her mom. Her mom was nowhere to be found. "Where's Mom?" asked Abby.

Mr. Walker hesitated for a moment and looked at his father-in-law. James Millener answered the question and said, "Your mom is in the hospital. She's not doing well."

Abby didn't know what to say or what to feel. She knew that her mom was sick, but it never really hit her how sick until she was not home to greet her. "What's wrong with her?" asked Abby.

"It's not good. It's some type of infection, and the doctors don't know what's wrong with her," said Christopher Walker.

Abby needed to be alone, so she went upstairs to her bedroom. As she walked through the door, Abby noticed that it was the same as she left it. Posters were around the room, and pictures were on her nightstand. She picked up the picture of the time she and her mom were sitting on the pier. Abby began sobbing, and her tears were like a waterfall.

After a while of crying on her bed, Abby decided to walk downstairs to see her father. Mr. Walker was eating a sandwich at the kitchen table. "Where is Grandpa?" Abby said.

He swallowed his mouthful of food before he answered. "He went home to change his clothes. He'll be back soon."

James Millener only lived a hundred yards away from Abby and her family. Mr. Millener had a house on Millener Farms since he was the one who purchased it several years ago. The whereabouts of Abby's grandfather was important, but not nearly as important as her mother. Abby wished to see her and wanted to know when that could happen. "When can we see Mom?"

"We can go when your grandfather returns. He wanted to see your mom today."

"When will that be?" asked Abby.

"Probably in the next thirty minutes," said Christopher Walker.

The front door swung open, and in walked James Millener. He nodded, and Abby and her father followed him out to the car.

When Abby arrived at the hospital, she was scared. Her mother had always been her role model and rock, and she didn't want to see her weak. Unfortunately, she didn't have much of a choice. Abby wished to see her mother alone, so her grandfather and father waited outside in the lobby. Abby walked into the hospital room and saw her mom lying on the bed, looking pale. "Hi, Mama!" Abby said, trying to maintain a tone of excitement.

Mrs. Walker looked up and saw her daughter standing beside her. "Sweetie, aren't you supposed be working? I didn't think the Army allowed you any breaks."

Abby didn't want to tell her mom the truth about why they let her leave. "They give you two weeks off every year. I wanted to come home and see you and everyone else," said Abby. Mrs. Walker had a huge smile on her face. She hadn't been this happy since her daughter left for the war.

Abby and her mom began catching up after the long absence. Abby's mom wanted to know everything in her daughter's life since she left. Abby revealed almost everything, except for the part about Eli and escaping a German execution. Abby's mom was an attentive listener and soaked in every moment of her daughter's experience. "I'm really glad that you're happy about your role in the war," Mrs. Walker said. She paused and went on to say, "How is Walter? Have you heard from him or heard how he's doing?"

"He's somewhere in France. I was able to see him briefly before he left for France. I'll be honest, Mama. I'm worried about him. He's on a dangerous mission."

Even though Mrs. Walker was ill, she wanted to console her daughter. "Walter is a resilient young man. He's coming home. You don't have to worry about him. He loves you too much not to come home," said Mrs. Walker. Abby felt better about the situation, although it didn't erase all her fears.

Judging by Mrs. Walker's deteriorating health, it was evident that Mrs. Walker would be forced to have a relationship with her daughter from heaven soon. She knew that she was dying. Mrs. Walker believed it was inevitable, even when Abby and the rest of her family still had a glimmer of hope. "Abigail, I need you to listen to me very carefully," said Ann Walker.

Abby proceeded to look at her mother with wide eyes. "I may not have much longer," said Mrs. Walker.

After the comment from her mother, Abby began to sob.

"Don't be sad for me. I couldn't have asked for a better life. I have a great family, great husband, and the best daughter."

"Mama, you'll be okay. We just gotta have faith," Abby said in tears.

"I need to tell you something before I go, because I don't know when that day will be. You need to listen."

Ann Walker began talking to her daughter the moment Abby's tears slowed down.

"Abby, I want to tell you how sorry I am about what happened before you joined the Army. I was wrong. I should have done more to stop your father's sabotage of your relationship with Walter. I apologize for that, and I'm hoping that you can forgive me one day," Abby's mom.

"Don't be sorry. Everything happens for a reason. I couldn't be happier right now. I feel blessed to serve my country. It's been the greatest honor of my life."

Ann Walker looked up at her daughter and smiled. "I couldn't be prouder of you, sweetie. When Walter comes home, I want you to cherish each other for the rest of your lives," said Mrs. Walker.

Abby began to cry again. She didn't want to lose her mom. The thought of not seeing her for the rest of her life began to sink in. "Mama, I just don't know what I'm going to do. I'm really scared about losing you," Abby said while looking at Ann Walker.

"Don't be. The hardest part of leaving is worrying whether you'll be okay. But with Walter in your life, I'm not worried one bit. He's a good man," said Ann Walker. Mrs. Walker looked at Abby and smiled. "I'll look down on you from time to time. I'll still always be there for you."

Abby took comfort in that. She realized that her mother didn't know about Eli. Ann Walker had always given Abby words of wisdom, and Abby wanted one last piece of advice. "I need some help with something," asked Abby.

"What is it, dear?" asked Mrs. Walker.

"Well, I met this young boy while I was in London. He has no family anymore. I want to adopt him," replied Abby.

"Do you think it's best for him to come to another country?" said Mrs. Walker while looking at Abby.

Abby didn't waste a second while responding to her mom. She knew in her heart that it would be the best thing for the young boy. "Yes," said Abby.

"Are you ready to become a mom? Are you ready for the responsibilities?" asked Mrs. Walker.

"I think I'm ready. War has made me grow up beyond my years. I'm not the same little girl that I was before I left," said Abby.

"I know you're not," said Mrs. Walker. "Then I think you should do it."

Abby and her mom sat there for a few more minutes. Both of them reflected on the memories that they shared and the good times that they had together.

"Where is your father?" asked Mrs. Walker.

"Dad and Grandpa are in the lobby. I'll go get them," declared Abby.

Abby treaded to the lobby of the hospital to retrieve the rest of the family. They all walked into the room together like a defeated football team following a heartbreaking loss. Mr. Walker grabbed his wife's hand and held it tight.

"I'm glad everyone's here," revealed Ann Walker.

"We wouldn't want to be anywhere else," said Mr. Millener.

After a few minutes of everyone gathering around Mrs. Walker, Christopher Walker asked if he could be alone with his wife for a few minutes. Abby and James Millener said their goodbyes and left for home.

When Abby and her grandfather pulled into Millener Farms, Martha, Abby's friend, was waiting for them on the front porch. Abby invited her inside, and they sat in the living room with two cups of tea.

"How have you been, Martha?"

"I've been really good. I'm studying at Ohio State, so it's kept me busy."

Abby couldn't stop smiling, because she was so happy to see her old friend. Martha asked Abby about the war. "It's hard seeing young men our age wounded. Sometimes there's nothing that we can do but comfort them. I wasn't prepared to deal with that," said Abby.

"Well, at least you're helping people. What you're doing is honorable."

Abby nodded, and the two continued talking. "Any boys in your life, Martha?" asked Abby.

"Not right now. I'm flying solo," said Martha.

"What about that boy Tom Willis? Didn't you go to a dance with him at the country club?" asked Abby.

"Yeah, we went out a few times. Nothing really came of it," said Martha.

"I'm sure you'll find someone," said Abby.

"Speaking of which, have you seen Walter's parents?" asked Martha.

"I haven't. I really should go soon," said Abby.

"Yes, you should."

* * *

A few days had passed, and Abby still hadn't seen Walter's parents. Time wasn't a factor; she had all the time in the world. She was just scared. She worried that his parents had uncovered the truth of the real reason Walter was sent to the war. There was no doubt Walter had been sending them letters home, and it seemed likely that he would reveal the truth.

Abby knew she had to face the music, however. She decided to hop in her car and drive over to Walter's house. When she was pulling up to his small brick house, her heart was pounding. She was worried about the reception from Walter's parents. Would it be good or bad? Whatever the case, she was about to discover it. She rang the doorbell and waited for Walter's parents to open the door.

"Oh my gosh, it's Abby. I can't believe it. What a pleasant surprise!" said Mrs. Wilson as she opened up her arms in order to hug the young woman. Mrs. Wilson was shocked that Abby was standing at the door. "Please come in, dear," said Allison Wilson.

Mrs. Wilson called the rest of her family to the living room. Mallie and Mr. Wilson arrived to greet Abby. "Abby, it's good seeing you," said Mr. Wilson.

"Welcome home, Abby," Mallie said.

The whole Wilson family was happy she was back in Ohio and wanted to know everything about her experience. While Abby was revealing her encounters during the war, Mrs. Wilson asked Abby if she would like to stay for dinner. Abby smelled the food coming from the kitchen. "Of course. I would love that," said Abby. "I can never say no to home-cooked meals now."

Abby then asked them if anyone had heard from Walter. "We received a letter a few days ago. Who knows when he wrote it," said Mr. Wilson.

"What did he say in the letter?" asked Abby.

Mr. Wilson turned to Abby and said, "He just told us that he was doing well and not to worry about him and he would be coming home soon. Although he did say he wouldn't be able to write for a while."

Abby knew that Walter must have written the letter before he left for Normandy. She decided to keep the thought to herself, because she didn't want to worry anyone in the Wilson family.

After numerous stories of her wartime experiences, dinner was ready. Abby, Mallie, Mr. Wilson, and Mrs. Wilson sat down at the round table in the dining room. Abby looked at the food and said, "This looks really delicious."

"If only Randall and Walter could be here," said Mallie.

Abby looked at Walter's sister and said to be patient. "Don't worry, they will come back, and we'll have a big celebration," Abby said. "When was the last time you heard from Randall?"

"About the same time Walter sent a letter home. Randall said he was doing well and that he couldn't wait to see me. He also said being in the war reminded him of the time Walter and Randall went to summer camp," Mallie said, smiling.

"I sure missed this pie," Abby said as she was taking a bite of apple pie. "Nothing tasted this good while I was in Europe."

Mrs. Wilson was flattered and said, "Thank you, Abby. It's my mother's recipe."

Just after she made that remark, someone knocked on the door. "Mallie, would you go see who could be at the door?" said Mr. Wilson. "It's quite rude. Someone interrupting our dinner like this."

Mallie stood up from her seat and walked over to the door. She opened it and thought she was dreaming. It was an all-too-familiar face, but she thought it was a mirage. "Hi, Mallie!" said Randall.

Mallie wanted to leap into his arms, but she saw his injured leg and a cane propping him up. Instead, she hugged him and they stood with their arms around each other for a long time. "I didn't know if you were coming back," Mallie said while in tears.

"I told you I was coming back," said Randall into her ear.

The two walked into the house, and Abby, Mr. Wilson, and Mrs. Wilson were astonished. As they looked at Randall, it seemed odd that he didn't look happy. He should be lighting up the room like a Christmas tree. On the contrary, Randall seemed sad and depressed.

Everyone in the house gathered in the living room. They all had so many questions to ask him but didn't know where to start. Mallie was so happy about the return of Randall she had forgotten about her brother. "How did you return so soon?" asked Mallie.

Randall lifted up his leg and showed them his wound. "It's hard to run, let alone walk. Since I was no use in battle to them, they sent me home," said Randall.

"We're glad you're home safe, son," said Mr. Wilson. Randall was like a second son to the Wilson family, so both Mr. and Mrs. Wilson were happy he had returned home. Mr. Wilson gave Randall a hug, and when he realized Randall was safe, he wanted to inquire about his son.

"Randall, where is my son?" asked Mr. Wilson, looking at Randall.

The tall and confident kid went mute. He put his head down and sighed. Randall would have put his tail between his legs if he were a dog. Randall didn't want to share the news with Walter's family.

Abby knew something was wrong when Randall was silent. She almost fainted and started sobbing. She sobbed uncontrollably, and it flowed like the Mississippi River.

As soon as Abby began crying, Randall rushed to her side. He parked himself next to her on the sofa and braced his best friend's girl. "Abby, he's still alive."

Everyone in the room had a glimmer of hope, but it was just that, a glimmer. They knew, if he was doing well, Randall wouldn't have been so distant.

"The last time I saw Walter, he was in a British hospital. Walter was in a coma, but he was relatively stable. The doctors think that he will wake up eventually. They just don't know when. It could have been the day after I left, or it could be a month from now. But they do believe he will pull through," said Randall.

Everyone in the house was quiet. The house was so silent the summer wind could be heard. "How was he hurt?" asked Mr. Wilson, holding a crying Mrs. Wilson.

"He was hurt saving my life. He shielded me from the straying bullets and was hit in the chest and leg," said Randall. "I'm so sorry. I wish it were the other way around and I had saved his life. I feel terrible."

Mrs. Wilson put her arm around her son's best friend. "Don't feel terrible, Randall. I know you would have done the same for him, dear. He's a fighter, isn't he? In my heart, I know he's coming home," said Mrs. Wilson.

Abby, Mr. Wilson, and Mrs. Wilson returned to the dining room so that Randall and Mallie could spend time together. The three of them didn't speak for a long time, because quite frankly, there was nothing to talk about. Nothing any of them could say could speed up Walter's recovery.

After a few minutes, Abby put her head down on the table. She was in pain. Mrs. Wilson scooted her chair next to Abby and put her arm around the young girl.

"Everything is going to be fine, dear, I promise," said Allison Wilson.

Abby wanted to believe her. Whether she believed her or not, Abby lifted her head and placed it on Mrs. Wilson's shoulder.

It was getting late and time for Abby to return home. She stood up from the table and hugged both Mr. and Mrs. Wilson. The young girl then proceeded to walk into the living room before she departed. Randall and Mallie were still on the couch together but were asleep. She didn't want to wake them, so she opened the front door and left.

Abby arrived home, and her father was waiting for her in the kitchen. "Did you enjoy spending time with Walter's family?" asked Mr. Walker.

Abby placed the keys on the table and said, "It was nice to see them. They're nice folks."

"I would hope they're nice. You'll be part of their family soon," said Mr. Walker as he turned toward his daughter.

Abby hoped her father was correct, and she was thankful he was beginning to accept Walter as a big part in her life. Abby began walking upstairs and turned back to give her father a kiss good night but didn't reveal Randall's update. She would tell him in the morning, because it was the last thing she wished to think about.

Before she went to sleep, Abby opened the door to her room and hopped into the soft bed. She looked over at her nightstand, and there was a picture of her and Walter. Abby began to think about Walter and hoped for a speedy recovery, or just a recovery. She hoped her mom was right about Walter coming home, because she wanted him more than ever, and quite possibly, she needed him more than ever.

CHAPTER 23

Walter Wilson was lying in a hospital bed across the English Channel. He returned to England alive, but by the skin of his teeth. It had been a couple of weeks since his valiant act of saving his best friend, and in those couple of weeks, he had been in a coma. The doctors were not confident he would be able to recover and return to the United States.

While he was unable to open his eyes, Walter was aware of his surroundings. Nurses and doctors hovered over him, and in his state, it seemed like they hovered like vultures. They monitored his health and did everything to ensure he remained alive. Even though he was unable to speak, he appreciated the medical care that was given to him.

On a sunny day, Walter woke up, and he woke up for good. As his eyes opened for the first time in weeks, his eyes wandered around the room. He saw many soldiers like him who were lying in similar beds to his own. *Am I still in France?* Walter thought to himself.

The last thing that Walter remembered was stepping in front of Randall to shield him from an oncoming bullet. He didn't know how he got to the bed, what happened to Randall, or about the other soldiers. One of the nurses was roaming around, replacing bedpans, so he attempted to gain her attention.

"Nurse," he said.

The nurse stopped removing bedpans and walked over to Walter. She strolled up to his bedside with a big grin on her face. It was always pleasant when a soldier pulled through. "Welcome back."

"Where am I?" asked Walter.

"You're in England," said the nurse.

"How did I get here?"

The nurse paused and touched Walter's arm. "You were wounded in France. We evacuated you to England. You're safe now."

Walter didn't feel safe. He was in a hospital bed, surrounded by wounded soldiers just like himself, who may not survive; he also didn't know if Randall, or anyone else, made it out of France alive. To make matters worse, there was a Barbie doll nurse telling him he was safe.

"Can you tell me what happened to my platoon? Can you tell me what happened to my friend Randall Moore?" asked Walter, hoping that the nurse would answer his question.

The nurse hesitated to answer his question. Walter wasn't sure whether she was holding out information or she just didn't know what happened. Either way, he wanted to know and began fidgeting in his bed out of frustration. "I don't know. I'll bring one of the doctors over to you. We will find answers for you, sir," the nurse said.

"What do you mean find answers for me?" Walter said. "I'm fighting for my country, and you're giving me the runaround. I want to know if my best friend survived!"

"Sir, I appreciate what you did. I'm trying to be as helpful as possible. I'll find out soon," said the nurse.

It was out of character for Walter to snap at someone trying to help. He just woke up from a coma and wanted answers. As a wounded soldier, he felt entitled to find out what happened to his friend.

When Walter saw the nurse disappear from his sight, he propped his body up on the bed and looked around; it was not a pretty view. There must have been hundreds of soldiers in the room, and most of them were either asleep or unconscious.

The longer he wasn't aware of what happened to Randall, the more worried he became. He couldn't afford to lose another brother, which was what Randall had evolved into for him over the years. Life wasn't fair, but hopefully it wouldn't be cruel.

Just as Walter was about ready to slouch back down into his bed, the man next to him woke up. It appeared he was just sleeping by the way he woke. The man in the bed only a few feet adjacent to Walter looked over at him. "Howdy there, partner. I see you awoke from you're hibernation, huh?" said the soldier.

"I certainly did. My name is Walter, Walter Wilson. What's your name?" Walter said.

The other wounded soldier didn't hesitate to respond. No one in his vicinity was in a state to hold a conversation, so he was eager about the opportunity. "Name is Doyle. Frank Doyle," said Frank.

"It's good to meet you, Frank. Where's your hometown?" asked Walter.

"El Paso, Texas, cowboy. My daddy is a rancher. I grew up on a farm down there. I counted down the days until my eighteenth birthday and joined the *Stars and Stripes*," said Frank, who didn't resemble a cowboy, with the exception of a Texas accent. He had short dark hair and a red birthmark that was present on his right cheek. "Where are ya from, cowboy?"

"Columbus, Ohio. Dad works in a factory, and Mom is a ballet teacher. It's a pretty simple life," Walter said, and when he said it, he missed home more than ever before. It had been a long time since he stepped foot on his native soil, and he hoped he would be able to soon.

"Oh, a good ole Midwestern boy. I love it. What unit did you serve?" asked Frank as he, too, propped up in his bed.

"I'm in the 82nd Airborne Division. I was in France for twenty-six days before I was wounded," said Walter.

"You boys really cleared the way for our landing. That was good work, cowboy," said Frank.

Walter paused as he saw one of the doctors walking by his bed. He was hoping he would find the information on his fellow troops, but he had no luck. The doctor walked right by his bed.

"I assume you stormed the beach," Walter said, turning his attention back to Frank Doyle.

"You assume correct. We were the first wave of soldiers to storm the beaches. I'm part of the 27th Infantry. We made our landing on Utah Beach, slick." Frank looked at the end of the bed and sighed. He looked at where his leg was missing. "I guess I should say I *was* part of the 27th."

Walter felt sorry for him. But he was thankful his leg was the only thing taken away by the Germans. Hitler's men certainly didn't cripple Frank's spirit, and for that, Walter was impressed.

"So do you have a cowgirl back home?" asked Walter.

"Not me, slick. No cowgirl waiting for me in El Paso. What about you? Do you have a cowgirl waiting for you?" asked Frank Doyle.

"Yes, I do," Walter said. He began thinking about Abby and couldn't stop thinking about her. His mind went back to the night when Abby told him that she would be waiting when he returned.

* * *

There was something that Walter's family possessed that the Walker family did not. It was a white-roped hammock that sat perfectly in between two oak trees in the middle of Walter's backyard. Abby and Walter would spend hours lying beside each other on breezy summer evenings.

A few days after the Fourth of July was one of those evenings spent swinging on the hammock. Relaxing was the theme of the night. They had dinner at Walter's house with his family and went straight to the hammock.

Walter climbed in first and stabilized it for Abby to join him. Not before long, the two were curled up next to each other like a pair of monkeys looking up at the sky full of stars.

"I could do this every night," said Abby.

"Me too, Abby. Me too," Walter said, whispering into her ear.

There was so much to talk about, yet for most of the night, they said nothing to each other. On most nights leading up to Walter's departure, they pretended nothing would change. Although it was just pretend, as they both were well aware their lives would change with a turn of 180 degrees.

The hours passed, and the crickets began chirping louder and louder. For whatever reason, Walter hated the sound of crickets more than anything. "I can't stand the sound of crickets," Walter said.

Abby chose not to respond to his comment; she had yet to have a meaningful conversation about Walter going to war, and she thought this might be the right time. The drawback to bringing up the war was the possibility of ruining a good night, which was something neither she nor Walter would have very often in the coming months or even years.

She turned on her side and kissed him on the cheek. "Walter, dear, are you scared?"

Walter didn't want to have a serious conversation. Not right now. Not tonight. "Of course I'm scared. I think these damn crickets are plotting against me. I may die from annoyance," Walter said with a smile.

Abby wasn't very amused, and that was evident through the stern look she gave him. "Walter, I'm serious. Are you scared?" asked Abby again.

Walter paused for a moment. He thought to himself, *Is that a serious question?* He acted tough around her, and he pretended that he wasn't scared of anything, but how could anyone not be scared? He had just turned eighteen, and nothing had prepared him for war.

"Yes, I'm scared. Am I afraid of dying?" Walter said, then paused. "Yes, a little bit. But I'm more afraid of the people I'll leave behind if I don't return. My family, Randall, Randall's mom, and most importantly, you."

It was the first time it crossed her mind that the love of her life might not return. She became scared, and terrified, but ceased to show it. She realized his primary objective was to come home and survive. He couldn't be worried about her.

Abby placed her arm around Walter and began rubbing his back. "Sweetheart, you'll come back to me. I know you will. And I'll be waiting for you. How could you not come back to the sound of these crickets? It's practically music."

Walter laughed, and her humor made him feel better about the night and about the war. He knew he would come home and Abby would be waiting for him. He would hear the crickets every single night if it meant returning home safe and having a gorgeous girl waiting for him.

When Walter looked over at Abby, she was smiling. "What are you smiling about?"

"Have you ever made love on a hammock before?" Abby asked.

"No, I haven't. But I always like trying new things."

"I always like trying new things, too, especially with you," said Abby, winking at him.

* * *

His mind shifted back to the hospital and to Frank Doyle. His daydream was over, and it was back to staring at hospital beds filled with wounded soldiers and bedpans.

While Walter was dreaming, Frank went back to sleep. He felt alone, even though soldiers surrounded him and doctors and nurses roamed the hospital ward. Hopefully, a doctor would tell him the extent of his injuries when he could return to duty and an update on his fellow soldiers.

Finally, his wish was fulfilled when a doctor wearing a white coat over his Army uniform shuffled to his bedside. "Private Wilson," said the doctor.

"Yes, sir," said Walter.

"How are you feeling?" said the doctor.

Walter just wanted this doctor to get straight to the point. No more small talk. No more conversations. Walter wanted facts. "I'm fine, sir. I had a good long sleep and feel well rested," Walter said, smiling.

"That you did, son," said the doctor.

Walter was annoyed. Why is this doctor saying everything but what Walter wanted to know? "When can I return to my unit?" asked Walter.

The doctor sighed, and Walter could tell that he was about to divulge some unpleasant information. "I'm sorry, son. You cannot serve in combat anymore. You were too badly wounded. Your shoulder shattered when the bullet hit you. It will take months for your shoulder to recover, and that's just the beginning."

Walter went from agitated to worried. "What do you mean the beginning?"

This time, the doctor didn't hesitate to respond. "Two bullets went through your ankle, and you lost a lot of blood circulation in that area. We almost had to amputate. It will take you a while to walk without some sort of cane."

Even though Walter was lucky to be returning in one piece with no limbs missing, he wanted to continue on with the war. He wanted to fight alongside his brothers.

Walter's attention changed to the status of his fellow soldiers, especially Randall. "What happened to everyone in my unit? What about Randall Moore? He is from my hometown," said Walter. His heart was pounding because Walter was terrified about the response.

"Randall Moore is fine. I treated him as well. He's back in the States as we speak," said the doctor.

Walter felt relieved. He felt like two hundred pounds of weight was lifted off his shoulders. Not only was Randall fine, but also he was back in the States. "I'm glad he's fine. What happens next for me?" asked Walter.

"The war is over for you, young man. You'll be flying home in the next few days," said the doctor as he placed his hand on Walter's shoulder.

When the doctor said he was going home, Walter had mixed emotions. He felt like he was letting down the other thousands of soldiers fighting for the same cause for which he almost paid the ultimate price. However, on the other hand, he was going *home*. He was going home! In a matter of days, he would be able to hug his family, shake Randall's hand, and hold Abby for hopefully the rest of his life.

CHAPTER 24

The dress code correlated with the weather. Dark clouds hovered over the little town of Arlington Heights. Ann Walker was dead. Abigail and her father were sitting down for breakfast. Mr. Walker turned on the radio. "It now seems inevitable that the Third Reich will fall. A few weeks ago, General Patton and the Third Army liberated Paris. The Germans have retreated to Germany to defend Berlin. It appears General Patton would like nothing more than to take down Berlin," said the radio announcer. Mr. Walker turned to Abby, saying, "Hopefully, our troops will be coming home soon."

Abby ate a spoonful of her cereal and responded to her father. "I sure hope so," said Abby. Christopher Walker looked at his daughter and asked if she had heard any news of Walter's condition.

Mr. Walker didn't get much of an answer; Abby just shook her head in the negative direction. She was miserable about her mom's passing and didn't want to entertain a conversation about Walter's health.

Mr. Walker finished his breakfast, and he turned off the radio. "We must go now. We don't want to be late for the funeral, and we still have to pick up your grandfather."

Abby finished her cereal, and they walked out the door. They picked up James Millener and drove to the old church on Front Street. The Front Street Church had been home to so many fond memories for Abby, from Sunday school to communion. Abby had always loved the church, but she could not have dreaded anything more than walking in through those large wooden doors. People would be wearing all black and looking at her with pity. She didn't want pity from anyone; she just wanted her mother back.

When Abby and her family walked into the church, some people were already sitting in rows of the cherry-colored benches. Everyone was in all black; some of the women were even wearing black netting and dark hats. Regardless of the type of attire, folks at the funeral looked at Abby, James Millener, and Christopher Walker with pity as they made their way to the front of the church.

As the pastor began speaking, Abby looked around and saw familiar faces everywhere. She even saw Randall and Mallie sitting in the back. Mallie was tearing up, and Randall had his arm around her, attempting to shield the pain. "God, I would do anything for Walter to be holding me right now," Abby said under her breath.

She knew that wasn't going to happen, so she turned her attention elsewhere. Abby recognized some people attending the funeral, but some of the others, she hadn't had the slightest clue. She wasn't sure if people came in support of her mom or her grandfather, who was the first mayor of the town. Whatever the case might be, she was at least grateful that they were present to pay their condolences and say goodbye to her mom for the last time.

After a couple of prayers were said, the pastor asked Abby's father to do the eulogy. Mr. Walker walked to the front of the church near the pulpit. He began talking about the life of Mrs. Walker from the time she was born to the day her life ended. In entirety, the eulogy took about twenty minutes.

As the eulogy commenced, Mr. Walker walked back to his seat and the pastor asked if anyone would like to share any memories of Ann Walker. Abby wanted to speak about her mother, but she hesitated to vault her two feet upright. She was afraid of sobbing in front of the whole community.

While Abby was hesitating, James Millener walked to the front of the church. He took a few deep breaths and then began speaking about his daughter. "Thank you, all of you, for coming to say goodbye to my beloved daughter. Her life was taken way too early, and I hope none of you have to bury your children. Children should always outlive their parents," James said. He took another deep breath in an attempt to not break down. He was filled with sadness, as well as he should be. "My Ann was a great daughter, wife, mother, and sister. She will be sorely missed, and I know that I will miss her every day."

James Millener proceeded to tremble back to his seat. Abby realized that it took great strength for her elderly grandfather to give that speech. She made the decision to speak about her mother when the pastor asked. "Anyone else care to share a few words?" said the pastor.

Abby stood up from her seat and walked with her nerves trembling to the front. The young girl hadn't been as scared since she was treating soldiers in Normandy, which seemed less terrifying than speaking in front of the entire town.

From the time she was little, Abby had always used humor to decrease the stress level. Her natural instincts kicked in, and she tried it. "Mom was almost banned from Hillsdale Market." Abby heard a few chuckles, so she continued with her story. "And it wasn't because she complained or argued about prices. Whenever we went to the market, we would be there shopping for hours. Mom would help customers pick out their groceries, and she would advise them on what to buy. Sometimes this would anger people who worked there, because she would be doing their job. The manager told her that was unacceptable. But if anyone knew my mom, she had none of it. By the end of the conversation, the manager was apologizing to my mother."

The people in the church laughed at the story, and Abby noticed that she began smiling. However, her smile turned to a frown, and tears started rolling down her cheeks. Abby went into detail about the first time she visited her mom while back from Europe. She explained that while on her deathbed, her mom wasn't concerned about her own well-being but rather the well-being of her daughter. During that visit, Ann Walker told her daughter that she wanted nothing but the best for her and, above all else, wanted her to be happy. "Even really sick in the hospital, Mama was so concerned about me. Mama knew she was living her last days, and all she could ask me was how I was doing and what the war was like. It meant the world to me, and I really appreciate her for that. She's always going to be in my heart."

Her effort to not break down failed, and she cried. She gazed into the room full of people, and they all looked at her with eyes of sorrow. At first, she didn't want pity from them, but throughout the course of the day, her thoughts changed. She returned to the Abby of Arlington Heights, Ohio, from the Abby of the US Army Nurses Corps. Even though her experiences of war would always be with her, she was ready to be an average, scared young woman.

As she was still sobbing, Abby saw her father rise from his seat. It appeared as if he would escort her back to the cherry-colored benches. He had just taken his first step into the aisle when the double doors opened. An American soldier dressed in uniform limped to the front of the church using a crutch. When he was standing close to the pulpit, Abby almost fainted. She couldn't believe it. Walter Wilson was back, and alive.

Abby sprinted toward Walter. The young nurse wrapped her arms around him and offered a long kiss. Several minutes earlier, she had asked for Walter to be with her during this difficult moment, and her wish was granted.

"I told you I'd come back," Walter said into Abby's ear. As he whispered into her ear, he could smell her perfume, the scent that smelled like tulips and roses. He missed that smell so much.

There was so much to say, yet nothing came out of her mouth. Walter escorted Abby back to her seat. While they were sitting down, Mr. Walker smiled at Walter and offered a handshake as a warm welcome. Walter shook Mr. Walker's hand and then used that arm to wrap around Abby.

The funeral continued as Ann Walker's friends shared memories. And when the last of her friends spoke, the funeral was finished. Abby and Walter, while holding hands, arose from their seats and convened with Mallie and Randall at the back of the church. Both of them were so excited to see Walter and nearly caused him to break another leg.

"Oh my god, Walter, I can't believe you're back!" said Mallie, smothering him with a hug.

While Mallie was hugging Walter, Randall managed to get a quick handshake in. "It's good to see ya, sport. I'm thrilled you pulled through."

As the friends were gathered, Mr. Walker walked up to them. "Walter, I'm so thankful you're back and able to be here for Abby." He then paused and looked at Randall. "Young man, did you drive here?" asked Mr. Walker.

"Yes, sir," Randall said.

"Excellent. Why don't you drive Abby back to Millener Farms? There's a gathering of family at my house. You, Mallie, and Walter are all welcome," said Mr. Walker.

The four friends talked for a few more minutes in the church and then walked to Randall's car. Walter and Abby hopped in the back seat of Randall's black Ford. They wasted no time kissing each other while Randall drove to Abby's house. There was lost time to make up for.

When they arrived at the Walker house, Abby and Walter climbed out of the car. "Hey, sport, I think Mallie and I are going to pass. Your parents are expecting us for lunch," said Randall.

"Are you sure?" said Walter.

"Yeah. I'll catch up with you tomorrow," said Randall, shaking Walter's hand. "I'm so happy you're back."

Walter walked around to the passenger's side window. "Mallie, I probably won't be home tonight. I'll see you tomorrow. I want to let you know that I missed you, Mom, and Dad," said Walter as he slid his arm in the car to hug his sister.

"I missed you, too, and I'm happy you're home. Does Mom and Dad know you've returned?" asked Mallie.

"Yes. I saw them before I went to the church. Have fun today, and I'll see you tomorrow," said Walter.

Randall and Mallie drove away from the Walker house while Abby and Walter walked inside. When they walked inside the house, Abby's extended family was present. Everyone from aunts, uncles, and cousins was munching on ham sandwiches and sipping on sweet teas. Everyone came up to Walter and sprinkled him with a warm reception.

"What a night-and-day difference to how they treated me before," said Walter under his breath. "I guess that's the reward of being a soldier returning home."

After a few hours, the party began dying down. People started departing, and Abby and Walter were both thankful. They were eager to spend time alone. When everyone had disappeared, the young couple opened the door and walked out.

"Where do you think you two are going?" Mr. Walker said as he opened the front door.

"Umm," said Walter.

"Dad, we don't need this right now. Walter just got back, and…," said Abby, unable to finish her sentence.

Christopher gave a smirk. He then reached in his pocket and tossed the keys to his new Cadillac convertible. "Be safe tonight," said Mr. Walker.

Abby took the keys, and they began loading up the car with pillows and blankets. It was a perfect night for the quarry. The temperature was in the midsixties, and the night was clear as glass. When they arrived, Abby put the blankets down on the ground about twenty yards from the water, while Walter looked for sticks to build a fire. Walter returned with sticks and had the fire in flames.

Abby and Walter were alone. No one was in sight. They cuddled together on the blanket under the night sky. Abby wanted to know about his injury but also wanted to be indirect about it. "Randall told me about what happened. That was really brave of you," said Abby.

"Yeah, it was. Randall would have done the same for me."

"How long was your stay in the hospital?" asked Abby.

"I was in the hospital for a few weeks. To be honest, I wasn't sure if I was going to return home or die overseas," said Walter. "You helped keep me alive."

"How did I keep you alive?"

Walter looked into Abby's blue eyes. "While lying in the hospital bed in England, I kept thinking about you. I kept thinking about you and the promise I made to return." He paused for a moment. "And then the weirdest thing happened."

"And what was that?"

"Right before I came out of the coma for good, I saw my brother. I think it was a dream. We were throwing the baseball, and he told me everyone was counting on me to come home. My mom, my dad, my sister, and you. He told me to come home, just like you did before I went to war."

Abby didn't know what to say; she just put her arm around Walter and told him she was happy he had returned. "Speaking of your parents, have you seen them yet?"

"I saw them before I came to your mom's funeral. My mom almost fainted, and she was in tears. My father was his usual self and tried not to display too much emotion. But I could tell he was thrilled. I did talk to my mom for a long time."

"I'm happy to hear that. What did you two talk about?" said Abby as she was rubbing Walter's back.

"I just told her that I wanted a clean slate with her. Whatever happened in the past is in the past. War changes a man, and I have a new perspective on life. I want a new beginning with her, and she seemed very grateful with that."

"I am happy for you. I think she deserves a second chance. I was over at your house when Randall told us what had happened to you. As I was crying over the news, she allowed me to cry on her shoulder. She was like a mother figure to me," said Abby.

Before Abby could get in another word, Walter leaned over and started kissing her. They kissed for hours until both Abby and Walter started stripping their clothes off. As their clothes were torn off, they made love.

Afterward, both of them were lying on the blanket, staring into each other's eyes. As they were lying intimately, Abby wanted to discuss something dear to her heart. "Walter, I need to talk to you about something," said Abby.

"What is it, Abby?" responded Walter.

"When I was in London before Operation Overlord, I went to a showing of *Pinocchio*. Our theater was bombed, and so was the city of London. I met a young boy named Eli. Eli's parents were killed in the bombings. He didn't have any family, so I took him in."

"You're so kind. That's why I love you."

Abby smiled, as she was hoping to get Walter's approval on adopting Eli. "So I really want to adopt Eli. He's such a sweet boy, and I've grown attached to him. He's also grown attached to me. What do you think about it? You'll have a big role in his life," said Abby.

"Do you even know where this boy is right now?" asked Walter as he sat up on the blanket.

"He's in London at some group home," said Abby.

"Well, are you sure you want to adopt a young boy? Do you think you're ready to take on that responsibility? And, how can you just take this boy away from his life in England?"

Abby didn't hesitate to fire back at Walter's questions. "Am I ready? Yes, I believe I am. Just like you, war changes a person. It makes people grow up real fast. I wasn't in combat like you, but I went to Normandy. I saw horrific things that no person should see. As for your second question, dear, I called the British Social Services a couple of weeks ago. They said I would have to fly back to England when it's safe to make the adoption final."

The young soldier who just returned was quite impressed with her answer. Yet he wasn't sold on the idea. Walter had a lot on his mind, so he wanted to contemplate the thought. "Let me think about it. I'm not going to say yes or no, but I want to let you know how I feel about it."

Abby couldn't complain because it was a fair request. Even though he didn't want to talk about the war, she wanted to tell him all about her adventure.

"I bet you won't believe me when I say this, but I almost didn't return from Europe," said Abby.

Walter didn't understand. Abby was a nurse, so she shouldn't have been in that much danger. Due to his curiosity, he asked, "Why did you almost not return home?"

Abby explained the story of how she and Gracelyn were almost executed by German soldiers. It was the most scared she had been in her life, which was the opposite of the feeling she had at this moment. She couldn't feel safer in the arms of Walter Wilson.

"German soldiers are the worst kind of people. They have no morals. I don't know what I would have done," said Walter.

"You would have been pretty lonely without your princess," said Abby.

"I would have been. I'm glad you're safe," said Walter as he kissed her on the forehead.

"Well, at least Gracelyn and I were able to drive in these cool Army vehicles called jeeps."

"Jeeps, huh? Did you enjoy your ride in them?" asked Walter.

Abby nodded and mentioned her conversation with Gracelyn and the privates about the civilian use of them. "We had this private who was convinced jeeps would be available to the public soon. How crazy is that? An average citizen driving jeeps—could you imagine that?" Abby said, giving Walter her opinion.

Walter was quick to respond, saying it could be possible but not likely. He didn't want to get into an in-depth conversation about jeeps, so he relinquished the simplest answer that came to mind. He was done talking for the night and just wanted to soak in the time with Abby. It had been almost a year since he was at peace. It had been a year since he was able to enjoy spending time with the person he thought about for the duration of the war. Walter just wanted to hold on to Abby for the rest of the night and for the rest of his life.

Before he fell asleep, he wanted to deliver his decision to Abby regarding Eli. He figured out what he wanted to say. He tapped Abby on the shoulder and said, "I have a decision for you about Eli."

Abby sat up on the wool blanket. She was ready to listen. "I really want to adopt Eli with you. We may not be as prepared as most people who become parents, but I think we can do anything together. But we can only adopt him under one condition."

Abby was taken aback because she wasn't expecting a negotiation. It was an adoption, not an arbitration hearing. There were no lawyers at the fire. "What's this condition?" asked Abby.

Walter pulled something out of his pocket. It was a ring. "Will you marry me, Abigail Walker?" asked Walter, getting on one knee.

Abby was speechless but managed to nod. Walter kissed Abby and told her that he loved her more than anything.

While Walter was about to fall asleep, he reflected on his life in the last year. His life was like a roller coaster. He fell in love with Abby, he was sent to the war, and now they were engaged. It might have been a roller coaster, but he wouldn't have changed a single aspect of it. Yes, he was forced to spend time away from his family, friends, and the girl of his dreams. However, he felt honored to have served in the United States military. He did his part to ensure that Hitler was stopped, and he was able to prove that freedom and civil liberties were more powerful than tyranny and fascism. Once his mission was complete, he was able to return home and live out a true fairy-tale ending. He couldn't wait for the challenges he faced with Abby by his side. Walter and Abby would be ready, as no challenge was tougher than being separated throughout a war, especially a war of the magnitude in which they fought.

CHAPTER 25

2015

It was almost time for the students attending Arlington Heights High School to be dismissed for the day. The elderly gentleman was very thankful he was able to finish his story by the time school ended. Once he was finished with the speech, he asked the crowd if they had any questions. One student raised his hand and asked, "Did Walter ever keep his promise? Did he deliver the letter to Bobby Hawkins's fiancée?"

Without hesitation, the elderly man nodded. "After the war, Walter traveled to Florida to deliver the letter in person. It was hard, but it was something he wanted to do," said the man.

He asked if anyone else had questions, and no one raised their hand.

The man strolled off the stage, and the principal returned to the podium. "Let's give another round of applause. We need to show appreciation toward your fellow Golden Bear!" said the principal. The entire student body gave him a standing ovation, which lasted for several minutes. He could tell the students appreciated the story, and that meant a great deal to him. The old man stood on his feet and waved to the students. After he began waving, the afternoon bell rang, which signaled the dismissal of the students. The students walked out of the auditorium, with the exception of his grandson, Paul Olsen.

Paul Olsen treaded down to the front of the auditorium to greet his grandfather. "Hey, Grampy. Thanks for coming in and sharing your story," said Paul.

"It was my pleasure. I'm just glad that your fellow classmates were attentive. I was impressed. When I was your age, I rarely paid much attention to speakers," said Paul's grandfather.

Paul laughed. "I guess we're just more mature today."

They walked to the elderly man's car in the visitor's parking lot. "Hop in," said the elderly man. Paul hesitated. He really didn't want to spend the afternoon with his grandfather. Paul was sixteen years old, and he wanted to hang out with his friends. However, he didn't want to disappoint his grandfather, so he jumped into the Ford Mustang. The man, who was in his mid-seventies, started the car and drove out of the parking lot.

A few minutes into the car ride, Paul asked his grandfather where they were going. "We'll be having an early dinner with my parents and your great-grandparents," said the man.

Paul nodded. "Good, I always like seeing them."

They arrived at the destination, and the two people from different generations walked up the driveway in front of the brick house. Before they knew it, they were standing in front of a pink front door. They heard a dog barking, and as the elderly woman opened the door, a golden retriever jumped on Paul with excitement.

"Oh, Sammy, stop that," Paul's great-grandmother said as she pulled the dog away from Paul. "It's so good to see you both. Come on in," said the woman, suffocating both of the men with a hug.

The three of them walked to the living room. "Sit down, sit down," said Paul's great-grandmother, who also went by GG.

Paul and his grandfather sat on the same couch, while GG sat on the chair across from them. Being a typical kid, Paul let his eyes begin to wander. GG witnessed her great-grandson looking at the kitchen. "I love that kitchen. It's been great to me over the years. I was able to cook and watch my kids play in the backyard," said GG. "Isn't that right, son?"

"That's right, Mom."

The three of them began talking, and GG asked Paul and his grandfather many questions. "Paul, have you started looking at college?" asked GG.

Paul had a few schools he wanted to attend. "Maybe Ohio State or Indiana. I want to play tennis in college. But I'm not good enough to play tennis there, so I may end up going to a small division III school."

"You should look into Ohio Wesleyan. Your grandfather and great-grandfather went there. They were Fijis," said GG. "Your grandfather played tennis there."

While GG and his grandpa were talking, he looked around the living room at all the pictures. Some of the pictures were in color, and some were in black-and-white. He saw his grandfather in the pictures with his brother and sisters. He didn't realize how much older his grandfather was compared to his siblings. Paul also noticed a picture of a young couple, and the man was in an Army uniform. His assumption was that the couple was of his great-grandfather and great-grandmother.

The sliding door swung open, and an elderly man, older than Paul's grandfather, waltzed in with a plate of hamburgers and hot dogs. "Silly me, it must be my old age. I forgot Grandpa W was outside, grilling," said GG.

Grandpa W placed the plate of hamburgers and hot dogs on the dining room table. The old man with balding white hair proceeded to sit down at the table, and the rest of the gang followed suit.

"Can you believe it? This man told me nearly seventy years ago that the only food he would make would be on the grill," said GG. She took a sip of her drink and went on to say, "and he didn't lie."

Everyone laughed at the table. "Dad always knew his limitations," said Paul's grandfather.

Just then, Paul made a discovery, and he didn't waste any time sharing it with the rest of the table. "Grampy, you're Eli from the story, aren't you?" said Paul.

"I am, Paul. That story I shared with everyone was the story of my parents and your great-grandparents," said Paul's grandpa, or Eli.

Paul was speechless. He couldn't believe it. The youngster was unable to produce any words. When Paul was able to regain his ability to formulate thoughts, he said, "So that means you're Abby, and you're Walter."

"That's right. I'm assuming your grandfather told our story at school today," said Walter.

"It's such a wonderful story," said Abby. "I hope everyone liked it."

"I think everyone liked it. He told us your story and how you fought in Europe and in Normandy," said Paul. "How did you adopt my grandpa?"

Walter smiled. "It wasn't easy. We flew to London after the war and spent months there fighting the British court system. Finally, they relented."

"And I'm certainly glad they did," said Abby Wilson as she smiled at Eli.

"We all are," said Eli.

"We are all in agreement, son. I'm really glad you shared our story," said Walter. "Throughout the war, I dreamed of having a life with your great-grandmother. And I was so fortunate to live it. Marrying Abby and serving my country were the two biggest honors of my life."

Abby smiled at him and realized that they lived through something special. Walter looked at his wife and said, "That princess over there made my life."

Abby tried not to shed any tears. Paul was intrigued, and he had so many questions for his great-grandfather. "Did Arlington Heights ever throw you a parade?" asked Paul.

Walter looked at Paul and said, "Yes and no. There was a float of all the World War II veterans during the Fourth of July parade. Many Golden Bears proudly served during the war. Some returned as heroes, while others paid the ultimate price."

The four of them continued to chomp down on the burgers. Paul was still curious about Walter and Abby's life, so he asked them more questions. "Were you still close to Randall after the war?" asked Paul, looking toward Walter.

"Of course. He married my sister, and he was my best friend. They both died a few years ago, but they had a good life."

Paul smiled and asked Walter if they lived next door. "We lived three houses away. Both of our wives put a three-house limit on the proximity," Walter said with a huge smile on his face.

"Did you have fun with him all the time?" asked Paul.

"We had our fun. There were times when we would go to each other's houses and had our wives watch the kids," said Walter. "But we had children, and we loved our wives. If we wanted that life, we couldn't sneak out all the time."

Paul was somewhat jealous of this old man. He thought about how awesome it would be to live near his best friends when they were adults. He would have fun the rest of his life if that ever happened to him.

"Grampy told me that you went down to Florida to see Bobby's fiancée," said Paul, hoping his great-grandfather would tell him what happened when he met Bobby's fiancée.

"Oh, yes, Samantha. She was a wonderful person. When I made the trip to Florida, I thought I had met Samantha's sister, because this blond-haired girl that resembled the person Bobby showed me was holding a baby boy. She told me that she was Samantha and she conceived a child with Bobby before he left for war."

"Why didn't she tell Bobby about the baby?" asked Paul.

"She didn't want him worrying about too many things. She thought it would be better if he only focused on the war. She married a man ten years after Bobby died. He was a nice man, but I don't think she ever got over Bobby completely," said Walter.

"You named my brother after Bobby, right, Mom?" said Eli.

"Yes, sweetheart. He was good man, and we wanted to honor him. We hoped your brother would be as selfless as Bobby Hawkins, and we were right," said Abby.

After hearing the sad ending of Bobby's life, Paul asked Walter about his friend who did make it through the war. "What happened to your friend Luke?"

"Luke was able to return home and reunite with his sister. His sister was so happy to get her big brother back," said Walter.

"Grampy told me that he was really smart. Where did he go to college?" asked Paul.

"His first choice was Columbia. He wanted to attend school in New York, but he chose to go to lowly Harvard," said Walter. Even with his old age, he didn't lose his sense of humor.

"Why didn't he go to Columbia?" asked Paul.

"He wanted to be near his sister in Boston. He figured he was away from her long enough during the war, and he wanted to see her grow up."

Paul nodded and asked what Luke did after college. "He became a really successful investment banker. He had a really nice house in Martha's Vineyard. Luke would invite your great-grandmother and me, along with your grandpa's uncle Randall and aunt Mallie, every summer to his house in Martha's Vineyard. Wasn't that fun?" Walter said while looking at his wife.

"I miss those days," said Abby. "It was so much fun. Lying on the beach all day. Drinking wine all night on the deck. I'll never forget those memories."

It was almost time for dessert. Abby brought out apple pie that had the natural, warm apple-cinnamon scent. "That smells really good," said Paul.

"It tastes even better. It's Walter's grandmother's recipe," said Abby.

As Paul was taking a bite of pie, he asked about Gracelyn and Wesley. "Gracelyn is still with us, but Wesley died about five years ago," Abby said.

"Did Wesley ever become a senator?" asked Paul, referring back to the story Eli told at school.

Abby shook her head no. "He thought about it but continued his career in the military. He ended up retiring as a general. He never regretted it. Wesley and Gracelyn had a great life together," said Abby.

The pie was delicious, and it disappeared within a snap of fingers. After they were finished with dessert, Eli and Paul thanked Abby and Walter for their hospitality and walked to the front door. "Come over more often," said Abby, speaking to Paul.

"Oh, I definitely will," Paul said.

Paul and his grandfather proceeded to stroll to the car and drive toward the home of Paul's parents. While on the way home, Paul thought about his great-grandparents' story. His great-grandfather and great-grandmother were able to put a stop to one of the cruelest tyrants in human history and allowed freedom to be triumphant. When that mission was complete, they were able to live happily ever after together.

The day ended when Eli pulled into his son's driveway. "It was great spending time with you. I'll see you later, Paul," Eli said to his grandson.

Paul gave him a hug and hopped out of the Mustang. During the walk up his driveway, he realized how blessed he was to live such a privileged life, and that was all thanks to his great-grandparents. He was lucky to be afforded the freedom that existed in America, and that wouldn't have been possible if not for all the people like Mathew Farr and Bobby Hawkins sacrificing their lives to uphold that freedom. He realized that anything is possible, and with hard work and determination, any dream can be fulfilled. Paul's example of that idea was Abby and Walter. Abby and Walter worked hard and served their country with honor and were able to live out their dream. He couldn't stop thinking about them because it truly was a fairy-tale ending.

ABOUT THE AUTHOR

Will Thieman grew up in Ohio, and studied history at Ohio Wesleyan University. While at Ohio Wesleyan, Will became an avid writer and passionate about everything related to history! When he's not writing, he loves to travel around the world.

CPSIA information can be obtained
at www.ICGtesting.com
Printed in the USA
JSHW030507140121
10919JS00001B/2

9 781647 017118